ULTIMATE
POWER

OTHER NOVELS BY STEPHEN FREY

The Takeover
The Vulture Fund
The Inner Sanctum
Absolute Proof
The Legacy
The Insider
Trust Fund
The Day Trader
Silent Partner
Shadow Account
The Chairman
The Protégé
The Power Broker
The Successor
The Fourth Order
Forced Out
Hell's Gate
Heaven's Fury
Arctic Fire
Red Cell Seven
Kodiak Sky
Jury Town

ULTIMATE POWER

STEPHEN FREY

THOMAS & MERCER

Published by Thomas & Mercer, Seattle

www.apub.com

Amazon, the Amazon logo, and Thomas & Mercer are trademarks of Amazon.com, Inc., or its affiliates.

ISBN-13: 9781503954083
ISBN-10: 1503954080

Cover design by Jae Song

Printed in the United States of America

For my beautiful Lily . . . I love you so much. You've always been there for me.

PROLOGUE

Charlotte, North Carolina

"He's in agony. Give him another shot."

"I already gave him—"

"Just do it, Doctor. I don't have time for your bullshit."

"Don't screw with me, Mr.—"

"And amp the dose."

"That much morphine could stop your brother-in-law's lungs literally in a heartbeat," Dr. Marshall warned, gesturing at the unconscious man lying on the narrow hospital bed between them. "Translated, Mr. Falcon, what you're asking me to do would kill him."

"Understand something," Falcon said as his brother-in-law gasped for a shallow breath. "I'm not asking you."

Marshall drew himself up defiantly. He was still six inches shorter than Falcon. "Maybe you scare people on Wall Street, but you don't scare me."

So the doctor had checked the Internet. Well, good for him. Falcon's IT bloodhounds had done their research, too. And they always found everything there was to find.

"The man my sister and two nieces loved as a husband and father is gone," Falcon said as his brother-in-law moaned softly. "The tumor attacking his brain won. He's got two weeks left at most. You told me that yesterday, Doctor."

"At my medical school graduation I took an oath to keep him alive no matter what, even if that's only for two weeks."

"Maybe this sounds harsh, but what's the point? He might as well be dead."

"'Might as well' doesn't count. It's black and white as far as I'm concerned. I care for life. I don't endanger it."

Falcon raised an eyebrow. "That's not what I hear."

The doctor shot Falcon a confused look. "What are you insinuating? I have nothing to—"

"He still feels pain," Falcon interrupted, gently laying a hand on his brother-in-law's shoulder.

"And I'm managing that pain as best I can. The last thing I need is your amateur diagnosis while I do. Stick to stocks and bonds, Mr. Falcon."

"How does compassion square with your graduation oath?"

"Excuse me?"

"My sister, Sally, comes to this hospital every morning and holds her husband's limp hand all day. When she finally gets home at night, she shuts herself in her bedroom closet and sobs between gulps of vodka until she passes out on the floor clutching the bottle. She closes her doors, but my niece, Claire, who I adore, still hears her mother crying."

"Yes, well—"

"Claire's sixteen. The front-row seat to her mother's meltdown is making a horrible situation a hundred times worse. Another twenty-four hours of this and they both might lose their minds. Sally and Claire need closure."

"They need to be stronger."

"My sister hasn't been to work in weeks. And, as far as I know, she's never touched alcohol except for a social glass of wine now and then. Claire's grades are in a free-fall, and she's always been an honor student."

The doctor shrugged indifferently. "Not my concerns."

"So you took the *other* oath."

"What other—"

"The Hypo*critic* oath. Look, I don't have a wife or children." Falcon kept going before the doctor could defend himself. "But I know when a family needs to move on."

"Care more about your brother-in-law. He's the one dying."

"They need mercy. Are you getting my message?"

"Loud and clear, but I'm no killer."

"No, you're worse. What you did to that boy in—"

The shrill ring of Falcon's cell phone interrupted the verbal battle. Penny Luzerne was calling from Manhattan, for the third time in the last fifteen minutes. He had to take her.

"Hello."

"Thank God I finally got you," Penny said in her heavy French accent. "I saw your text, but I can't execute a trade this big until we talk, until I actually hear your voice. You made me promise to always follow that procedure."

"Yes, I did," Falcon agreed, closing the door to the hallway and standing in front of it. Marshall had moved to the end of the bed, a livid expression on his face, but he stopped when Falcon made it clear he wasn't allowing the doctor to leave.

"Let me get this straight, Monsieur Falcon. You want me to sell our *entire* position in Gillette Energy?"

"Immediately."

Penny was just twenty-five, and she'd been with Falcon for only six months. But of his three dozen subordinates in his $30 billion hedge fund group, he trusted her most. As much as he relied on analytics to make his investment decisions, he trusted his instincts when it came to people.

"That's a half billion dollars' worth of stock, Monsieur."

"And have those boiler-room brokers across the Street work the trade. Not our people on five."

"A sell order that big could crater Gillette's share price ten to twenty percent, maybe more. It could drag down the entire sector."

"Maybe."

"If we did it in a series of transactions over a few weeks, it might work out better."

Propose the hedge, Falcon urged silently.

"And those guys across the Street, they front run," Penny reminded him. "We've caught them at it more than once."

Show me something, Penny.

"They'll dump any shares of Gillette they hold ahead of ours. Gillette's at forty-four right now, but our average sell price could end up below forty when that much supply shows up at the Stock Exchange."

Falcon shook his head when Dr. Marshall found an ounce of his courage and edged closer. The doctor stopped in his tracks when their eyes met.

"And that could drag down the price of other energy companies." She hesitated.

Even from six hundred miles away, Falcon saw her idea bulb flash on.

"Should I call the guys on five and have them sell a contract for us that bets on a drop in energy stocks across the board?" Penny asked. "We have a little ExxonMobil in the vault but nothing else. Should we short the entire industry?"

That's what Falcon had been waiting for. She was learning fast. She was a keeper.

"Yes. But check with our energy I-bankers before you call the guys on five. See if they're leading any big debt or equity offerings in the next two weeks. And make sure you get the contract inked before you pull the trigger on the Gillette sell. Sell the Exxon, too. When the press hears about us dumping Gillette and Exxon, which you know they will, *you* take the avalanche of calls. Nobody else in the department talks to the reporters but you, Penny. Understand?"

"*Oui,* Monsieur Falcon."

"Don't tell them we're down on energy stocks, but don't deny it, either. Your 'no comment' will be ten times more effective. They'll blog about how a well-placed source says Sutton & Company is negative on the entire sector. For a few weeks, energy stocks will take a hit across the board because of who we are. But by the time it starts to recover, we'll have sold the contract and locked in our gain on it. We'll make five times the money on the sector short than we'll lose by dumping Gillette fast. Even at an average sell price of thirty-eight on Gillette, we still make a hundred and fifty million. That's a forty percent gain in eight months without even counting the contract profit. I'll take that." He chuckled knowingly. "So will Sutton's twenty-five partners."

"You always have a plan, don't you, Monsieur Falcon?" Penny murmured, realizing this had all been a lesson.

"Do me a favor, Mademoiselle Luzerne."

"*Oui?*"

"Call me A.J. from now on."

"Ah, *oui* . . . sir. I-I mean A.J."

Falcon chuckled again. "OK, I've got to—" He grimaced as he interrupted himself to indulge his only vice. It had been his father's only vice as well. "What's the line on the Giants playoff game with the Cowboys?"

"Giants are giving five in Dallas."

He'd trained her well. She had the answer at her fingertips. At bonus time in a few months, Penny was going to be a very happy young woman. "Put a thousand bucks on the Cowboys for me." He was a huge Giants fan. But giving five points in a road playoff game was too tempting. "Keep that to yourself, Mademoiselle."

"*Oui.* Where are you?" she asked. "More important, when are you coming back?"

He hadn't told her he was going to North Carolina. Not even why he'd left Manhattan in the first place. He kept his personal life personal.

"Soon," he answered, glancing at Dr. Marshall, who was still standing at the end of the bed. "Very soon."

"Good. I . . . Well, maybe I shouldn't say this . . . but I . . . I . . . miss you when you're—"

Falcon cut the call and slipped the phone back in his pocket. Marshall had finally found all of his courage. He was moving toward the door.

"Get out of my way," he demanded, stopping just out of Falcon's reach.

Falcon pointed at the box in the doctor's hand. "Put it down."

"You're not killing your brother-in-law."

"And you're not leaving here with that box of mercy."

Marshall placed the syringes down on the foot of the bed and drew his cell phone like a sword. "I'm calling security right—"

"You do, and I'll tell the AMA everything about that incident last month." The thermonuclear detail had been buried deep, *very* deep. But, as always, his IT bloodhounds at G2-DATA had detected it. They'd found the nurse. "The one you can't have them or anyone else knowing about."

"Excuse me?"

"I'll tell them everything you did to that teenage boy in the recovery room while he was coming out of anesthesia. How you bribed the nurse who caught you. And I know that boy wasn't the first." He had no proof there were others. He was just guessing. But he could tell by the doctor's terrified expression he'd scored another direct hit. "You're an awful man."

Always bring an Uzi to a sword fight. Falcon's father had taught him that.

The doctor swallowed hard and tugged at his shirt collar. That fast he'd started to sweat. "What . . . uh . . . what are you talking about?" he asked, his voice going high-pitched.

"Spare me the indignity of defending yourself. Get the hell out of here."

Marshall muttered something as he brushed past Falcon into the corridor—leaving the needles behind.

When he was gone, Falcon locked the door. He'd call the AMA later. Marshall's medical career was finished.

Minutes later, Falcon unlocked the door and leaned into the hallway.

"*Sally!*" he shouted down the corridor. "*Claire!*"

They'd just slipped bills into a vending machine, but they turned and raced toward him the instant he called.

Sally was already crying. Claire was right behind her mother, cheeks drawn and pale.

"It's time to say good-bye," Falcon said gently but firmly.

"He needs Dr. Marshall," Sally gasped.

"No, Sally." Falcon held his sister's arm. "He needs you."

She stared up at her brother for several excruciating moments, then sobbed and burst past him into the room.

Falcon glanced down at Claire with every ounce of sympathy. As her father had fallen gravely ill over the last year, Falcon and Claire had gotten close. Despite the intense demands on his time running his massive hedge funds, he called her at least every other night. And he'd visited them in Charlotte as often as possible.

He wasn't a man easily swayed by emotion. But the sight that met his emerald eyes caused his heart to rip so hard he had to put a hand to his chest. It was all he could do to keep his expression strong, to be the rock he knew she needed at this most horrible moment of her young life.

Tears poised precariously on Claire's lower lids, and her lips trembled. But it was the lost look in her eyes that crushed him. It was a lost, vacant stare, as if she were peering into the valley of death herself. As if at sixteen she was facing her own mortality.

Falcon couldn't meet her gaze for long. He couldn't remember the last time someone had stared him down.

He turned to walk away so she and her mother could have privacy. "No," Claire whispered, "don't leave me."

And then she was in his arms, sobbing, pressing her face hard into his chest. "I can't handle this by myself, Uncle A.J. Hold me, *please*."

When she looked up at him through her tears, he suddenly felt like he had a daughter.

It was the most powerful feeling he'd ever known.

◆　◆　◆

Brooklyn, New York

"What's wrong, Billie?" Paul Fellini asked.

"Nothing," she answered, voice barely audible.

Paul glanced suspiciously toward her boyfriend, Vito, then gestured to her. "Look at me, Billie."

Billie had been gazing off at a ninety-degree angle when Paul entered the cramped kitchen of the Brooklyn row house. As captain of the Bayside Crew, he was here to give Vito an order, but it was Billie he'd been eager to see. She hadn't looked him in the eyes yet, though, and he was worried. Usually, she hugged him as soon as she saw him. And he'd never heard her voice so low and empty of emotion.

Something was definitely wrong. He'd never trusted Vito—with business or personal matters. As far as Paul was concerned, the kid was a punk who should have no future with the Gambino Family. But Vito was related to the underboss of the entire Family.

That meant Paul had to deal with him.

It didn't mean he had to like him.

"Billie."

Still, she wouldn't look over.

Billie Hogan was very, very pretty, exactly what Paul was into—long jet-black hair, exotic features, and a figure sent from heaven—or hell. He hadn't decided yet. Maybe it didn't matter. He already knew where he was going.

She had a great personality, too, usually up and positive—though not tonight. Tonight she was down, *way* down.

Something was very wrong.

As much as Paul wanted to, he hadn't made a play for Billie, hadn't even flirted with her . . . well, not too much. Even though Vito was just a low-level soldier and would probably never be made, and the vibe Paul had always gotten from Billie was a good one, like she wanted him to step outside the lines, he hadn't. You didn't do that with other men's wives or girlfriends in the Family, even if they were subordinates. Those were the rules, and if you broke them you'd pay—brutally.

Billie would have to end it herself if they were to ever have a chance. And why wouldn't she? She was way out of Vito's league. What the hell was she doing with this little weasel?

"Billie."

"She's fine," Vito spoke up sharply. "Stop bothering her, Paulie."

"What'd you say to me?" Paul snapped in his heavy Brooklyn accent, moving across the kitchen to where Billie stood. *"Huh?"*

Vito held up both hands. "I'm sorry, I'm sorry. I was out of line, Paulie. I don't know what's wrong with me tonight."

"Hey, you," Paul said to Billie softly. "Meet me halfway."

Finally she looked up at him. But she made sure her hair was hanging over the right side of her face.

Gently, he moved it. She turned away immediately, but he'd seen the deep black-and-blue bruise covering her cheek and neck.

"You bastard," Paul hissed, lunging for Vito.

Vito tried to run, but Paul caught him before he made it out the back door.

Within a minute, Vito's face was beaten unrecognizable.

As Vito lay on the floor whimpering, Paul grimaced. This would be a problem when the underboss heard about it.

◆ ◆ ◆

New Orleans, Louisiana

Officer Huey Breaux sped through the night into a poverty-stricken neighborhood northeast of the French Quarter.

A summer mist, the last remnants of a powerful system of thunderstorms that had pounded the entire Gulf Coast a few hours earlier, sifted down through the darkness and the delta-bound foghorns onto dimly lit streets.

Bleary-eyed and overweight from a steady diet of fried clams and oysters, Breaux leaned over the steering wheel of his police cruiser as far as he could and squinted as he counted down the deserted streets.

"Independence . . . Congress. Come on, *come on.* There, Gallier."

He fishtailed right onto Gallier Street, and then raced into the thin mist between two lines of dilapidated homes.

"Middle of run-down town at two a.m. on a DV SOS," he grumbled, reaching beneath his seat for the half-full fifth of Jack Daniel's. "Third time this week, and I need a goddamn raise." He swallowed a comforting dose of corn mash whiskey and then wedged the bottle between his thighs. "I hate the graveyard shift," he muttered, wiping his lips with the back of his hand.

Out of nowhere, a young man wearing a bright-white T-shirt and baggy, low-hanging jeans appeared like a specter out of the mist directly in front of Breaux's cruiser. He wrenched the steering wheel hard right at the last second and slammed on his brakes, sending the bottle of Jack tumbling to the floor between the brake pedal and the accelerator.

"*Geeeod damn it,*" he hissed, thrusting open the door. He whipped his service pistol from his holster as he climbed from the vehicle and aimed at the fleeing figure. "Freeze-frame, boy, or I shoot!"

The young black man instantly turned into a statue at the edge of Breaux's visibility.

"Hands up high, where I can see 'em."

The young man dutifully raised both hands as Breaux jogged up behind him, breathing hard after only a few strides.

"What's your name?" Breaux demanded, keeping the pistol trained on the young man.

"Kelvin James, sir."

"What you doing out here at two a.m., Kelvin James?" Breaux demanded.

"Walking home from work."

"Where's work?"

"The Burger King a few blocks over. I man the drive-through."

"That BK Lounge closes at midnight on Thursdays. Don't try fooling me."

"Yes, sir."

"What are you doing out here?" Breaux demanded again, taking one step closer. "Tell me the truth this time, Mr. James."

"I *am* telling you the damn truth, Officer. We were cleaning up after we closed. Every Thursday night we clean the whole place corner to corner. I just got out of there. I swear. You can check my time card. You can ask my super. She's probably still there."

"On your knees."

"But I—"

"*On your knees!*"

Kelvin dropped to his knees, hands still raised above his head.

Breaux took a deep breath to calm himself. His pulse was going mad, spurred on by the whiskey he'd gulped in the last twenty minutes to make it through his shift. He glanced around one more time to make certain they were alone.

◆ ◆ ◆

Tulip, Mississippi

Tulip, Mississippi—a rural town of four thousand people located fifty miles east of the capital city of Jackson—had always been a lightning rod when it came to issues of race.

True to form, someone or some group had decided a hundred years ago to erect a statue in a pretty park in the small downtown area—a statue of Robert E. Lee, the Confederacy's most beloved general.

To some of the town's population, the statue was a tribute to a great man.

To the rest, it was a poignant symbol of all things horribly wrong with the United States.

A month ago, the Tulip town council had sided with those who believed it wrong to honor a man who'd led the fight to keep slavery alive. They'd voted to have the statue removed.

In the morning, the statue of General Lee riding his beloved horse, Traveller, would be destroyed. The equipment was parked a hundred yards away. The crew was sleeping in a hotel down the block.

But there were those who would not give up the statue easily.

Fifty young white men marched toward the statue through the night carrying torches and bottles of bourbon. They were clad in khakis, white Oxford shirts, and blue blazers. They sang "Dixie" as they walked in step.

Upon reaching the statue, they circled it at ten feet out, standing several deep around it.

When they finished singing, the leader—a tall, lanky fraternity president from the University of Mississippi—climbed the statue so he was standing beside Traveller.

"We will not allow this beautiful symbol of the Confederacy to be torn down and discarded like some ordinary piece of junk!" he shouted, raising his torch. "Will we, boys?"

"No!" came the thunderous response. "Never!"

"We'll form a barrier around it and never let it be destroyed!"

Another roar of agreement rose.

"Our forefathers fought and died for this great man, for us! It's the least we can do to keep the memory of him preserved for the next generation to—"

The young man was interrupted by spits of gunfire, then a barrage. Several boys on one side of the statue fell, screaming in pain.

Out of the darkness charged twenty young black men.

CHAPTER 1

Six months later
Manhattan, New York

Falcon sped through the possibilities—*again*. But he came up empty—*again*. They should be congratulating him, not dragging him to the mountain to grill him.

He sat by himself in a small conference room on the forty-seventh floor of 61 Wall Street, the firm's worldwide headquarters. Forty-seven was sacred ground at T. U. Sutton & Company, the planet's most powerful investment bank. If you weren't one of its twenty-five partners, you weren't welcome here—unless you'd been summoned to explain a misstep.

Falcon wasn't a partner. He was just thirty-one. No one made partner at Sutton in front of forty. And he'd been summoned.

Remove emotion from the equation. Don't be distracted by getting even, at least not in the short term. Always keep the ultimate objective top of mind. Then, when the issue has been decided, take your revenge and take it hard. So the enemy is afraid to retaliate—even if they survive. His father's counsel was with him constantly.

Every other iconic Wall Street partnership that mattered— Goldman Sachs, Morgan Stanley, the now defunct and disgraced Lehman Brothers—had yielded to greed and gone to the public for equity years ago. Thanks to those IPOs, the former partners had stashed vaults of cash in their pockets. But now they had public shareholders in their shorts.

Sutton & Company had always been private, never owned by more than twenty-five men. And it had never suffered the disgrace of begging the Feds for bailout billions. The firm had remained rock solid since its founding several years before the Civil War.

Even Sutton dealt with some regulation. But by remaining private, its partners cloaked most of what they did from the outside world—which gave them a massive advantage while they managed client billions, advised on high-profile mergers and acquisitions from New York to Hong Kong, and raised debt and equity for cash-hungry companies large and small.

Most critical of all, by staying private, the partners could move money around the globe in the world's darkest shadows, without so much as a whisper.

Outsiders didn't know who was a partner and who wasn't. In fact, most of the firm's forty thousand employees didn't know.

Falcon did. Late one night he'd found a list.

"Mr. Falcon."

Falcon glanced up from his cell phone. At the doorway stood James Lee Wallace III, the slim, stoic, snow-haired senior partner and CEO. Years ago he'd been nicknamed "Three Sticks" by Sutton's rank and file for those three Roman numerals standing tall behind his name. But no one ever called him that to his face. He was "Mr. Wallace" to all but his twenty-four partners.

Even to some of them.

"Follow me," Wallace ordered in his gravelly, West End Richmond drawl. He was First Family of Virginia and traced his genes directly back to General Robert E. Lee. "And turn off that damn phone. I don't want any interruptions."

Falcon stood up and trailed the lanky older gentleman down a deserted hallway hung with tasteful paintings of nineteenth-century

Richmond. Despite Wallace's order, Falcon used his phone to finish placing a bet on who would win professional golf's US Open. The tournament started tomorrow, and he had a good feeling about the winner.

Summer was a downtime for gambling. No football, no basketball, and he hated betting on baseball. It was too boring to watch, so he couldn't go through the ups and downs of his wager while he viewed the game.

Everyone needed distractions. Gambling seemed to him the most victimless.

"In here," Wallace said, gesturing at an open doorway.

Falcon pushed the "Send" button on his phone and then slipped it in his pocket just as Wallace turned around to usher him inside the large, ornately decorated office.

Philip Rose, Sutton & Company's chief financial officer, sat in a leather wingback on one side of the office's wide desk. Rose had fought as a marine in the first Gulf War. He still kept his cherry-blond hair high and tight.

In a matching wingback on the other side of the desk sat Michael Mattix, the firm's chief operating officer and head of all merger and acquisition business at Sutton. His hair was dark, highlighted by just a few distinguishing grays. In his late forties, Mattix was still in tremendous physical shape, still one of Wall Street's best squash players, regularly beating men half his age. He'd won a national championship at Princeton three decades ago.

Wallace pointed at an uncomfortable-looking wooden chair positioned before the desk like a witness stand, then sat down between his lieutenants. "It's almost eleven o'clock, Mr. Falcon. I'd apologize for keeping you so late. But, according to our security people, you rarely leave the building before midnight. That is, the three to four months a year you aren't circling the globe for us raising those billions you manage in your exceptional hedge funds."

That intro didn't sound like the start of a grill session.

"Such dedication," Mattix spoke up. "Of course, you've got no one at home to bitch about your hours."

"Why is that, Mr. Falcon?" Rose asked. "Why is there no trophy wife complaining because you're never around? Not even a girlfriend chirping. You're thirty-one, damn good-looking, and doing very well for yourself at the most prestigious investment bank in the world. Objectively speaking, you're quite a catch. Yet you're completely unattached."

"Well, eHarmony owes me a big refund."

Rose and Mattix laughed.

Wallace didn't.

"Women should be beating down your penthouse door," Rose continued after checking Wallace's impassive expression.

"First of all, my penthouse is a one-bedroom on the twenty-seventh floor of a forty-two-story building. Second, I don't need to explain why—"

"He's consumed by his work," Wallace interrupted. "By *our* work."

Falcon eased into the uncomfortable chair. He'd been at Sutton for seven years but had never met Rose. Rose hadn't stood up or offered a handshake when he'd entered the office—so neither had he.

Michael Mattix, on the other hand, had been Falcon's unofficial mentor since the day he'd joined the firm. They weren't close. They had lunch once a month or so. But, especially during Falcon's early days at Sutton, Mattix had always been someone he could count on for advice. And that advice had always been rock solid.

They'd played squash several times in those early days. Falcon always made sure to lose by two or three points. He valued advice much more than victories on a squash court.

"But it would be good if he were married," Rose said, "and if he had children."

"Why?" Falcon asked.

"What we do is stressful, A.J.," Mattix answered paternally. "You and I have talked about that. Having a wife and kids at home can help. You'll need their support at some point, as a balance to everything that happens around here."

Falcon still had no idea why he'd been summoned. He was managing $30 billion of principal hedge fund money for the firm. Each fund comprising that massive sum was already up more than 30 percent halfway through the year despite most markets stumbling sideways for the last eighteen months. The annual management fee on that sum was $300 million.

Even more lucrative than the fees, the profit share Falcon charged each investor on the gains had stashed another $900 million into Sutton coffers since January 1, so $1.05 billion in total this year. He was making the three men in front of him—and the other twenty-two partners—insanely wealthy . . . *by himself.*

He chuckled softly.

"What's so funny?" Wallace demanded.

"Last I heard, the divorce rate in this country was more than sixty percent," Falcon answered. "That doesn't sound very supportive, not to mention it's damn expensive."

"The divorce rate is a whole lot higher at Goldman Sachs than it is here at Sutton," Wallace said.

Falcon looked up and caught Wallace's piercing gaze for a moment.

Maybe that was it. Maybe these men sitting before him like a grand jury had found out what Goldman was offering him to jump ship: $5 million a year along with performance bonuses that could push his annual income into the eight-figure zone.

"Why do people call you A.J.?" Rose asked. "Why not A.B.? Your first name is Andrew, but your middle name is Blake."

"I'm Andrew Junior. I've been A.J. since day one."

"Your father was a legend in this city," Mattix spoke up.

"Then he jumped out that fortieth-floor window a few doors down Wall Street," Wallace added.

"Who says he jumped?"

An uncomfortable silence settled onto the office.

"Are you implying he was thrown out that window two years ago?" Wallace finally asked, as if the notion were ridiculous.

"He had no reason to jump."

"Your dad was bankrupt," Mattix reminded Falcon gently. "He made a huge bet on Argentina. When that country nationalized all foreign assets, his wager destroyed him. Creditors were closing in on your father from all sides."

"Sure," Falcon retorted defiantly, "if you believe the press."

"Do you have specific evidence to the contrary?" Wallace asked, leaning forward.

Falcon didn't know Wallace well. Despite making the man billions, he'd only met the senior partner a few times. Those meetings had taken place downstairs on twenty-seven, on Falcon's floor, when the European Union was first fracturing and Wallace wanted to make certain Falcon's international hedge funds were secure, not suffering massive redemptions the way many others were. They'd only met those few times, but Falcon still recognized the intensity hiding in the older man's poker face.

"No," Falcon admitted, "I don't."

The office went stone silent again.

"Your sister, Sally, lives in Charlotte, North Carolina," Mattix spoke up. "Her husband died of a brain tumor six months ago. Sally has a daughter. Her name is Claire, and you're especially close to her."

Falcon held Wallace's gaze a few moments longer, then shifted to Mattix. "I'm her godfather. Now will someone please tell me why I was called up here—"

"Sally was facing a mountain of medical bills when her husband died. They didn't have enough medical insurance. You saved her financially. You paid off everything."

"She's my sister. Of course I did."

"You're a generous man, Mr. Falcon. Last year you gave two hundred thousand dollars to the St. Jude Children's Research Hospital. And you did it in Claire's name."

They must have his tax returns—which didn't surprise Falcon. These men could probably get their hands on anything.

"Claire's sixteen," Mattix said. "You taught her to snowboard in Deer Valley last winter. You taught her to fly-fish in Montana last month. Claire worships the ground you walk on."

"What is this?"

"On the flip side, you had a run-in with the law while you were at the University of Virginia, down the hill from Mr. Jefferson's Rotunda."

"I had a few beers one night, and I shouldn't have been driving." Falcon wasn't going to deny the accusation—or run from it. "But it's been almost a decade." He never denied or ran from a mistake. "That incident is no longer relevant."

"*We'll* decide what's relevant," Rose snapped, the way he probably had to hundreds of marine cadets.

"And what isn't," Mattix added quietly.

"Is there anything else we should know about?" Wallace asked. "Is there anything that could embarrass us?"

"Embarrass?"

"Anything, Mr. Falcon?"

Then it hit him. He caught his breath as his eyes widened. He hated ever giving away what he was thinking, but he couldn't help it this time. The realization was overwhelming, even for him. He wasn't here because anything was wrong. It was just the opposite. All was right.

A Sutton partner, Harry Sullivan, had died last week of a heart attack while trophy hunting in Kenya. Falcon was about to be proposed to the partnership to replace Sullivan.

Wallace eased back and folded his arms across his chest. "Well, gentlemen, Mr. Falcon just figured out why we called him up here tonight."

"I'm only thirty-one," Falcon said quietly. "It's never happened to anyone on my side of forty."

"How do you know?"

Falcon shrugged. "I just do."

"Well, it hasn't happened yet," Wallace warned. "You've still got a ways to go tonight. The vote must be unanimous. Don't get ahead of yourself, Mr. Falcon."

CHAPTER 2

Camp David, Maryland

"I can't believe these numbers," Katrina Hilton spoke up angrily as she read the report, running her slender fingers slowly through her long, blonde hair from her forehead all the way to the back of her neck—twice. "They're terrible, Dennis."

Dennis Jordan grimaced. She always did that with her hair when she was *really* stressed. As her chief of staff, he always felt responsible when she did. "I know. I'm sorry."

"Are we sure about them?"

Jordan nodded grimly. It was all he could do. There was nothing to say. "Two more points down since last week."

"It's late, Madam President. Please get some sleep."

"How can I sleep when thirty-eight percent of Americans approve of the job I'm doing? And *sixty-two* percent of them can't stand me?"

"It's not you personally. It's terrorism, the economy, the wealth gap, unemployment." He rushed to defend her, ticking off the usual suspects. "And everything's on ten different news networks twenty-four hours a day. People are bombarded with doomsday scenarios constantly. So they blame you because they have to blame someone."

"The reporters bash me constantly, Dennis, like I'm blind to the problems, like I'm not doing everything possible to make the world a better place."

"They bash you because bashing sells. Viewers love to hate and they hate to love. They love bad news and they yawn at good news. TV news producers know that very well. It's all about the money for them. You can't take these numbers personally."

"That's exactly what I was hired by the people to do, Dennis, to take these numbers *very* personally. The blame stops with me."

He marveled at the way she always shouldered accountability for everything. She always had. She always would.

"You've got a long day ahead of you tomorrow," he reminded her.

She dropped the report loaded with disturbing statistics down on the coffee table and moved to the window of the Camp David cabin. "Every day's a long day for us," she said as she stared into the darkness of the western Maryland forest. "That's the job and that's the way it should be."

"Yes," he agreed, "but we need to be on *Marine One* by seven a.m. to get back to DC for your meeting with President Cruz of Mexico. And it's almost midnight. He'll hit you hard on the GOP's proposed immigration policy. He'll demand more financial help from us. He's a pushy man. You need your rest."

"Sixteen months to the general election, and I'll never keep the Oval Office with these numbers," she said, gesturing at the report. "Four more years is a pipe dream for us right now."

President Katrina Hilton had escaped a trailer-park childhood outside Austin, Texas, with guts, guile, and a million-dollar smile to become the first female president in US history, and she was only in her midforties. Jordan had known her for more than twenty years, since before she'd taken the first of her three high-tech ventures public and made all her employees—including him—rich.

She was scary smart. Her charisma was lightning-bolt dazzling. Her swagger was authentic. This woman was the real deal. She could handle anything. Her confidence never wavered.

So he hated seeing her like this.

The worst part was that he couldn't argue it. Her approval rat. was a disaster. He could say all the right things, but she'd never le. herself be deluded. She was too good for that.

"It's time to take drastic action, Dennis. What do I do?"

"You really want to talk about it now?"

"I have to."

Jordan motioned for her to sit on the couch as he eased into a chair across the table. "It's all about the wallet and the purse. It always is in this country. Hell, it's like that everywhere, and it has been since time began, Madam President. You know that."

"You can call me Katrina when we're alone," she said as she moved across the room. "I won't throw you in jail like Putin would in Russia."

"As I was saying, Madam President, if you want to reach the people, then make their lives better. The most powerful way of doing that is by getting them more dollars. It's that complicatedly simple."

"I can't cut their taxes, not without an offset. The twenty-trillion-dollar deficit I inherited won't allow that."

"So raise their incomes. Make the solution even more personal and powerful. Put them in position to pay *more* taxes because they're bringing home *more* money."

"My predecessor raised the minimum wage, and the unemployment rate took off like a rocket. He paid a dear price as a result." She held out her hands. "I'm not making the same mistake."

"I'm not talking about a few dollars here and there. I'm talking about a major initiative. Attack a fundamental problem that's ravaging this country."

She shook her head like the list was so infinitely long it made no sense to guess. "Which one?"

"The rich getting richer at the expense of the middle class and the poor. Wealth being concentrated more and more at the top of the food chain. Everything is more expensive for most people every day, but the average Americans' paychecks haven't budged in years. So they've borrowed until their credit cards are maxed out, and now what do they do?" He gestured at her. "That's why people are angry. That's why your numbers are bad. It isn't you. It's the situation. So fix it."

"How?"

"Start by going after the most evil cartel in the world. Torch it and scatter its ashes to the wind. While you're at it, tax the hell out of the rich based on their wealth, not just on their income. And do it *before* they die. And for God's sake, *cut military spending.*" He hesitated, to allow her several moments to take it all in. "The middle class and the poor will reap the benefits. We'll see a fundamental shift in wealth immediately. And it won't be some quick fix like an arbitrary increase in the minimum wage that's canceled out almost immediately by unemployment and/or inflation. You'll be a savior to average Americans, and your popularity will soar. By the next election, the disapproval numbers in that report on the table will be a footnote no one remembers. You'll win in a landslide this time. It won't go down to the wire like it did three years ago."

"I'm from Texas, Dennis. So are you. We can't go after the big oil companies. We can't go after that cartel. We could never go home again. We'd be shot the second we stepped back in our state."

"I'm not talking about *that* cartel. I'm not talking about Big Oil."

She ran her fingers through her hair again. But this time only once . . and more slowly. "Which one, then?"

Jordan's mahogany eyes glistened. "Wall Street."

Charlotte, North Carolina

"Hi, Mom," Claire called as she hurried into the kitchen from outside. "Work let me go early, so I'm home for the night."

"Good, then it's just the two of us tonight."

Sally glanced at her daughter as she closed the cabinet door, and the image almost made her cry. Claire was growing up so fast. It seemed like just yesterday she was that tiny, helpless baby they'd brought home from the hospital wrapped in a pink blanket. Now, at sixteen, she was beautiful with that shimmering dark hair and those laserlike emerald eyes. She reminded Sally so much of A.J. that Claire was like his female clone. And she had his same shining charisma.

"I'm baking fudge brownies," Sally said, holding up the box of mix she'd just pulled from the cabinet. "Let's make it a girls' night. We'll watch a tearjerker on Netflix while we binge on brownies and French vanilla ice cream."

Claire made a face. "Too many calories."

"Give me a break, honey. You're rail thin. One night won't hurt."

"OK, but I need something from my room. I'll be right back." Claire started for the stairs, then hesitated. "I almost forgot."

"What is it?"

"Uncle A.J. texted me this morning. He wants to take us to Bermuda next month."

"Seriously?"

"He told me I could bring a friend if I wanted. How cool is that?"

"Very, but that's your uncle."

"Is it OK, Mom? Can we go?"

"I need to check with my boss, but I think it'll work."

"Can I text A.J. back that it looks good?"

"Sure."

Sally smiled as Claire took off. A.J. had called earlier to discuss the trip. But she'd let Claire think she was the point person on this. Her brother had become a wonderful father figure for her girl. With her husband gone, it was crucial for someone to fill that void, even from six hundred miles away.

She put the brownie mix down on the island counter and opened the refrigerator to get a quart of milk. When she closed the fridge door, the carton slipped from her fingers and exploded on impact with the floor, splattering her legs beneath her shorts. She didn't notice.

Three huge, black-clad men loomed in front of her. And they weren't here on a religious mission to preach conversion. They were here on a hunting mission. She'd never been as terrified in her life.

Run or fight? The two options flashed through her mind.

Fighting would be useless.

She turned to flee, but they caught her and slammed her to the floor, shoving a gag deep down her throat.

"It's not you we want," one of them hissed. "It's Claire."

Sally tried desperately to scream. But nothing escaped her lips save a muffled moan.

"Do not call the police when you wake up," the man warned. "If you do, Claire dies. Do you understand? *Do you understand?*"

Sally nodded as her tears began to flow . . . and then everything went to black.

◆ ◆ ◆

Camp David, Maryland

"Wall Street," Jordan repeated hungrily. "That's where it all starts. There and with the Pentagon," he added. "We take down both of them, we take the next election."

"Why don't you pick a couple of tough opponents," Katrina said. "I mean, we'll roll over Wall Street and the DoD in a few days."

Jordan chuckled despite the disastrous numbers contained in that report lying on the table. Katrina always maintained a balanced perspective on everything. She always made him feel better when she was the one who ought to be feeling bad.

Going into his interview with her two decades ago to become CFO of her fledgling high-tech company straight out of undergrad at the

University of Texas, Jordan figured he didn't stand a chance at getting the job. And not just because he'd earned his diploma only a few weeks before and, therefore, had no real-world experience.

Yes, he'd walked across the commencement stage twenty-three years ago at the top of his class with a degree in finance. But he was black and gay. She was white and establishment. It wasn't going to work.

The first two strikes—no experience and being black—were obvious. Being gay didn't even matter.

So he was astonished when she hired him on the spot at the end of their hour-long conversation.

Her decision made more sense when he found out she'd been dirt-poor at the starting line—just like him. She wasn't establishment at all.

It made even more sense when she told him his first day on the job that she liked that he was gay—though they'd never discussed his sexuality during the interview.

She was a beautiful, vivacious woman, and she was fed up with men constantly coming on to her. Criminally several times, she'd confided in him. Though she'd never pressed charges because she had no faith the police would believe her, much less do anything. She had to completely trust the people she worked with the closest, especially the one handling the money. That he was gay made her feel secure. That he was black showed the world she was progressive.

She'd been straight up about why she wanted him. She hadn't sugarcoated it. It was a business decision, all calculated to promote her image. But he liked that. He'd always know where he stood with her.

He'd been impressed by her brains, insight, pragmatism, and, yes, her beauty. He still was, even more so now. But, as she'd pointed out, he appreciated her looks the way art lovers appreciated a great painting. There was no sexual tension between them.

As she'd boldly predicted, they'd quickly become a force in the business world. Their winning partnership had continued onto the state political stage, then, just as quickly, into the national spotlight.

He'd dedicated his life to her. She'd made him rich in return—and not just on the money scoreboard. He was the top adviser to the most powerful person in the world—so it was up to him to put out this bonfire.

"The middle class and the poor hate Wall Street," he continued. "It's ingrained in their DNA even more deeply than hating Big Oil for prices at the pump. They figure it's a rigged game, and why shouldn't they?" Jordan shook his head bitterly. "During the real-estate crisis, the Feds bail out the major banks with hundreds of billions in gifts. And what do the senior executives who groveled to Congress for those emergency bailouts ultimately do with the money? They pay themselves hundreds of millions in bonuses. Ordinary people throw up their hands and shout, *WTF!* Forty percent of my fifty-thousand-dollar-a-year salary goes to save these criminals. And the bastards laugh at me while they build mansions on Nantucket . . . *with my money.*"

"It's so true."

"Most people figure the housing crash was Wall Street's fault."

"It was," Katrina agreed firmly. "IOs, POs, interest-rate swaps, and all the rest of those devil-made derivatives that tanked the markets and killed the little guy's home value were dreamed up by a bunch of slimy investment bankers. So they could line their own pockets with more gold while the rest of the nation went on food stamps. And then they turn around and profit on the disaster they created."

"Once in a while one of them gets nailed for insider trading."

"But he ends up playing bocce ball for eighteen months at some minimum-security prison in Connecticut. When he's released, he lives like a king on the millions he stashed in Antigua before he was convicted."

"And," Jordan kept going, "Middle America assumes that for each slime bucket who has to spend a little easy time away from home in a twenty-by-thirty cell, thousands more clean up on insider trades and never get caught." He nodded confidently. "We'll take back everything

Wall Street ever made off average taxpayers and give it back. We'll destroy the Street." His expression turned steely. "You'll be a hero, Madam President. And Congress won't get in your way. They won't dare. They'd never be reelected if they did. It's the perfect plan at the perfect time."

Katrina stood up and walked to the window again. "We took three companies public, Dennis. We used Wall Street. There could be blowback."

"You always made sure your employees shared generously in your wealth. Nobody will blame you for using Wall Street. You were living the American Dream. That's all. Helping the investment bankers is what aggravates the average person. It's being perceived as one of them that really grinds the gears of the middle class and the poor." He gestured to her. "You won't be perceived that way. You never took campaign money from them, not even in the state elections. We were always careful about that."

"How do we attack?"

"We go after the big boys first," he answered firmly. "Goldman Sachs, Morgan Stanley, J.P. Morgan, Citibank, and the other money centers." His eyes narrowed. "And then there's that one firm that's still private. That firm at 61 Wall Street that still operates behind a curtain."

"Sutton."

"*Yes,*" Jordan agreed hungrily. "T. U. Sutton & Company."

"Is this personal for you, Dennis?"

"What do you mean?"

"Sutton didn't exactly roll out the red carpet when you were putting together our underwriting syndicate for our last IPO . . . the big one."

He clenched his jaw but said nothing.

"One VP in a cramped conference room," she continued, "and five minutes later he's showing you the door, telling you he doesn't think the 'fit' is right. They didn't even have a partner meet with you. While, if I'm remembering correctly, every other firm on the Street put on a parade and had their most senior executives beg you for our business."

"Madam President, this is not personal. I'm—"

"I want it to be personal, Dennis. I want you going after them with a vengeance. This is a tremendous initiative. I don't want us stopping until we've turned Wall Street from a bastion of capitalism into an empowerment zone." She looked back out the window into the darkness. "Can you imagine what would have happened if my opponent had won the election?"

Jordan was quiet for a moment, remembering how Katrina had beaten him by so razor-thin a margin he hadn't formally conceded for a week after election night. "I'd be riding in the back of the bus and eating in a different section of the restaurant than you. And the generals at the Pentagon would have gotten even more money to buy their war toys."

"We can't ever let that happen. We must reach out to those in the middle class who left us on election night and bring them back for good. And I believe your plan will do that." She smiled. "I don't know what I'd do without you."

Jordan glanced down. She'd never said anything like that before. "Thank you, Katrina," he whispered.

"Do you know what T. U. stands for?" she asked him.

"It's the name of the founding partner, Thomas Underhill Sutton."

"That's what everyone thinks."

"That's not right?"

"A person I know swears there never was a Thomas Underhill Sutton. He claims T. U. actually stands for 'The Untouchables.'" She turned to face Jordan. "And we're going to prove him wrong." She pointed at her chief of staff. "How fast can you put together our specific plan of attack?"

Jordan grinned slyly. "I already have, Madam President. I put it together a month ago."

CHAPTER 3

Manhattan, New York

"How much money are you managing for us now, Mr. Falcon?" a partner to Falcon's left asked.

"More than thirty billion of principal." Twenty-four men sat in large leather chairs that formed a perfect arc in the dim light before him. Aside from Wallace, Rose, and Mattix, he recognized Charles Cain, who'd long been a mentor to him, and a few others. He wondered how soon he'd be able to match the rest of the faces to the names he'd found on that list a few months ago. "That thirty billion is up four and a half billion so far this year." This was the Sutton partner room. Located at the top of the building on the seventieth floor, it was huge.

"That's three hundred million a year in fees," the same partner pointed out.

"And," James Wallace spoke up from the middle of the arc, "that thirty billion should be forty billion of principal by year-end with all the new investors lining up around the block to get into your funds. Correct, Mr. Falcon?"

"Easily."

"That's another hundred million a year in fees for us."

"Assuming no black swan events," someone else said.

"*Despite* any black swans," Wallace shot back, "Mr. Falcon's hedge funds have proven resilient in the face of major market upheavals, like Brexit."

"What's the vig percentage on the ups?" another partner asked from the flickering candlelight. "Twenty?"

"Yes."

"What did you say that thirty billion is up so far this year?"

Falcon did a quick scan of the men assembled before him. Physically, they all looked very similar. "Fifteen percent. Four-point-five billion."

"That's nine hundred million more to us," Wallace called out, "and we're only halfway through the year."

Impressed whistles filled the large room.

"How many people in your group, Mr. Falcon?"

"Thirty-six."

A chorus of even louder whistles erupted.

"That's *it*?" someone muttered incredulously from the far right of the semicircle.

Falcon could almost hear them doing the calculation in their heads. "That's everyone . . . including me."

"That's more than eight million a year an employee, not including the ups," Wallace said, "for anyone who didn't bring a calculator tonight. With the ups, it's almost twenty-five million per. That has to break the all-time revenue-per-worker-bee ratio. The idiots in the manufacturing world we get rich off are lucky to get that number up to three hundred grand per."

It was raucous laughter's turn to fill the room. Greed was on the warpath.

"It's time to vote," Wallace announced, "unless anyone else has a—"

"He's only thirty-one," Rose interrupted. "Is he too young, James? Tradition . . ."

"Traditions are made to be broken," Wallace replied sternly, "especially when the candidate is so outstanding . . . and Goldman Sachs is pounding on his door."

Falcon's eyes flickered to Wallace's. So Jimmy Three Sticks knew about Goldman.

"Anyone else have anything?" Wallace demanded like he'd personally kill anyone who did.

Someone on the left took a deep breath, as if preparing to ask something. But Wallace shot him a withering glance.

The man buckled.

"All in favor, say 'aye.'"

The room filled loudly with *aye*s.

"Nays?"

Silence met this request.

"The ayes have it," Wallace proclaimed proudly. "Mr. Falcon is the newest partner at T. U. Sutton & Company."

When Falcon stood up, the first man to shake his hand was Michael Mattix. "Congratulations, A.J.," he whispered as he leaned in close. "Tonight the real work begins." His smile faded. "But be careful while you do it, *very* careful. I can't stress that enough."

Over Mattix's shoulder, Falcon caught Wallace staring at them intensely.

Thirty minutes later, Falcon descended the marble stairway leading from Sutton's main entrance down to Wall Street. For a brief moment he thought about turning right to visit the horrible spot where his father had slammed into the pavement two years ago.

Then he thought better of it and turned left—he still couldn't go there—heading west through the summer night toward Broadway. He could have called a Sutton car to take him home to the Upper West Side. But he wanted to walk alone through the darkness of Lower Manhattan to process what had just happened.

It was after 2:00 a.m. The normally bustling area was deserted.

After Mattix turned and walked away, Wallace had placed a hand on his shoulder and smiled broadly. It was the first wide smile Falcon had ever gotten from Jimmy Three Sticks.

The older man had explained the bottom line of the vote in one brief sentence.

"You are now worth a hundred million dollars, Mr. Falcon."

The amount wasn't liquid, Wallace had quickly cautioned as the world momentarily blurred before Falcon. It wasn't as if a $100 million wire would hit his bank account in a few hours. The $100 million represented his initial share of Sutton & Company's equity. But, Wallace had assured him, that $100 million he was suddenly worth would almost certainly grow into the billions by the time he retired in fifteen or twenty years to enjoy his spoils. And the firm would make it liquid then.

Of course, the value wasn't completely illiquid, either. Wallace had made clear that if Falcon wanted $5 to $10 million in cash in the coming weeks "to buy a few things for fun," that could easily be arranged.

"A hundred million dollars," Falcon muttered, stopping to put a hand on the wall of the New York Stock Exchange to steady himself. It was mind-blowing. "In one night, my God, it's almost too—"

"Mr. Falcon."

Falcon whipped around and came face-to-face with a short, slim man. Beneath the brim of the small man's plain baseball cap were round wire-frame glasses. He seemed as dangerous as a newborn lamb. But, as Falcon's father had always warned him, looks could be deceiving.

"How do you know my name?"

"It doesn't matter," the man answered, holding out a piece of paper.

"I charge for autographs," Falcon said, holding up his hands. "Besides, I don't have a pen."

"Take it," the man demanded, bristling. "Don't make me tell you again."

"What is it?"

"An address in the Adirondack Mountains. Take it if you know what's good for you and your family."

"My family? What does *that* mean?"

"It means you need to be at that address by midnight tonight. And do not bring anyone with you or tell anyone else about this. We'll know if you do."

"What the hell?"

"We want information about your partners."

"My partners?" How could this man already know? There had to be a mole among the other twenty-four.

"You'll be meeting with Danny Sykes."

"I'm not into meetings. They're for pussies."

"It's a long drive, Mr. Falcon. There will be dire consequences if you aren't on time." The man walked up Wall Street a few strides toward the Trinity Church and then turned back. "Call your sister, Sally," he instructed. "She has important information for you. And remember, be at that address by midnight."

"Who are you?"

This time the man didn't turn back.

Falcon took several steps after him, intent on getting answers. But two more men emerged from the shadows, blocking his path. One pointed a pistol at him.

"Call your sister," the one aiming the gun ordered, "now."

Falcon dug his phone from his coat. He wasn't arguing with that end of a gun.

"Hello," a low voice answered groggily after the fifth ring.

Sally sounded as if she'd been sleeping, but she'd always been a night owl like him. "Sally?"

"Oh Lord," she muttered, "my head."

"Are you all right?"

Her sharp shriek pierced Falcon's ear.

"Sally, it's A.J." He could hear her breathing hard; it sounded as though she were running. "What's going on?"

"I . . . I—*oh no!*"

"Sally!"

"She's gone!" Sally shrieked.

"Who's gone?"

"Claire! They took her just like they said they would. Oh God, help me, A.J.! My baby's gone."

Falcon glanced up Wall Street. The three men had disappeared into the darkness.

CHAPTER 4

North Woods, Wisconsin

Wisconsin's North Woods—fifteen miles south of Lake Superior—were a far cry from the corridors of ultimate power he was intimately familiar with. But every few months General George Fiske allowed himself a brief respite from the enormous pressures he dealt with inside those Washington, DC, corridors on a minute-by-minute basis.

This time it was a remote club outside a tiny town secluded inside a vast pine forest. Ninety days from now it might be a place in downtown LA. In six months it could be a city in Eastern Europe. It didn't matter to him as long as the subject satisfied his requirement—and the situation satisfied his need.

Fiske lived for this. It allowed him the distraction that enabled him to deal with everything else. To hate himself personally so he didn't have to hate himself for his profession.

"Does she fit your requirement?" John Brady asked as he eased into the big, beer-stained chair to Fiske's left as the loud, grinding music played on. As usual, Brady was clad in ordinary clothes—not his colonel uniform. These clothes that enabled him to blend into the rest of the world. "Do you like my choice?"

The pretty young woman with the long, blonde hair tumbling to the small of her back was still wearing tiny white shorts and a double-D bra above her seven-inch red heels as she moved seductively around the intimate stage. It didn't matter that Fiske hadn't seen everything about her yet. He'd fallen for her immediately. Now he couldn't wait for the endgame. Just the thought of it made his heart race.

"Yes," Fiske answered. He was wearing civilian clothes tonight, too. It felt odd. Unlike Brady, Fiske wore his uniform at least five days out of seven.

Brady glanced around casually. Making certain none of the other patrons could tell he was analyzing each of them intimately in an instant, prepared to kill if necessary. On the lookout for anyone who wasn't who they appeared to be. He was a slight man, belying the deadly force he led and wielded at his discretion—thanks to Fiske.

"This place is too small," Brady muttered under his breath when he was satisfied that they were all just the average Americans he protected on an hourly basis. "I don't like it, sir. Someone might remember us."

Fiske and Brady had known each other for twenty years. For the last ten of those, they'd waged a high-stakes game of Russian roulette between the United States and the rest of the world, refereed by the imminent possibility of mutual destruction. They detested each other personally, but they believed passionately in the same patriotic ideal: the United States *must* remain the lone superpower—at any and all cost. Because no other country on the face of the earth could possibly rule the way the United States could—powerfully and fairly, at least for the most part.

Perhaps their hatred of each other actually intensified their trust, Fiske figured as he watched the young woman slink around the small stage like a cat on the hunt for a mouse.

"No one will remember us as long as you've done your job," Fiske said, "as long as you've identified a situation that fits my need. But thanks for protecting me."

"I'm protecting myself," Brady snapped.

"So, what's the situation?"

"Her boyfriend's been beating her. He gets drunk while she's here stripping. Or 'dancing,' as all these girls so pitifully call it," Brady added snidely. "Isn't that just another shining example of women deluding themselves about their reality? Like any man here really cares if that girl up there dances."

"Focus," Fiske ordered. Life was hard. Sometimes delusion was a necessary ingredient of survival's recipe. Unlike Brady, he'd maintained a little general sympathy despite his intense military training. "Tell me more about the situation."

"When she gets home, he takes his jealousy out on her after he takes her cash. He's been arrested for assault twice. So tomorrow night will seem like the logical progression to the dumb-ass local cops. It'll be a lock, especially after we're done rearranging his single-wide."

"He's a drinker. Good."

"Yeah, but tomorrow night he'll have something extra in his vodka."

Fiske was convinced that Brady and his four assassins were the most talented killers on earth. They slipped through only the world's darkest shadows. They never slept in the same place twice. They used different names every day.

Fiske figured they didn't as much as leave footprints in the snow. They could get to anyone, *even if the target knew they were coming*. This mission in northern Wisconsin was a walk in the park for these men. Very soon the bastard in the beat-up single-wide on the other side of this forgotten town would be in jail on a murder charge he had no way of beating. Very soon he'd find himself behind bars for the rest of his life.

And so be it. Fiske needed the distraction Brady's men would provide as desperately as the world needed him. The young man in the single-wide was simply a sacrificial lamb to an only slightly lesser god than the real one the planet would disintegrate without. That was how Fiske saw it. And that was all that mattered.

"Next week," Fiske spoke quietly, "you'll visit me at the Pentagon." The young woman was slowly bringing the tiny shorts down her legs as she bent over, leaving nothing inanimate in their wake except a thin, lacy thong. No one else in the bar would remember anything except what was happening onstage. Men were predictable animals when attractive women were involved. "We have a challenge on our hands."

"Oh?"

"A *major* challenge."

Brady leaned in slightly. "What's the problem?"

Fiske held his breath as the woman straightened up, turned to face the audience, and slowly, ever so slowly, removed her bra. Excitement surged through him when he saw her full breasts for the first time. He was forty-nine, but this *never* got old. It never would.

"What's the problem?" Brady asked again, raising his voice this time to display his irritation at being temporarily ignored.

Fiske glanced over warily. Brady seemed bored by the stripper, by the whole affair, which Fiske found fascinating. Brady wasn't one of the predictable male majority who could easily be lured and manipulated by beautiful women. Instead, Brady reveled in hunting human beings, male or female—and the tougher the hunt the better. The kill at the end of the hunt was just a minor detail. It was the tracking and trapping that got him off.

Yes, John Brady was a different animal, a *very* different animal, Fiske knew all too well . . . which was why Brady's wife had cheated on him . . . with Fiske . . . among others . . . which Brady knew . . . and why Brady had killed her . . . which Fiske knew and could prove.

Two administrations ago, the Fiskes and the Bradys had attended one of many Washington inauguration balls for a beloved and revered president who, instead of slashing military spending during his reign, had doubled it. In a quiet moment, while they were alone during the festivities, Brady's wife had whispered to Fiske how much she'd always fantasized about him.

Completely unable to resist the advances of an attractive woman, Fiske had arranged for them to meet at a hotel in Reston a few days later. Rebecca Brady had turned out to be an extraordinarily passionate and sexually expert woman—unlike Fiske's wife, who'd become cold and distant in the bedroom as he'd spent more and more time at the Pentagon or traveling.

Fiske and Rebecca had pursued their affair for several months. And, during one of their interludes after sex, she'd confided to him that she believed her husband suspected her of cheating. She'd tearfully admitted to Fiske that he wasn't her only dalliance—thanks to her husband showing no interest in her physically in a decade.

She'd further admitted that she'd secretly installed cameras in the house, and the recording was being fed to a cloud account, to which she'd given Fiske the password. She'd confided to him that she was scared for her life. Her husband didn't want to make love to her. But he didn't want her making love to another man.

Fiske had discounted Rebecca's fears as just misguided emotions going haywire. But when she'd gone missing three months later—a month after he'd stopped seeing her—his interest had been piqued. Not because he cared about what had happened to Rebecca—because he cared about being able to manipulate a direct subordinate.

He'd checked the recording in the cloud account and, sure enough, Brady had murdered Rebecca. He'd strangled her in their bedroom, then, apparently, disposed of her body. Probably in a wooded interstate cloverleaf, as he'd admitted to Fiske he'd done several times before because no one ever went there.

As a senior Pentagon official, Fiske had used his considerable influence to persuade police detectives to look in other directions for answers to Rebecca's disappearance and probable murder. Away from the husband, who was the obvious place to start.

Then Fiske had told Brady what he had and how he'd come to possess it. They'd never spoken of the affair again.

"Let's get out of here," Fiske said, rising from his seat at the back of the room just as the young woman began twirling around the floor-to-ceiling pole in the middle of the stage clad in just her thong and silly-tall heels. "Come on."

When they reached the door, Fiske hesitated and nodded back at the stage. "How old is she?"

"Nineteen."

Sexual excitement surged through Fiske's body again. "Good. I like them young."

Brady set his jaw grimly. "Oh, I know you do."

"Remember to wear your uniform when you come to the Pentagon to see me next week," Fiske reminded Brady as they moved out into the warm Wisconsin night. "You didn't last time and that raised eyebrows. We cannot draw attention to you for any reason."

"I don't even know where my uniform is anymore."

"Find one," Fiske growled, turning to face Brady. "Do you understand me, Colonel?"

"Yeah, yeah."

"What did you say to me?"

Brady kicked a pinecone across the dirt parking lot. "Yes, General," he finally muttered, saluting quickly after checking the area to make certain no one was around.

"That's better." *Mutually assured destruction*, Fiske thought. Brady had saved assassination orders from Fiske—Brady had shown him one. But Fiske had the absolute proof that Brady had murdered his wife. It was a stalemate. "Now get me that girl."

"Yes, sir."

As Brady turned to go, Fiske's phone buzzed. "Hello. Yes, General Lewis. Well yes, of course. I understand, sir. I'll take care of it immediately."

Brady had almost reached the rented SUV when Fiske ended the call.

"John," Fiske called in a low voice. "Come back here."

"What is it?" Brady asked after trotting back to where Fiske stood.

"I have a job for you in Montana. Something I need taken care of immediately."

Brady gestured around. "What about this?"

"Send one of your men to New York—a civilian operation, so that's all it will take. The rest of you stay here and prepare the girl for tomorrow, then get to Montana."

Brady nodded. "Yes, General Fiske."

CHAPTER 5

New Orleans, Louisiana

The four-bus convoy of three hundred freedom fighters and all their gear rolled through southern Mississippi's early morning, reaching the Louisiana state line just as the tip of a fiery, burnt-orange sun climbed above the horizon over their shoulders. They'd left Richmond, Virginia, yesterday beneath gloomy skies. So they took the azure blue breaking clear above them just as they reached the target state as a sure sign they were doing God's work.

The three hundred members of TARC—The Alliance to Reform Communities—were tired but excited when their gleaming silver motorcade finally pulled to a halt in a parking lot of New Orleans's warehouse district. It was time to make a difference.

"Everyone off," Talia Seven Feathers exhorted as the buses emptied, and for the first time the three hundred TARC members experienced a thick July humidity saturating the Gulf Coast. "Come on, let's go!" Talia was a broad-faced, full-blooded Apache who wore her long, jet-black hair in a ponytail pulled tightly together by colorful rubber bands. "Gather round, people!"

Roscoe "Bones" Harris grinned as he watched Talia amass the troops. She was a firecracker. No. More a stick of dynamite, he figured as his cell phone began to play "Shakedown Street." They'd come tantalizingly close to having sex twice in the past few months, but she'd rebuffed him at the last instant both times. He was twenty years her senior. But he was confident he'd finally close the deal on this trip, as long as the trip was a success, as long as they *really* pissed off the right people. He just hoped her passion between the sheets would match her passion for civil rights.

He pulled the vintage flip phone from the front pocket of his threadbare jeans beneath his Grateful Dead T-shirt, and a thrill surged through him when he saw the name.

"The target is 127 Gallier Street," Talia shouted, swiveling her head about so each of the three hundred could hear. "It's seven thirty, and I want you in front of that house no later than ten o'clock. But don't be there any earlier than nine fifty-five. It's a thirty-minute walk from here, so you've got plenty of time for breakfast. And *remember*, groups of four or less walking around, absolutely no more than four of you together. We *do not* want attention until we get to Gallier, until the TV cameras are turned on. But if you're stopped by the law, use the fake IDs I gave you in Richmond. Understood? Good!" she yelled without awaiting an answer. "Now get out of here!"

Muffled assents arose as the group dispersed in all directions, and Bones came jogging toward her.

"What is it?" Talia called out when he was still twenty feet away.

"You won't believe it."

"*What?*"

"We know who murdered Kelvin James."

"Who?"

"Huey Breaux."

"Who is—"

"*Officer* Huey Breaux . . . of the New Orleans Police Department."

"Is he white? Please tell me he's white, Bones."

"He's white with a record of harassing blacks. He's our perfect villain."

"Are you sure on this, *absolutely* sure?"

"Paul just called from Richmond. There's no doubt about it. We found an eyewitness."

Talia grabbed Bones's arm with her stubby fingers as she dropped to her knees in front of him, then raised her arms, clasping the stubby fingers into fists of joy. "Hallelujah, Bones, hallelujah. It's a sign from heaven."

◆ ◆ ◆

Richmond, Virginia

"They made it to New Orleans," Paul Treviso announced, putting his phone down on the spindly conference room table at TARC's Richmond headquarters after ending the call with Bones. "They'll mass on Gallier Street at ten a.m., in front of the Kelvin James house."

"Do we have appropriate media coverage?" asked Reverend Chalice B. Taylor, TARC's CEO.

Chalice was a massive African American man who'd made a mint as an all-pro NFL tight end, then founded the Ministry for Better Tomorrows when he'd retired from football seven years ago. He'd never invested a dime of his NFL millions into the ministry or TARC. He'd never had to. The money side of things had always been taken care of for him.

"Is the press prepped and ready for the big game?"

"Count on it," Paul answered, trying to sound normal, trying not to give away any of the suspicions he suddenly harbored. "I made sure of that myself. I called all the right people at the TV and radio stations personally."

"Good man," Chalice said approvingly. "As the chief operating officer of TARC, you shouldn't be mired in too many details, Paul. But this is a very important project for us. I mean, they're all important, but this one is especially high profile."

"The press will be at the James house in force by nine thirty this morning, Chalice. They're salivating."

"Excellent."

At first, everything here at The Alliance to Reform Communities had seemed normal to Paul. TARC's stated objective was to fight law enforcement injustices against the poor and the disenfranchised in the United States. By targeting specific incidents of injustice—primarily cops shooting and murdering innocent people—and setting up protests to bring attention to those horrible incidents, TARC was making certain the world heard about police crimes so that steps against the offenders and their conspirators could be taken. TARC people were first on the ground at a hotspot, quickly stirring up a hornet's nest of anger and fury at the authorities. Then they slipped out of town before they could be detected, allowing locals to take up the cause. Reverend Taylor's goal was to remain in the shadows at all times, to shun publicity for what they were doing. Seeing the injustices being exposed was thanks enough, he always sermonized. More to the point, he didn't want attention because he didn't want retribution from those who hated what TARC was doing, who hated TARC's goal of exposing the guilty.

Paul wasn't a man who cared deeply about social causes. But TARC had proven a perfect place to land after he'd been forced to run from the Gambino Crime Family. The Gambino underboss had put out a hit on him after Paul had beaten Vito into a coma from which, Paul had heard, the kid still had not awakened. Paul had fled New York City and changed his last name from Fellini to Treviso. He'd been introduced to Reverend Taylor through a trusted friend in the sports world and settled into Richmond as COO of TARC.

But now that he'd been here at TARC for a few months, he was starting to question things—especially after the shocking telephone call he'd received from Washington, DC, from an individual representing one of the most prominent lawmakers on Capitol Hill.

"What about the locals?" Chalice asked in his booming James Earl Jones voice. "We need to get our three hundred people out of there as quickly as possible, especially the leaders on this one. We can't have

Talia and Bones captured. The other side is getting smarter about what's going on. We need the locals taking over our causes even faster."

Paul rolled his eyes. Chalice constantly reminded him that their role in inciting these protests couldn't be exposed. "I know all about how we—"

"What's your problem?" demanded Donnell Thigpen tersely from across the spindly table. He was TARC's chief financial officer. "I don't like your tone or that look you just gave Chalice."

"It's Reverend Taylor to you, Donnell," Chalice spoke up.

"OK."

"What?"

"I mean, yes, sir," Thigpen said dutifully.

Until two years ago, Thigpen had been an NBA power forward, though his basketball career had been nowhere near as celebrated as Chalice's football glory. As far as Paul could tell, Thigpen had no financial training whatsoever, though that didn't seem to matter to Chalice.

"Paul's just getting fired up," Chalice said from the head of the table. "All athletes do that once in a while, Thiggy. You know that."

Paul caught Thigpen's quick grimace at the nickname. Thigpen hated it, and that had to be obvious to Chalice. It was to everyone else at TARC.

Still, Chalice kept using it.

"He ain't no athlete."

"*Isn't* an athlete, Thiggy. 'Isn't,' *not* 'ain't.' And eighty-six the double negatives. You embarrass me when you speak like that. You sound ignorant, like some Kentucky redneck. I will not have that kind of language here at The Alliance to Reform Communities. Do you understand me, Thiggy?"

"Yes, sir," Thigpen answered, chin dropping.

"I do have a question," Paul spoke up.

It was time to start gently digging. The caller from Washington was offering Paul a carrot but was also waving a big stick. Of course, Chalice could wave a big stick, too. He knew about the Gambinos, too.

"What is it?" he asked, raising one eyebrow slowly.

"How did we find this eyewitness down in New Orleans?" Paul asked. "And how did he or she happen to see Officer Breaux shoot Kelvin James in the back of the head in the dead of night? Was this person wearing night-vision goggles? And why didn't this person report the murder right away?"

Chalice and Thigpen chuckled sarcastically at Paul's last question.

"You still don't get it, Whitey," Thigpen spoke up.

Paul hated Whitey as much as Thigpen hated Thiggy. "Hey, *do not* call me—"

"He's making a good point, Paul," Chalice interrupted. "Sometimes you still don't get it. And it's because you're white. Our witness is a young woman of color. She felt she and her family would have been vulnerable to a blitz from the New Orleans Police Department if she ratted out Officer Breaux for shooting a seventeen-year-old black man in the back of the head at two o'clock in the morning, then leaving him dead on a side street."

"And she doesn't feel that way now?"

"We're going to protect her," Chalice answered. "As soon as we're done with this meeting, I want you to arrange round-the-clock security for her and her family."

"It just seems awfully convenient that right as our three hundred people get down to New Orleans, we find a witness," Paul said quietly. "Protesting the fact that cops down there haven't done enough to follow up on Kelvin James's murder is one thing. But accusing a local cop of being Kelvin's killer is quite another. In fact, it's a showstopper. By the time I'm finished setting up round-the-clock security for that young woman of color, she'll be national news. So will the cop."

"Sometimes we get lucky," Chalice said with a smug smile. "Don't let me think you aren't as committed to our goals as you were when you started here."

For Paul, TARC was simply a safe harbor in a bad storm. But he'd done an excellent job of convincing Chalice otherwise. "I'm just as committed to righting social injustice as you are, Reverend." He hesitated. "I just want the truth."

"You let me worry about the truth, Paul."

"Where does the money for TARC come from?" Paul kept going, his voice dipping low as he gestured at Thigpen without looking over at him, without taking his eyes off Chalice. "How does Donnell pay for three hundred people staying in New Orleans for the next several days? How does he pay for the two other protests we're starting next month in Los Angeles and Washington, DC?" He needed to start getting some answers. Otherwise that caller from Washington had threatened to call the Gambinos. How that person knew about the Gambinos hadn't been made clear. "And the seven others we started since the beginning of the year. We have bare-bones offices with stick furniture here at HQ. But we're spending tens of millions in the field to support our protest operations. I know you made a lot of money playing football and making all those Pro Bowls. Still, it doesn't add up."

Chalice pointed a long finger at Thigpen. "Leave us, Donnell."

"Yes, sir."

That quickly, Chalice and Paul were alone in the small conference room.

"Kneel before me, Paulie."

"What?"

"Do it," Chalice ordered, pointing at the floor beside his chair. "Pray with me, son."

Paul had a bad knee from an old high school football injury. So it took him a few moments and a groan to drop down and bow submissively as Chalice placed his fingers on his head. Refusing to pray when ordered to do so by the reverend was a mortal sin at his ministry. Paul knew better than to ignore it.

"Bring this lost sheep back to me, Lord," Chalice implored in his booming voice. "He was a thief and a murderer, a hit man for the Gambino Crime Family in New York City who the Feds and the cops never caught. I thought I'd reformed him, Lord, by giving him a place to hide, an important job to do, and my counseling. But I don't know anymore. Don't make me take that step I don't want to take. Please don't make me take it, Lord. I know he has more good left in him, more to accomplish with me here at The Alliance to Reform Communities, more better tomorrows. Don't make me hand him over to the Feds. Or his former Family," Chalice added ominously as he slipped a finger beneath Paul's chin and tugged it up so he was staring down into Paul's face. He held his massive hand before Paul's lips. "Kiss it, Paulie. Show me your loyalty like you once showed it to your underboss." Chalice's eyes narrowed. "I know how much he wants to find you, Paulie. He wants you back even more than the Feds do. Now, show me your loyalty."

Paul took Chalice's hand and kissed the back of it. He had no doubt Chalice would follow through on his threat if Paul showed any further disloyalty. By probing TARC's finances, he was risking his freedom, perhaps his life. But if he failed, he'd be at the mercy of that blackmailer from Washington . . . whose boss was more powerful than all the other players put together.

How had his life suddenly gotten so complicated?

"Good man," Chalice said, rising from his chair. "Sometimes you need reminding of what I know and what I could do to you."

"Yes, Reverend."

Paul's phone pinged with a text as Chalice exited the room. He picked it up and scanned the small screen.

Contact made, it read. We'll find out where the trail leads. Don't worry.

If Chalice wouldn't confess the truth, Paul had his own methods of finding out where the money came from. He was risking everything by digging, but he had no choice.

From now on, he'd play things better. He'd be that lapdog to Chalice he'd been when he started. Even to Thigpen if that was necessary. He'd find what that person in Washington wanted so he could start his life over again—with Billie.

When Paul returned to the phone's home screen, it hit him: he had no personalized screen saver. Translated: there was nothing in his life he cared enough about to be reminded of.

He navigated to his texts and took a deep breath while gazing at the selfie Billie had sent him a few hours ago. He smiled . . . an innocent, childlike smile he hadn't smiled in what seemed like forever.

Maybe there was something he cared about enough to put on his screen after all.

◆ ◆ ◆

New Orleans, Louisiana

"Justice for Kelvin, justice for Kelvin!" three hundred people chanted as they amassed before the James house.

The small three-bedroom ranch was in a state of disrepair. Siding was coming off in many places, the roof sagged, and the front stoop was crumbling. It was home to a single mother and her six children. Not seven now that her eldest—Kelvin—had been murdered.

"Charge Breaux with murder!" someone shouted above the chant.

"Charge the cop with murder, charge the cop with murder!"

The three hundred smoothly altered their chant. As if they'd made that kind of a transition thousands of times before—because they had. They were professionals. In fact, they'd nicknamed themselves the Riot Actors. They parachuted into a neighborhood, lit a protest bonfire, then slipped back out of town after Paul had arranged for enough locals to take up the cause—and before the authorities realized the Riot Actors were from out of town.

"How did you find the eyewitness to Kelvin's murder?" the Barbie-look-alike TV reporter asked Talia Seven Feathers as the camera rolled with the angry, sign-wielding crowd as a backdrop. "How do you know Kelvin James was murdered by Officer Huey Breaux?"

"Oh, we found the eyewitness all right. And we know for certain Officer Breaux murdered Kelvin James."

"Yes, but how do you know—"

The reporter was cut short by the sound of screeching tires. Multiple SWAT trucks skidded to a halt on the street, and Kevlar-covered officers wielding guns and clubs poured out.

As the three hundred hired protesters screamed and tore off, Bones grabbed Talia's wrist and dragged her away from the cameras.

"We gotta get out of here!" he shouted, pulling her between the James house and an equally broken-down home to the left. "Come on!"

Bones glanced over his shoulder as they sprinted off together. Four officers in riot gear were chasing them, ignoring easier prey.

"They're following us!" he shouted.

"They saw me talking to the reporter! They figure I'm in charge!"

"We can't get caught! They'll link us to TARC!"

They darted left down a narrow alley littered with broken glass and used heroin needles. Weighed down by gear, the four officers were still gaining ground. Just inches a stride but still gaining. The sound of their big black boots crushing glass was getting louder.

"This way!"

Bones grabbed Talia again and led her across the crabgrass-covered ground between two more houses, then dashed left around one of them and tumbled behind a huge boxwood bush beside the front stoop. Seconds later, the officers raced past.

He was about to jump up and head the other way.

But it was her turn to take the lead.

She slipped her fingers to his jaw, pulled his lips to hers, and kissed him passionately.

CHAPTER 6

Upstate New York

Despite the circumstances, Falcon felt himself relax during the long drive from Manhattan to upstate New York—particularly the last hour of it as he sped deeper and deeper into the vast, barely populated Adirondack Mountain Range.

He was an avid fisherman, and his casting arm twitched with anticipation at having so many blue-ribbon trout rivers so close at hand. Beautiful waters, these in particular, haunted him. It was in these mountains and on these secluded gin-clear rivers where his father had taught him the art of fly-fishing, of making a rainbow rise to a tiny fly imitation, of fooling one of nature's most beautiful creatures.

And it was a chance to escape a city that imposed claustrophobia on each and every resident. Even those who claimed to love living in its concrete jungle—which Falcon definitely did not. He would have gladly traded the Upper West Side for a cabin in Montana or Wyoming. But he had no choice. Manhattan was the epicenter of the financial universe, and the virtual galaxy extended only so far.

He'd shut off his phone to mask his movements, so no one could track him from cell tower to cell tower. The satisfying consequence was that no one could reach him. So he had a few hours to himself.

But every time he began to enjoy the solitude, he thought of Claire being held by captors and how terrified she must be. And that horrible thought caused him to jam the accelerator down and drive faster.

He was driving his jet-black Shelby GT500. He didn't get to enjoy it often. But he kept the classic '67 Mustang in mint condition at a private garage a few blocks from his apartment so it was ready and waiting nearby the few times he did.

He wasn't a car buff. The Mustang had been his father's favorite mode of transportation before he'd gone out that Wall Street window.

Fortunately, Falcon had managed to hide the car from the creditors as they were closing in—and not for its significant monetary value. He'd hidden it because it was his most prized connection to his dad. He felt close to his father every time he slipped behind the steering wheel and brought the powerful engine roaring to life. He remembered riding in the Mustang on weekends as a boy, of having Senior all to himself during those times.

As Falcon whipped around a tight turn on the winding mountain road, he met the blinding high beams of another vehicle. It was the first one he'd seen in twenty miles, and he quickly flicked off his bright lights—though the other driver didn't.

"Prick," he muttered as he shielded his eyes, flicking on his high beams again the instant the other car was gone. He'd barely missed a big buck deer a few minutes ago, and he wanted no part of a collision with another one. More important, he was closing in on his objective and didn't want to miss it.

"There," he said, nodding at the break in the trees rapidly approaching on the left. "Gravel driveway nine-point-six miles past Murphy Falls . . . like the note says."

He pulled to a quick stop when the Mustang's wide tires crunched gravel. Far ahead, the driveway disappeared between pine trees lining both sides of the narrow valley falling to the rocky strip. If someone wanted to trap him—at least so he couldn't escape on wheels—it wouldn't be hard.

The image of Claire's beautiful face rose to his mind like a daffodil blooming as he gazed out over the hood. He'd spoken to Sally several times since the confrontation with the three men outside the Stock Exchange. He hadn't told her about them or why he'd called her at two o'clock this morning. He'd simply vowed to find Claire after Sally began sobbing a few seconds into the call.

"This is where it starts," he said under his breath, teeth gritted, giving the Mustang its reins after turning his phone back on and checking his watch. It was five to midnight. "I will find her. And people will pay."

Minutes later, he eased to a stop in front of a solitary two-story cabin built at the end of the gravel driveway and the edge of a small clearing. The first-floor windows were brightly illuminated. After checking his phone and committing to memory the most important data points it displayed, then turning the phone off again, he climbed out of the car into the chilly night air of the mountains.

Halfway up the slate path, the front door opened. "I'm here to see Mr. Sykes," he called out to the person who'd emerged from inside.

The young woman standing on the porch smiled slyly. "I'm Danny Sykes."

"It's nice to meet you, Danny. Where's my niece?" He saw no reason to beat around the bush. And he made certain to show no surprise at being met by a woman. "I want to see Claire *now*."

"Who's Claire?"

"The person you'd better hand over in the next few seconds," he snarled, starting toward the young woman.

Who calmly raised a shotgun from beneath her knee-length windbreaker. "If I were you, I'd stop right there."

Falcon did, ten feet away, because it made no sense not to. He turned his head slightly as he gazed at her. She had long, dark hair that framed her pretty, exotically featured face as it cascaded down her shoulders and glistened in the light shining through the open doorway and windows. He could see her flashing eyes were sapphire. And there was a crazy look in them that had turned even fierier when she pointed the gun at him.

"Don't even think about drawing the pistol I'm betting is wedged into your belt at the small of your back," she warned him. "We know about your concealed weapon permit."

"I don't—"

"And your gambling habits." The eyebrow went even higher. "I know all about you."

Falcon prided himself on reading people quickly. So far he was enjoying the first chapter of this manuscript despite both barrels of the gun pointed at him. Or maybe because they were. The young woman standing on the porch was startlingly attractive and had a fascinating edge to her. He'd never met anyone like her.

"Well, well, well," she said, keeping the gun leveled at him, "Andrew Blake Falcon Junior in the flesh. You're the first man in T. U. Sutton history to make partner before the age of forty. Of course," she added, her tone turning acidic, "there's never been a female partner."

"How do you know I'm a partner?"

"How do you think?"

"Twenty-four possibilities." He assumed he could delete Wallace and Rose from the list. But maybe not Michael Mattix. The whispered warning from Mattix after the vote was still echoing in his mind. "And I can rule out two of them."

"You never know, Mr. Falcon. Maybe Jimmy Three Sticks is our mole."

She seemed to be enjoying this. "Where's my niece?" he asked again, watching her eyes flicker around, as if she were on the lookout for something—or someone. "Where is Claire?" Maybe she thought he'd brought someone else along.

"I'm here to talk about something other than your niece."

"Then I'm out of here," he called, turning back toward the Mustang.

"She's safe," the young woman spoke up loudly. "But she's not here. She's still in North Carolina."

Falcon stopped and turned deliberately back around.

"And if you don't do what we want, she dies. It's that simple."

"That's pretty cold." He paused. "Billie."

The young woman's eyes flashed wide open and the crazy look in them turned to confusion, then, for an instant, to fear.

"How do you know my real—"

"If you've studied me so thoroughly, you know I invest in many things, Billie, mostly publicly traded stocks and bonds. But sometimes, when I know it's a sure thing, I go the venture route to seriously juice my returns. I see lots of cutting-edge technologies. Entrepreneurs come to me constantly with new ideas. I back a few. Only the ones I'm sure will make me serious money." Falcon gestured over his shoulder at the Mustang. "Before I got out, I checked the texts and e-mails on your phone."

"What?"

"Thanks to a little Silicon Valley company I invested in last month that isn't going to be little much longer."

"How can you—"

"If I'm within a hundred feet of your cell phone, I can see anything on it with mine. And let me just say that's quite the selfie you took in the mirror and then sent your boyfriend earlier tonight. I really liked the way you had your hair." She'd been nude in the photo. "At least, I *hope* Paul is your boyfriend."

"My God, I can't believe you—"

"What do you want to talk about?" he interrupted again. "Get to the point."

Her eyes narrowed as she nodded. "Good, Mr. Falcon, that's what I wanted to hear."

"Well, do me a favor while you're listening, Billie."

"What?"

"Call me A.J."

The first chance he got, he'd put his tech-superior information bloodhounds on the case and have them track down the person behind every last number and e-mail on Billie's phone—the technology allowed him to see the data *and* capture it on his phone. He'd have lots to go on by this time tomorrow, and that thought comforted him. He was going to find Claire.

"And lower the gun. We both know you're not going to shoot me."

"You have no idea what I'm capable of . . . A.J."

She was crazy, for sure. But she wasn't going to shoot him, at least not tonight. That wouldn't serve her purpose, whoever she was or whoever she represented—and was why he hadn't hesitated to describe the technology his phone was armed with. He'd wanted to deliver the shock-and-awe factor. Judging by her expression, he had.

"Come on, Billie, tell me what you want to know." She seemed to wince every time he said her name. "I need to be on Wall Street in a few hours."

Baltimore, Maryland

Police cars tore through the early morning of Baltimore, a city skewered by racial tension long before the Freddie Gray disaster. Emergency lights flashing and sirens screaming, the cops raced for the Inner Harbor, the city's prime tourist district. A multiple stabbing horror show had been called in, and Baltimore was addicted to its tourist revenue. The city could not afford bad publicity—not when it came to this area of town.

The first responders squealed to a stop, jumped from their cars, and sprinted for the location of the alleged stabbing, drawing their pistols as they burst into the bright lights of the area near the permanently docked historic warship USS *Constellation*.

"This way!" the sergeant shouted over his shoulder, motioning to his men. "Follow me!"

Moments after the men in blue streamed into the light, Quentin Jefferson—a decorated marine sniper—began firing his assault rifle from the sharpshooter's nest he'd constructed on the fifth floor of a parking garage overlooking the Inner Harbor.

The sergeant was the first to die—from a single bullet through the heart.

Then the others began to fall.

When the nightmare was over, the black sniper had assassinated six white police officers. Jefferson was dead, too, his body riddled by seventeen bullets, the last of which had blown his head apart.

When the assault team made it to where Jefferson lay, there was a note pinned to his blood-drenched shirt. It was addressed to the officers.

◆ ◆ ◆

North Woods, Wisconsin

The young woman stood before General Fiske in the same seven-inch red heels she'd performed in last night on the intimate North Woods stage thirty miles north of here. Except for the shoes, she was naked.

While she sobbed, Fiske inhaled deeply to calm himself, titillated by her anguish.

He'd immobilized her ten minutes ago, after his third orgasm. Her wrists were cuffed together above her head. The cuffs were chained to a hook in the ceiling so she was forced to stand on her tiptoes. And each ankle was secured in place by a wrought-iron shackle. He could do *anything* he wanted to her. Sex had been good, but this was the best part by far. It always was.

He shook his head, disgusted with himself.

Disgusted but excited. He never felt more alive than he did at this moment—when he was playing God.

So far Brady and his crew had executed tonight's mission perfectly. They'd kidnapped the woman without anyone noticing right before she went into the club, dropped her off here after sedating her so she couldn't get away from him or resist during sex, then headed back to the tiny town and the single-wide trailer to complete the mission. At this moment they were framing the girl's passed-out boyfriend, planting obvious and incriminating clues around the trailer. Sentencing him to life behind bars for a crime he wouldn't commit.

"Please let me go," she begged pitifully. "I've done everything you told me to do."

"Ordered you to do," he hissed.

"Sorry, sorry, *ordered*. I forgot I was supposed to say 'ordered.' Just please set me free."

"I'm about to do just that," he replied.

"Oh, thank God," she whispered, another sob racking her body. This time it erupted from immeasurable relief instead of mortal fear. "I promise I won't tell anyone about tonight."

"No, you won't," he agreed as he threaded a rope around her neck and then tied the ends together so the rope formed a loose noose. "You *definitely* won't."

"What are you doing?" she screamed, frantically trying to twist and turn away. "I thought you were setting me free."

"Oh, I am," he assured her as he slipped a short piece of PVC pipe into the noose and began to turn, creating a twisting knot that slowly approached her soft throat.

"Don't kill me; please don't kill me!"

He loved her screams—which no one could hear from this lonely basement in the middle of the woods. Earlier this afternoon, Brady and his assassins had killed the six family members who were vacationing here and stacked their bodies in the attic.

"I'm setting you free forever," he added. "I wish someone would do the same for me."

As she begged and struggled, Fiske leaned forward so his face was only inches from hers. He wanted to see from close range the exact moment the light in her eyes extinguished. He wanted to watch her struggle all the way to the end, even though she must have known her death was close at hand and that there was absolutely nothing she could do about it. This was the only thing that truly excited him anymore.

He swallowed hard with anticipation when the knot reached her throat and she began choking. When she was dead, he'd have sex with her one more time. He always felt most guilty for that, though not nearly enough to stop himself.

Someone definitely needed to catch him. Someone definitely needed to stop him. Because he sure as hell couldn't stop himself.

He was about to finish her off when his cell phone rang. So he loosened the noose and stuffed a gag down her throat. She was a fighter. She wouldn't die until he wanted her to.

"What is it?"

The man on the other line was someone Brady didn't know about yet but who shared their vision of America's supremacy. "Baltimore exploded right on time."

"And?"

"Six white officers are dead."

"What about Jefferson?"

"Dead, too."

"Excellent. The only witness is gone." He glanced at the young woman. He thrived on the desperation in her eyes. She had no say in the matter. He would make all her choices from here to the end. "Make sure our right-wing allies in the press bark about this thing for weeks. Make sure the world knows all about Mr. Jefferson."

"Yes, sir."

"And make sure we demand action from President Hilton. Ask her point-blank what she's going to do about blacks killing white cops in America. She won't do a damn thing, of course, and we must make very sure white America sees that very, very clearly."

"Yes, sir."

"Don't bother me again tonight unless the North Koreans launch nuclear weapons."

"Yes, sir."

Fiske put the phone down, pulled the gag from the woman's mouth, and wiped the tears from her face. "Now," he said, "where were we, young lady?"

CHAPTER 7

Upstate New York

Falcon sped through the steep-walled canyon, twisting and turning along the narrow, winding road. He had a four-hour-plus drive back to Manhattan ahead of him, and it was already past 2:00 a.m. He wouldn't have time to go back to his place on the Upper West Side to shower and change because he had a crucial 7:00 a.m. meeting at Sutton & Company. The Asian investor he was sitting down with had more than a billion dollars to deploy. And the man had made it clear on a call last week from the other side of the globe that he was leaning toward putting all of it into Falcon's soaring hedge funds. Whales like this didn't come halfway around the globe to be delayed.

Falcon wasn't tired. He'd always been able to skip a night of sleep and be fine the next day. Still, he rubbed his eyes hard as he sped along—out of disbelief. What Billie had told him seemed crazy, more like impossible. Her claims about Sutton made no sense. That they'd have a connection to . . . Well, it seemed utterly irrational to him.

He'd have to be very careful trying to get the information that would prove it. If what Billie claimed was going on turned out to be true, the people who were keeping the secret would probably think nothing of going to great lengths to keep the conspiracy quiet. Because if the connection actually existed, there had to be a very dark purpose behind it.

He took a deep breath. He needed to get the numbers and e-mails from Billie's phone to his IT bloodhounds ASAP—so they could unearth the full names and addresses behind the numbers and e-mails—even if he had to ice the Asian investor for a short while. That billion-dollar investment would translate into at least another $10 million a year of income to Sutton—but rescuing Claire took priority over *everything*. He had no faith that these people would release Claire even if he did get them the proof they were searching for so desperately. He had to assume Claire's safety was in his hands . . . and his alone. *That* was why he had to get Billie's phone to his people immediately. With the information on Billie's phone, he was confident he could save Claire.

But could he save his Sutton career? Would he want to if what Billie had told him turned out to be true?

The instant he spotted the headlights in the Mustang's rearview mirror, he realized the car was coming at him fast. Now he had to decide if whoever was driving the car was coming *for* him.

The vehicle raced up behind him but then remained a hundred feet back, pacing the Mustang. Falcon accelerated from seventy to eighty to ninety, but the trailing car stayed right with him.

When Falcon reached a hundred miles an hour at the top of a long straightaway, the car behind him darted left into the oncoming lane.

Falcon slammed on his brakes, and the other car went flying past— slamming on its brakes, too.

Whoever was driving was definitely coming *for* him.

Falcon executed a quick three-point U-turn—as did the other driver—and sped off in the direction he'd just come from . . . with the other car in pursuit. He could have jumped out of the Mustang when he slammed to a stop and fought, or tried to hide in the forest. But there might be several people in the sleek Mercedes that had careered past a few seconds ago. He wasn't into those odds—despite being armed— especially in the dark, when people equipped with night-vision, infrared capability could spread out in the woods and track him down.

He was constantly thinking worst-case scenario in pressure situations. His father had trained him to always think that way, to always anticipate an enemy's move. Then what they did was no surprise and you could react to their move instantly.

As he raced ahead, he reached beneath his seat, grabbed the Beretta .9mm from its hiding place beneath the seat, and slipped it under his left thigh. Billie had been exactly right. The gun was wedged into his belt at the small of his back as he'd moved up the slate path toward the cabin. He'd chambered the first round and slipped it there as he was climbing from the Mustang. And he hadn't removed that chambered bullet after getting back in the car to leave. The gun was still ready to fire.

He'd put it beneath his seat before heading up the long gravel driveway toward the main road after leaving Billie—who'd assured him several times that Claire was fine and wouldn't be harmed as long as he cooperated.

The speedometer needle pushed past a hundred again as he hurtled through the night, his focus flashing constantly from the windshield to his mirrors. Any oncoming vehicle could be working with the car chasing him. He had to be aware of that. What he couldn't figure out was why. Why were they trying to run him down if they so desperately wanted information from him?

A pickup truck whipped by going in the opposite direction without incident as the Mustang screamed past the top of the gravel driveway into uncharted territory. He was heading deeper and deeper into the Adirondacks, away from where he wanted to go.

The Mustang might be faster flat-out, he figured. But it didn't have the modern suspension the Mercedes did.

Within thirty seconds, his enemy had caught him on the winding road.

Falcon kept blocking his pursuer by darting left and right as the Mercedes tried to pass. But as they swung around another tight turn, the chase car managed to get around the Mustang and speed up beside Falcon on the passenger side.

Again he slammed on his brakes.

Again the chase car did, too. But its front end suddenly swerved right, and the tire dipped into a deep ditch between the road and the valley wall as the car fishtailed. The Mercedes plunged down and cartwheeled once violently.

Falcon skidded to a halt, grabbed the .9mm, climbed from the Mustang, and sprinted for the battered Mercedes—on its side in the ditch—pistol leading his way.

At twenty feet, he stopped in the middle of the road, legs straddling the double yellow lines. The Mercedes engine was still roaring, and he could smell gasoline. He moved deliberately through the darkness, both palms clasped around the gun's composite handle.

But there was no need to shoot. The man behind the wheel was dead. His head lay against the steering wheel, eyes and mouth open and bloodied. The man in the passenger seat was slumped forward. He looked dead as well—at least unconscious.

"Help!" someone yelled in a muffled voice.

Falcon stepped back quickly, bringing his pistol up just as flames shot out from beneath the side of the hood.

"Help me! *Please*, somebody help me."

The screams were coming from the trunk, Falcon realized, recognizing the female voice. It was Billie's.

He tried opening the driver-side door so he could pop the trunk as the flames reached higher and higher, licking at the windshield. But it was jammed shut from the crash, and this was a Mercedes coupe, so there was no backseat door.

Falcon dashed to the back of the car and desperately tried to open the trunk, searching for a button to push or a way to pry it open. The front of the Mercedes was now engulfed in flames.

Billie shrieked in panic. She could undoubtedly smell the flames.

Falcon slipped the pistol into his belt, grabbed a softball-size rock from the ditch, bashed the latch repeatedly, and finally forced the trunk open. He reached inside, scooped up Billie, and sprinted toward the Mustang with her in his arms. They reached a safe distance just as the Mercedes exploded, illuminating the area with a gigantic fireball.

Falcon set Billie down gently on the asphalt behind the Mustang so they were protected in case there was a second fireball. She was bleeding badly from a deep gash on the side of her head. And, as he untied her wrists, he saw that her left forearm had been broken in the crash. The lower half of it was bent at a sickening angle.

"I'll get you to a hospital."

"No," she gasped, "there'd be a record of me checking in, and then they could find me."

"Who are *they*?" Her arm must be killing her, but he had to know. "Who could find you?"

She gazed at him desperately. "I don't know."

He clenched his jaw. She was a good liar. "OK, let's go."

He helped her up, eased her gingerly into the passenger side of the Mustang, and sprinted for the driver side. He'd figure out something, some way to take care of her. But right now he had to put distance between them and the cabin. Billie was involved with Claire's kidnapping, which he hated her for.

But at this point, she was his only connection to his niece.

◆ ◆ ◆

North Woods, Wisconsin

"Open up!" the Wisconsin state policeman shouted as he banged on the single-wide's front door. He stood to one side of it to protect himself in case the man inside started shooting. His partner was covering the back door in case the guy ran. *"Open up!"*

The cop had tried peering inside the trailer through the windows, but all the curtains were drawn. The neighbor who'd called in the report claimed to have heard a woman screaming. And the guy who lived here had already been arrested twice for beating his girlfriend bloody. The silence didn't bode well.

The cop stepped in front of the door and bashed it in with one swift kick. At the same moment, his partner kicked in the back door, and the two officers met in the living room. At the chair in which the young man was passed out, an empty plastic cup lay on its side on the floor just beneath his outstretched fingertips.

"Keep an eye on him," the cop called to his partner as he headed toward the back.

The young woman lay sprawled on her stomach on the floor of the first bedroom, arms extended above her head. She was naked except for one red high heel.

He knelt down beside her and pressed two fingers to her neck. Dead.

Fifteen minutes later, the ambulance arrived, and the cops guided the young man who'd been passed out in the chair to the back of their cruiser, wrists cuffed tightly behind his back. It took both of them to get him from the trailer to the cruiser because he could barely walk, he was so drunk—they thought.

They had no idea what was actually coursing through his veins—in addition to the vodka. Or that the young woman had been murdered elsewhere and her body brought to the trailer thirty minutes ago.

Brady smiled thinly as he watched from inside a grove of pine trees while the officers struggled to stash their obvious suspect into the back of the cruiser. He knew exactly what was coursing through the young man's body. He also knew the young man was just beginning his journey into a life behind bars at a state penitentiary—but he felt no sympathy or remorse. The kid was a slimeball. In fact, Brady was the "neighbor" who'd called in the supposed disturbance.

"And that's that," he muttered as he hustled off through the trees. His team—minus the man he'd sent to New York City at Fiske's direction—was waiting for him in an SUV parked on a dirt road half a mile away.

He and his men had to get to that time-sensitive job in Billings, Montana—the one Fiske had been contacted about while they'd stood outside the strip club. Then he had to get back to Washington to meet with Fiske at the Pentagon.

He'd find a uniform somewhere.

◆ ◆ ◆

Near Charlotte, North Carolina

She'd been fighting the ropes binding her wrists behind her back for hours. Praying harder and harder as she slowly made progress that the men who were holding her here—wherever *here* was—wouldn't open the closet door and discover that she almost had her hands free. Once she did, she'd whip off the blindfold, quickly untie her ankles, and *run*—even though they'd taken her shoes off her. She was positive she hadn't heard a lock click on the closet door the times they'd brought her the stale crackers and water.

Claire caught her breath and froze the instant she thought she heard someone walking heavily down the hallway outside the room. There were three men involved. She recognized each of their voices as they took turns checking on her and warning her not to try anything stupid, that they'd kill her if she did. At least they'd allowed her privacy in the bathroom the two times they let her use it. They told her the window was nailed shut just in case she was thinking about escaping.

They'd untied the ropes around her wrists those two times but ordered her to keep the blindfold on while she was alone. She'd obeyed. They seemed extremely nervous when they spoke, and she didn't want anything setting them off.

A toilet flushed, and this time she was certain she heard footsteps. But this time the heavy, plodding strides were coming at her.

When the room door creaked loudly, she lay down on the floor so she was facing out, so her wrists were hidden behind her. A rush of cool air eased over her when the closet door opened. She breathed deliberately and deeply, feigning sleep.

"The pretty young thing sleeps," the man muttered. "If your uncle doesn't come through," he hissed, "I'm gonna have some fun with you before we kill you." He chuckled meanly. "Maybe I will even if Uncle A.J. does come through."

When he was gone, she resumed her battle against the ropes, more terrified than ever.

Slowly but surely, her palms came closer and closer to slipping through the nooses. Finally, her left hand was free, then her right. She ripped off the blindfold and then the bindings around her ankles.

Her heart pounded wildly as she slipped from the closet and stole through the darkness to the window—which was nailed shut. She glanced outside into the night but could see nothing. It was so dark she couldn't tell if the house was in a neighborhood or in the middle of nowhere. She'd been blindfolded and bound during the long ride from her house, so she had no idea where she was. But it didn't matter. Anywhere was better than here.

She moved to the room door and reached for the knob but pulled her hand back just as her fingers were about to touch metal, as though she'd just been shocked. The door would creak when she opened it, alerting the men.

Claire stood like a statue at the door for what seemed like forever. Terrified to open it. Petrified not to.

But it was the only way out.

She turned the knob and whipped the door open, hoping that by doing so fast, there might not be any noise. But it still creaked loudly on its hinges.

She sprinted down the dark hallway into the living room and tripped over a chair. She tumbled to the floor but was up instantly. The men were suddenly shouting to each other from somewhere behind her.

She hurled open the front door and raced down the porch steps, across a dirt driveway, into a huge field of knee-high grass, and toward the tree line and a thick pine forest where she could hide from these men.

In the dim moonlight, she could see no other homes around—just this lone farmhouse in this little valley. No one who might hear her if she screamed.

As she sprinted across the field as hard and fast as she could in her bare feet, Claire heard dogs barking wildly behind her—and her heart shattered. She wasn't going to make it anywhere near the tree line before the dogs caught her. And it wouldn't matter if she did because the dogs would track her down.

In a few minutes she'd be back in that closet—or worse.

Still, she ran.

◆　◆　◆

Manhattan, New York

As Michael Mattix sat up on his side of the king-size bed, the dim light of dawn seeping through the penthouse window, he glanced proudly over his shoulder at his trophy wife's gorgeous silhouette. Monique was lying naked beneath the silk sheet, breathing softly while she slept. In the low light, he could still make out her exquisite shape. She was an auburn-haired supermodel half his age who possessed a sex drive exceeding even his own.

Monique had been sent to him from heaven, Mattix was convinced. Part of the reason he'd allowed himself to be manipulated by the aide representing that high-ranking Washington official, to set them up with someone at Sutton who could get the information they sought, was because he had to be thankful and pay heaven back for his trophy. There needed to be a social conscience somewhere at Sutton's highest level. And because it wasn't going to be him who actually did the dirty work.

Giving them Andrew Falcon's name had made him feel better about his divorce, too, as though there was a higher purpose for abandoning so abruptly his first wife of twenty-one years.

And then there was the real reason he'd cooperated with the senior DC politician: the undeniable proof of his insider trading three years ago—on which he'd made $7 million, enough to pay for that house in the Bahamas—which he'd managed to hide from the divorce judge and his ex-wife. The insider trading problem had sealed the deal when the aide had presented the evidence to him so matter-of-factly.

Take what I'm offering or you go to jail.

He'd taken the offer.

The divorce from his first wife had cost him an arm and a leg. But even after two years of senseless legal wrangling to gain his marital freedom, he still tipped the net worth scale at more than half a billion—though most of that was his illiquid ownership of Sutton. However, the sex he was getting constantly from the most beautiful female creation he'd ever laid eyes on made the exorbitant price of his liberty worth every hundred million.

What he should do at this moment was stand up, get dressed, and go directly down to Wall Street in the back of his chauffeured limousine. The mergers and acquisitions group he ran at Sutton was set to close three blockbuster deals by the end of the week. In the aggregate, the mega-transactions totaled more than $100 billion. That meant at least a billion dollars in success fees for him and his twenty-four partners, who now included A.J. Falcon.

Mattix had given Falcon that quick, cryptic warning at the partnership meeting, when Falcon had been voted in. He couldn't help himself. After all, he had been the man's mentor for seven years. But Wallace had shot him that long, cold look afterward, and he'd instantly regretted whispering what he had to Falcon. He just hoped he wasn't reading too much into that look from Wallace.

Negotiations were still ongoing in each of those huge takeover battles they were trying to close. High-stakes poker games were still being played. Mattix would have many complex decisions to make today in order to best represent Sutton's three sell-side clients, in order to ease hostilities and make everyone wildly rich in the process. He needed to get downtown.

Mattix began to stand up but then eased back onto the bed. Ten minutes wouldn't make a difference. He chuckled softly. Besides, it wouldn't take ten minutes. More like two. He was already primed.

He caught his breath as he turned toward her, startled. Instantly, his heart was in his throat, pounding madly.

Monique was kneeling before him on the mattress, hands on her thighs. "Don't ever do that to me again, Michael," she purred in French as his shoulders sagged in relief. His nerves had been on alert after thinking about that look Wallace had shot him. "Don't ever leave me in the morning without fucking me."

Monique wasn't from France. And her name wasn't really Monique. Mattix had thoroughly investigated her before turning his life upside down. He let his dick go only so far before he put his brain back in charge. At his core, he was a strategist.

Monique's real name was Katy Gundersen, and she was from a small farming community in central South Dakota. She was actually of Scandinavian descent and had taught herself the broken French she used during their lovemaking by studying it on the Internet.

She'd never studied a foreign language in high school. In fact, she'd never even graduated from high school. She'd been discovered quite by accident, walking down Main Street in her tiny town one chilly October morning, by the husband of a New York City fashion maven who was hunting pheasant and had been entering a greasy spoon for breakfast before heading out to the fields to blast birds. A week later, Katy was Monique and Monique was strutting down catwalks instead of high school hallways.

Monique put her soft arms around Mattix's neck and kissed him passionately, pressing her full, natural breasts to his chest as she slipped her tongue deep into his mouth. She ran her long nails down his chest and stomach, and he gasped when her fingers closed around him.

"You love it," she murmured into his mouth, "you love what I do for you."

"I'm addicted to it, to *you*," he readily admitted, slipping a finger inside her. She was already so wet. "Like an addict to heroin."

"Good," she gasped, "that's what I want. I don't want you even *looking* at anyone else."

She'd told him during their first intimacy that she needed to come at least once a day or her body would rebel. She was upfront with him that during the times he was away, when he was traveling on Sutton business, she took care of herself. He hadn't liked that revelation at first. But, he figured, it was better for her to do it than give someone else a chance.

Now she turned him on by doing it. She'd moan and gasp to him on the other end of the phone while he listened in his hotel room, sometimes while he was in meetings. And she sent pictures and videos of herself doing it—all so he wouldn't be angry with her. She was a problem solver. He loved that about her.

"Lie back," she ordered.

Who was he to object?

When he was on his back, she crawled between his legs and went down on him. Within seconds, he was on the edge.

"Not yet," she murmured. "I get mine first. Then you get yours."

She knew him so well.

She moved slowly up his body, running her tongue up his stomach and chest to his neck, before mounting him. As they found their rhythm, she arched her back and began to moan in time with his thrusts. She pulled his fingers to her long, pink nipples and urged him to twist them gently. Her moans quickly turned to screams when he did it exactly as he knew she craved.

How quickly Monique climaxed amazed Mattix. It had always taken his first wife at least fifteen minutes—if she even could. And that was when she hadn't had it in a month.

Fifteen seconds later, Monique's screams reached their peak—he wondered if they awoke the people in the apartment below during these early-morning romps—and then she slumped onto him, breathing hard, cooing in his ear.

"Your turn," she finally murmured when her strength returned.

She started moving up and down on him. But after a few moments, he pushed her down, gently but firmly, so she was between his legs again. "I want your mouth," he whispered.

"I like that," she whispered back. "I like you taking control when I'm finished, taking what *you* want now."

So he took a fistful of her long, thick, silky hair in his hand, forcing her so far down on him she gagged, finally releasing her when she began to struggle. *God, how I adore this,* he thought as he allowed his head to fall back onto the pillow, as he allowed her to work her magic.

"I have a surprise for you, Michael," she said as she worked.

"What?" he managed through his teeth, clenching them in pleasure.

"My friend Jasmine is coming to New York from Paris next week. You met her last month at the London fashion show."

"I remember," he gasped, picturing the exotic, doe-eyed, long-legged Latina. "What about her?" But he already knew. Monique was crazy, and he couldn't get enough of her insanity.

"I told her I want to give you an early birthday present. The best birthday present you've ever had," she whispered. "I told her you need two supermodels all weekend to do anything you want with."

He felt himself losing control instantly at the thought. "But . . . but you said I wasn't to even . . . to even look at . . ."

"As long as I suggest and initiate, it's all right."

He had only moments left, and he grabbed her head with both hands and pushed it down just before he exploded.

The instant his orgasm went into overdrive, her teeth clenched down on him. He twisted and shouted, pulling her hair as violently as possible to get her to stop, ripping long strands from her head in the process.

But it was no use.

As he endured the final stages of his orgasm through the awful pain of her bite, he suddenly realized why it was no use.

◆ ◆ ◆

The assassin dropped the pistol with the silencer attached onto the mattress and clamped Mattix's throat tightly with both gloved hands. He'd shot the beautiful young woman in the back and blown her heart to bits with one well-aimed bullet just as Mattix had gone over the edge, causing the woman to clamp down on Mattix in an excruciatingly painful death bite, like a hunter's snare clamping down onto a wild animal's leg. It was beautiful, as beautiful as the young woman had been only moments ago.

Mattix grabbed the assassin's forearms, tufts of Monique's shredded hair still entwined in his fingers, desperately trying to pry the other man's hands from his neck. But he was no match for the man behind the black ski mask.

"I want you to die slowly," the assassin hissed. "I could have shot you like I shot your wife. But I want you to suffer." He tightened his grip one more turn as Mattix choked pitifully. "I want you to suffer so badly, you fucking traitor, you fucking Benedict Arnold."

Mattix's body finally relaxed when his breathing ceased. But the assassin maintained his grip for a full sixty seconds after Mattix's eyes turned to the thousand-yard stare.

When it was done and the assassin was certain Mattix was dead, he rose up and pulled his phone from his pocket. It had vibrated while Mattix was dying.

He glanced at the now-illuminated screen. Brady and the rest of the team were already heading for Billings, Montana. He needed to hurry if he was going to catch the first flight west out of Newark and make the mission on time.

CHAPTER 8

Washington, DC

"Thank you all for coming to the White House this morning on such short notice," Katrina said authoritatively but graciously after breezing into the press room and moving behind the waist-high dais bearing the presidential seal. "I realize it's an inconvenience, but you'll be very glad you pried yourselves out of bed at the crack of dawn when you hear what I have to say." She gave the room the million-dollar smile she was famous for. "So let's get right to it. The initiative I'm announcing this morning is called Prosperity for All, or PFA for short, and it has three major components." She made eye contact with as many of the assembled press corps members who were packed into the room as possible. "First, the wealthy will finally pay their fair share. They'll be taxed at much higher rates not only on their incomes but on their wealth as well. *Before* they die," she added forcefully. "*Well* before . . . and we're talking rates of sixty to seventy percent at the appropriate income levels."

An audible murmur rose from the room.

"At the same time, I'm going to lower tax rates on Middle America and the poor. A family earning fifty thousand dollars a year shouldn't be sending forty percent of their income to Washington."

She was using Jordan's line: simple but effective. It was an exaggeration, but she was making a point.

"The second component of Prosperity for All involves the military. I'm going to cut the Department of Defense's annual budget from its current one trillion dollars down to two hundred billion."

A much louder rumble rolled through the crowd of reporters. It was one thing to hike tax rates on the rich while lowering rates for Middle America and the poor. That ship had sailed into oblivion and back many times through the course of history. But slashing the DoD budget by 80 percent was different.

In all the ways that mattered, Katrina had just declared war on the Pentagon, on her own protectors and enforcers. It would seem a foolish move to the press and public, to anyone who wanted to hurt the president. But Katrina knew what they didn't. Katrina had the Black Book.

"With all due respect, Madam President," a young reporter spoke up, "the Department of Defense's annual budget is only seven hundred billon."

Katrina couldn't have asked for a better setup, and she wondered if her chief of staff had spoken to the woman about making the remark. "Only?" she asked in a leading tone.

The entire room—save the young reporter—broke into hearty laughter.

"Not when you take into account other department shares, it isn't," Katrina explained. "There's another three hundred billion spread around, mostly at the Energy Department, which you obviously aren't familiar with. Take cues and learn from your more experienced comrades."

The wet-behind-the-ears reporter had just been schooled. Several of the older press members nodded to each other knowingly.

"Now," Katrina continued, raising her hand and her voice to signal quiet, "we'll stair-step the military cuts down over several years. But make no mistake, *we will make them*. It's time to stop spending America's money on things we don't need. It's time to stop giving the Joint Chiefs so many toys they don't need. It's time to take that eight hundred billion we'll save every year by reining in DoD nonsense and give it to the people who need it to survive."

"What about the shooting in Baltimore last night?" a reporter yelled from the back. "What about the six police officers who were gunned down in cold blood?"

"*Third,*" Katrina went on, ignoring his attempt to derail the thunder of her announcement. "We'll make Wall Street accountable for all their past sins."

"What exactly does that mean?" someone called out from the left. "How will you make them accountable?"

"Take the real-estate crash as an example," she replied. "The federal government gave New York City I-bankers billions to save themselves from the mess they'd created. So what did the money men do with all that bailout cash? They took it and used it as capital to profit on the cleanup of the very mess they'd created." She went on another eye-contact mission. "I can't stand carpetbaggers, and that's exactly what they are. It's a glaring example of how Wall Street has ripped off Main Street for decades and decades.

"So how will I make them accountable?" she asked. "I will engineer much tighter regulation over the money manipulators. And next time they make massive amounts of cash on something that stinks, I'll take it and channel it to people who need it." She shook her head. "Let's get real for a second. What investment bankers do isn't brain surgery. They match a buyer and a seller and take a profit on the trade. They're basically bookies. The reason they make so much money at it is because they operate like a trust—worse, like a cartel. Like OPEC or, more accurately, like the Mexican drug lords."

"The Baltimore cops were assassinated by an African American ex-marine," someone else yelled.

"I'll get to that," Katrina responded tersely, glancing at Jordan, who was standing against the wall to her left.

"Focus, people," Jordan called out loudly, stepping forward. "I don't want to have to excuse anyone from our press conferences. Permanently," he added ominously. "Am I making myself clear?"

The room went deathly silent.

"Good, I'm glad we got that straight." He nodded to Katrina. "Go ahead, Madam President."

"Thank you, Mr. Jordan," she said as she looked back out over the reporters. "Prosperity for All will generate more than two trillion dollars a year of new tax revenues. And we'll cut eight hundred billion from expenditures. In short order, PFA will turn our annual deficit into a healthy surplus. In addition to helping people in need, we'll also start paying back the twenty trillion dollars of debt we owe the world." She smiled. She couldn't help herself. This was too good a line not to use. "I'll turn Wall Street from a bastion of capitalism into an empowerment zone and, at the same time, the Pentagon into a much smaller reality. Prosperity for All will go down in history on the same level of importance and influence as Roosevelt's New Deal." Her smile turned into a steely glare, to quickly convince anyone who thought they might find a crack in all this that there were no cracks to find. "I've already spoken to Congressional leaders. PFA will happen." Not technically true, but it would be.

"What about the Joint Chiefs? Have you spoken to them?"

"I'm the commander in chief," Katrina reminded everyone. "The Joint Chiefs take orders from me, as do the combatant commanders. I don't need to speak to them. Check your protocol."

"But there will be blowback. I mean, from a trillion down to two hundred billion? Can we even make military payroll at that level of funding?"

"The annual military payroll is one hundred and fifty billion," Jordan spoke up. He always had the figures at his fingertips. "We're fine."

"But," Katrina followed up, "I will reduce the number of active personnel in the military. We don't need a million and a half troops, not in this high-tech day and age." She held up her hand again to quiet another rumble racing through the crowd. "Let me be very clear on something. I will not put those who have served this country so bravely in a bind. No one will be discharged from the military until he or she has a private-sector job waiting at equal or greater pay. And I will make certain the private sector offers each and every one of them that job."

"So you're going to force corporate America to hire military personnel?"

"What about the white cops in Baltimore who were assassinated by a black man?"

Katrina bristled. After the killings in Baltimore early this morning, Dennis had recommended that she delay her announcement of Prosperity for All, at least for twenty-four hours. Now she was wishing she'd listened to him.

"What happened in Baltimore this morning was a terrible tragedy. But let's not turn it into a racial issue. A deranged individual with military training mercilessly murdered six men. The gunman *happened* to be African American and the policemen *happened* to be white."

"But there's a report that the gunman left behind a note identifying himself as a member of a group called War on Whites. The note claims that others of WOW will keep luring police into public places with false claims and then shooting the white officers who respond. It says that ambushes like these will become commonplace."

"The Twitter mongers are trying to incite racial combat," Katrina snapped as harshly as she dared. As president, she had to walk the thin line between anger and rage. There had indeed been a note, pinned to the shooter's shirt. But tens of millions were watching this press conference. Sometimes avoiding the truth was necessary in order to avoid chaos. "We all know what their agenda is. Don't help them."

"It's the third ambush incident of this kind in the last three months," a reporter yelled. "The third time we have a black shooter gunning down white police officers who were called to a false alarm. It already is commonplace. Police forces are saying you don't have their backs. They're saying they're going to stop responding to emergencies in public areas until they're absolutely certain it's not an ambush. What happens when it is a real emergency but the police hesitate for fear of an ambush? People's lives are at stake here, police officers and regular people. What are you going to do about it, Madam President?"

Katrina stared at the reporter for several seconds, wishing Dennis would throw him out. Of course, that would only inflame his colleagues at the network.

"Let's get back to Prosperity for All," she finally said. "Let's get back to what will change America for good and forever."

CHAPTER 9

McLean, Virginia

"Turn it off," General Lewis ordered tersely, jabbing angrily at the sixty-inch flat-screen bolted to the far wall of his home study. A study prominently decorated by his long and distinguished military career. In addition to the flat-screen, carefully arranged battle prints of America's twentieth-century wars and his medals and ribbons also hid the plain white walls. "Get that woman out of my home immediately, General Fiske. I won't sit here and watch another minute of her."

"Yes, sir." Fiske picked up the remote lying on the table in front of him and detonated the president's early-morning news conference.

"Katrina Hilton is an embarrassment to this country," Lewis muttered, "an *eight-hundred-billion-dollar* embarrassment. If she's in her right mind, how can she possibly propose to cut our military spending by that much every year?"

"Maybe she's not in her right mind."

"That kind of DoD budget slash would quickly put the entire globe at the edge of chaos," Lewis charged ahead, "into a clear and present danger. For Christ's sake, what controlled substance is she smoking when she's alone in the Oval Office?"

"Maybe she's not alone."

Lewis's gaze shifted deliberately from the now-darkened screen to Fiske's grim expression. "You mean her COS, Dennis Jordan?"

"Yes, sir, that's exactly who I mean."

"The FBI has files with pictures of them smoking pot . . . the night they took their big high-tech company public."

"That was a long time ago."

"It's still illegal in Texas."

"I'm not sure anyone would care at this point, sir."

Lewis grinned thinly. "Perhaps we could catch them at it now."

"Perhaps."

The two generals were meeting at Lewis's home in McLean, Virginia, twenty miles west of the Pentagon. Lewis's order to meet here and not at the Pentagon on a weekday meant something very interesting could be developing, Fiske understood. Like the first few sinister circulations of a low-pressure system that ultimately formed a catastrophic category-five hurricane, this meeting held destructive potential. It was a hurricane that could ignite Fiske's passionate psychopathic desires in the most incredible way possible, perhaps even satisfy them—at least for a while.

"The problem is, smoking marijuana is now lawful in the District of Columbia," Fiske reminded Lewis.

"Another social disaster."

"So it wouldn't be illegal even in the unlikely event we caught them—not in Washington, anyway."

"Maybe if she was in the residence it would be legal, but not if she and Jordan were in the Oval Office. Smoking marijuana is still banned in public places, and I believe the Oval Office qualifies as that. The Oval Office is owned by all of us."

"You're right again," Fiske murmured under his breath.

It seemed as if Lewis always was. Over the years, Fiske had grown accustomed to Lewis's constant ability to one-up—almost.

In his early fifties, General Bradley Lewis was director of the Joint Chiefs of Staff. He was the soldier who made certain everything ran smoothly at JCS. He was a Marine Corps three-star general who reported directly to the vice chairman of the Joint Chiefs, the second-highest ranking officer in the US military. Lewis was a classic square-jawed, broad-shouldered, no-nonsense marine who always figured it was better to go through something than around it. He was the prototype.

For Fiske, it was as though he were looking straight into a mirror when he looked at Lewis—physically and psychologically. The only tangible difference between them seemed to be a single star. Fiske had only two.

But that would soon change, according to Lewis. He'd made that clear a few weeks ago.

Lewis had become Fiske's mentor a decade ago and had made certain his protégé was well taken care of ever since. Fiske had no doubt about getting the next star soon, as long as Lewis was around. In his role at the Joint Chiefs as director of intelligence, Fiske reported to Lewis.

"She could bring this country down," Lewis muttered disgustedly after taking a sip of black coffee from his Marine Corps mug, "if we don't do something about it."

The image of Katrina Hilton tied up before him arose in Fiske's mind out of nowhere, nearly taking his breath away. Her hands were secured above her head, her ankles shackled, moaning as she stood on tiptoes straining against the rope, naked except for her heels, exactly as the young woman in Wisconsin had been.

That woman was dead, and her boyfriend was sitting in jail for life for a crime he didn't commit during a night he couldn't remember—all thanks to John Brady. If Fiske had his way, President Hilton would suffer the same fate as the stripper.

He gazed out the den window into northern Virginia. Wouldn't it be something if Brady could actually deliver Katrina Hilton to him the same way he had that young woman? Knowing Brady as well as Fiske did, that possibility didn't seem to be out of the realm of reality.

"I agree, General Lewis. She still doesn't understand how our enemies think. If they saw that much of a decrease in our military spending, they would attack us sooner or later."

The urge to play God was growing stronger every day for Fiske. It was becoming his obsession, and he wasn't going to wait another three months this time. When Brady came to see him at the Pentagon, he'd order his personal assassin to arrange another situation.

"Before we get to the specific reason I asked you here this morning," Lewis spoke up, "is there anything going on in the world I need to know about? Anything I need to tell the vice chairman?"

"I checked with the major agencies on the way over, sir. National Security, Homeland, CIA, ONI, and, of course, DIA." Fiske ticked off the intelligence networks he was in constant contact with. "It's the same as yesterday, the same as every day." He'd briefed Lewis two mornings ago on a secure line as he'd headed to Reagan Airport in his street clothes to catch a commercial flight bound for Minneapolis and then Wisconsin's North Woods. "Our friends in Europe headed off an ISIS attack at the Brussels Airport. And the guys protecting New York City arrested some idiot at the Lincoln Tunnel tollbooth. He was driving an Enterprise rental truck loaded with dynamite."

Lewis shook his head. "It's just a matter of time before New York's going to take another major hit. The radical Muslims are obsessed with it. And we can't count on always stopping them before the bomb goes off."

"And President Hilton wants to cut our defense budget by eighty percent in the face of that."

"That's exactly why I had you come here this morning. So we could talk about that problem in complete privacy, George."

Fiske glanced up. Lewis rarely called him by his first name. This wasn't just getting interesting. This was getting real. A shiver shot up his spine. "Yes, sir?"

"She's gone too far this time," Lewis said firmly, nodding at the darkened television screen. "We can't let her cut our budget to two hundred billion a year. Society as a whole would end, at least as we know it. The whole idea is insane."

"Do you really think Congress will pass this PFA thing?"

"She and Jordan have been very cunning about it."

"You mean by linking Pentagon cuts to tax increases on the wealthy, tax cuts for the middle class, and the war on Wall Street."

"She's going to bribe white, rural, middle-class America to her side with tax cuts that the rich and the military will pay for. And you and I both know how popular a war on Wall Street will be with the average Joes in the Rust Belt—in Michigan, Ohio, and Pennsylvania. I don't know what she thinks she can really do to those pricks in Manhattan. But just saying she's going to try will send the liberal media into a lather. How does Congress *not* fall into line with that plan?" Lewis asked. "They'd never get reelected if they didn't."

"And she's got Peppermint Patty in her hip pocket," Fiske pointed out. Patricia Stiles was the first African American ever to be Senate majority leader. "I hear she and President Hilton are lesbians."

This time Lewis's eyes shot to Fiske's. The Marine Corps coffee mug stopped halfway between his lap and his lips. "Seriously?"

Fiske was instantly sorry he'd said that. It seemed as if an affirmative would make the other general's decade. And for a moment he considered going for it. "Well, I heard a rumor," he finally mumbled.

"Oh." Lewis took his sip of coffee, making it clear he knew what that meant. "President Hilton is being cagey about this. She'll win the next election in a landslide if PFA gets legs. Most of the time people care more about their wallets and their purses than they do about national security."

"Until the bombs and the bullets actually start to fly," Fiske pointed out. "Then they care about being protected."

Lewis grimaced. "But then it's too late, as we know all too well."

Fiske thought long and hard about asking the question on his mind. This single inquiry could set in motion an unprecedented chain of events—events that, if executed improperly, could land him in prison at any moment beside the kid who Brady had drugged last night.

Worse, it could land him in front of a firing squad.

So he started softly with a leading comment.

"We recently had a brief conversation about a way to block this path President Hilton is leading us down."

"After your mole in the West Wing contacted you about what Jordan was planning. And thank God your mole did."

Three years ago, people Fiske and Lewis knew very well had taken extreme measures to try engineering a victory for the opposing presidential candidate, a hard-line conservative. Given Katrina Hilton's platform in her time in the Texas state legislature, they had anticipated what she might try to accomplish in the White House. When their candidate had been defeated, by the narrowest of margins, they had taken pains to establish Deep Throats inside Hilton's administration. And, as Lewis had just remarked, thank God they had. They hadn't been caught flat-footed by this morning's press conference and the president's announcement in front of the cameras.

"Yes, sir. Well, uh . . . I mean . . . well . . ."

"Speak freely here, General Fiske. You don't have to worry about anything you say inside these walls. That's why I asked you to come to my home this morning."

Fiske swallowed hard and glanced around. Not much in the world scared him. He'd seen plenty of combat, been shot twice, and lost the little finger on his left hand to an IED blast in Iraq.

But this was different. He was about to dive into as deep an ocean of conspiracy filled with the biggest sharks as had ever existed—and he was the first one diving in. He believed very strongly in what they were considering. Still, this was not a decision to be made lightly.

"We must do it this way, General Lewis." Fiske's heart was suddenly beating hard—out of fear and anticipation. He could barely believe what he was saying. "Just assassinating her won't stop what she's putting in motion."

"You'll get no argument from me. The vice president would keep everything going if President Hilton were gone."

"Exactly."

"Though I think if we decide to go down this road, we still may want to consider taking her out. No need to provide the enemy with a living martyr. No need to provide anyone with any inspiration."

Fiske nodded. "You're right, of course."

"So give me the basics of Project Sundance," Lewis ordered, "as you see it unfolding."

When Fiske was finished, perspiration drenched his entire body. He could feel it dripping down his back beneath his uniform when he finally relaxed into the comfortable leather chair. But now that Sundance was out in the open, at least between the two of them, he felt better. Now there were two of them swimming in this ocean of ultimate conspiracy that was filled with megalodons.

"We must get the Black Book, General Fiske, as quickly as possible. You didn't mention that as part of Project Sundance."

Fiske hated not knowing something in front of Lewis, especially when it came to something that sounded an awful lot like he should. He was, after all, director of intelligence for the Joint Chiefs. "Of course we'll get it, sir." He regretted his response immediately. They were good friends, but Lewis never missed an opportunity to assert his dominance.

"Do you know what the Black Book is, General Fiske?"

This time Fiske didn't hesitate. He didn't want to dig the hole any deeper. "No, sir," he admitted contritely.

"Where did you go for the last few days?" Lewis asked.

It wasn't unusual for Lewis to do this, to avoid the answer to an important question by suddenly turning the conversation in a completely different direction. He seemed to enjoy keeping people on edge and in the dark. Fiske had seen him do it to other subordinates many times. However, this was the first time he'd experienced it. It was no fun, especially given the nature of the conversation's new direction.

"I had a meeting in Minneapolis." Fiske had to be careful about his lie. Lewis could easily check on where he'd gone, so he had to at least be honest about the airport he'd flown into. "It was a cover location." That was code for both parties in the meeting needing to be outside their home territories to avoid being recognized together. It implied a high degree of secrecy, and Fiske hoped Lewis would leave it there. "That's why I took a commercial flight. You understand, sir."

"Are you having an affair, George?"

Lewis had just used Fiske's first name for the second time in a single meeting. This was unprecedented. "Of course not." Fiske made certain not to go overboard with his defense. That would be incriminating.

"I hope not. You know how much Betsy and I care about Carol."

"Yes, sir, but—"

"I understand a man's needs, especially as he closes in on fifty."

"Yes, sir."

"And as long as you weren't considering divorce, as long as it was just a distraction, I wouldn't typically have a problem with it. Divorce could throw off your career path. The powers that be don't like divorce on a high-ranking officer's record. Everyone understands the need to have distractions. It's natural for men. It keeps us young at heart and strong." Lewis shook his head. "But divorce is a no-no. Understand?"

"Yes, sir."

"I want to see you get that next star."

"Thank you, sir."

"But Project Sundance puts everything on a different level. We can't do anything that attracts attention in any way other than performing what appear to be our normal, everyday duties. Nothing that gives anyone any excuse to investigate us, especially the press. Do you understand me, General Fiske?"

It made Fiske feel better to have Lewis address him formally. "Yes, sir." However, what he was thinking about made him feel worse.

As much as he hated to admit it, Fiske was thinking back on last night and how much he *craved* it. Even as Lewis was warning him, even as he promised that he understood, he was thinking about the next time. How he wanted Brady to identify another situation immediately so he could take another woman's life into his hands. So he could play God again.

"This afternoon I intend to raise the possibility of Sundance to the next level."

Fiske's eyes snapped back to Lewis's. "To the vice chairman?" This was incredible.

Lewis nodded. "So if you don't hear anything more about me after tomorrow morning, if I suddenly disappear into thin air never to be heard from again, you'll know why."

◆ ◆ ◆

Richmond, Virginia

"It was close," Talia described.

"*Very* close," Bones echoed from his foldout metal chair in the TARC conference room. "It was like the cops were targeting Talia and me. Like they knew we were the protest leaders and they wanted to arrest us way more than they wanted to arrest any of the others."

"Well, you have to admit I was the only one talking to a reporter when they crashed the party," Talia said, slipping her hand to Bones's for a moment. "Then you grabbed me and saved me."

It was a subtle touch, but Paul caught the gravity of it and understood immediately. Talia and Bones had been intimate in New Orleans last night before catching the first flight back to Richmond this morning.

"That was a pretty clear sign I was a leader."

"I don't know." Bones wasn't convinced. "Maybe I'm just paranoid, but they seemed laser-focused on getting both of us. It was just those four cops coming after us at first, but then there were more. We had to dodge at least three more groups of them before we got out of the area. None of the other three hundred came our way that I could tell. So what were all those cops doing chasing us?"

That Talia and Bones had become intimate didn't surprise Paul. They'd been working together in high-pressure, dangerous situations for more than two years. Intimacy was simply a natural by-product of the experience. But now he had to separate them. He couldn't have their relationship infecting their decisions.

"How many of the three hundred did the cops end up detaining?" Talia asked.

"Seventeen. I've gotten all but two of them out."

"Thank God for fake IDs."

"Yes," Paul agreed. "Thank God."

"Are the buses already headed back?"

"I got out everyone I could right away." It seemed to Paul like Bones never changed clothes. He was always wearing that same Grateful Dead T-shirt and those same ratty jeans. "They all spent the night in Houston."

"Houston?"

"I didn't want them coming back in the direction of Richmond in case the Feds got on their tail. So I had all four buses take four different back roads west, none on I-10. All four buses went to different hotels, too. And I'm having them take different routes back to Richmond today and tomorrow. As far as we can tell, no one's tailing them."

"Sounds like I'm not the only one dealing with a bad case of paranoia," Bones said with a wry smile. "Right, Paulie?"

"There's nothing wrong with a certain level of it," Paul chided. Being in the mafia had taught him that very well. "It keeps us on our toes."

"OK," Talia spoke up, "then here's my contribution to the paranoia fest. Is what we're doing ultimately good or bad?"

Paul raised an eyebrow. Talia always said what she thought when she thought it. She never held back. It could be annoying, but more times than not she had a good perspective. He didn't like her being bold enough to ask this question in front of Bones, though. He would have preferred she be more discreet and wait for a private moment. This was why relationships between colleagues were dangerous.

"Of course what we're doing is good." Paul had a prickly feeling he knew where her train of thought was headed, and he didn't want anyone else suspecting the same thing. That could get in the way of his agenda. "What are you talking about?"

"We find a cause to support, where we feel a social injustice has been committed."

"Yes."

"In a situation that hasn't had the legs to get publicity on its own."

"Yes."

"We try to make things right by starting a very loud protest."

"Of course we do."

"And most of the time, we do. We bring the establishment to justice."

"Yes."

"At least in the short term, at least in that specific situation."

"Make your point, Talia."

"It occurs to me that President Hilton barely won the last election. It also occurs to me that the reason the election was so close was because a lot of nonurban, mostly white middle classers deserted President Hilton at the polls."

"That's what the data suggest," Bones chimed in.

"So?"

"So during the campaign, her opponent cited many of the protests we started. Which almost always involve white police officers unjustly targeting and abusing blacks. Like in New Orleans, where Officer Breaux killed Kelvin James. On the campaign trail, the other candidate constantly talked about how we were just doing it to stir up trouble. That what we were really trying to do was steal the country."

"And?"

"Maybe our protests and the publicity we get from them contributed to all those rural middle-class whites deserting our party at the polls. Maybe it got them furious because, well . . ." She hesitated. "Well, because we don't always have a lot of evidence behind what we're claiming." She saw Bones cringe. "Well, it's true, Bones. Don't deny it. I'm not saying we're wrong. I'm just saying a lot of times we don't have much proof. And the media always helps us, and you know that infuriates certain members of the white middle class." She held her hands up defensively. "I have zero sympathy for most whites. They murdered my ancestors and they stole my land. All I'm saying is, I don't want to think that what we're doing here at TARC is actually hurting our cause. You know?"

"We do good things," Paul said, "but don't try convincing yourself we influenced the election."

"But the other guy, who I basically consider Satan's angel, referenced us over and over in his speeches. And he talked about the specific protests we started. Just like whoever they put up against President Hilton in the next election will."

"I don't think you have to worry about us being cited this time," Bones spoke up. "This time it'll be about that War on Whites group."

Paul gazed at Bones, who was staring back unflinchingly. Until Paul's eyes dropped to his cell phone in his lap and the sexy picture Billie had sent him last night. Why wasn't she answering any of his calls or texts since then?

◆ ◆ ◆

Washington, DC

"Sometimes I really hate the press," Katrina fumed as she sat down behind her desk in the Oval Office.

"Easy, Madam President," Jordan said gently.

"Easy? *Really?* Did you see what happened in there? Were you not at the same press conference I was?"

"Of course—"

"I'm sorry," she interrupted. "I shouldn't be taking it out on you. It's just so frustrating. All they wanted to talk about is what happened in Baltimore."

"Not all of them, just the right-wingers. Just the ones who can't stand that you're sitting in the chair you're sitting in."

She smiled at him. "What would I do without you?"

"Well, I—"

"Call Patty Stiles, Dennis. Please get her over here as quickly as possible. The three of us need to strategize."

"Yes, Madam President."

CHAPTER 10

Connecticut

Falcon watched the doctor set Billie's arm after sewing up the gash on her head. The doctor had injected her with a local anesthetic for the stitches and given her a fast-acting oral sedative for the arm.

She still shrieked when her bone snapped back in place.

Falcon winced himself.

"She'll be OK," the doctor assured Falcon as they moved out of the bedroom where Billie was resting and into the hallway. "That splint I put on the break will stabilize her arm. It's a crude fix, but it'll work. Now she needs rest."

"Thanks, Jason. I appreciate you coming all the way out here from the city on such short notice, especially at this hour of the morning."

It was only a few minutes before 8:00 a.m.

"But what she *really* needs," Jason continued firmly, "is to get to a hospital so the technicians there can check to see if she has any internal injuries. That crash sounded pretty horrible. There's just no way of my telling if anything's wrong where I can't see."

Falcon had described the crash briefly, how Billie's injuries had occurred. "She isn't complaining about anything else hurting."

"You never know, A.J."

"I understand."

"So . . . *then* . . . ?" Jason asked in a leading tone.

"So then thanks again for coming out here so fast."

"Are you really willing to take that responsibility?"

"Yes, I am."

"That's not the Andrew Falcon I know and love."

"So be it. Desperate times call for desperate measures."

Jason Sanchez was a longtime friend of Falcon's who had a fast-growing private practice in Manhattan.

This wasn't Manhattan. This was the middle of the Connecticut woods.

Falcon had turned on his phone as he was coming out of the Adirondacks only long enough to place two calls—one to Jason and the other to his IT bloodhounds in Manhattan. At least one of the bloodhounds was always minding their high-tech midtown office—even at three o'clock in the morning—in case a client . . . like Falcon . . . had an issue . . . like Falcon's . . . at three o'clock in the morning.

Jason owed Falcon for staking him the initial six-figure outlay required to break away from the large practice he was working for at the time and start his own practice. He constantly promised Falcon he'd be there for him if the time ever came that Falcon needed a favor. So, after groggily answering his personal number on the fourth ring, Jason had gotten out of bed and driven to Connecticut to tend to Billie.

Falcon would have preferred to buy a place on a Montana trout river, but that didn't make sense given how rarely he'd get out there. So he'd settled for a cabin on a Connecticut trout stream instead. It wasn't Montana, but it was still pretty nice. And it was only ninety minutes northeast of Manhattan. At least once a month he drove the Mustang out of the city on a Saturday or Sunday and fished the cascading stream running behind this secluded cabin. For the big rainbows and browns that stalked the deeper pools.

It had always served as the perfect getaway.

Now it was the perfect hideout.

"What's going on, A.J.?" Sanchez asked in a low voice so Billie couldn't hear. "Who is that woman? Why are you desperate?"

"You don't want to know," Falcon answered, ushering Jason down the hallway and toward the front door.

He didn't have time for conversation. He figured every hour Claire was being held doubled the danger of her situation, doubled the odds against his saving her, doubled the possibility that her captors would do something rash to her. Thirty-two hours had already passed since she'd been taken, and he felt the time ticking down quickly to a moment when he wouldn't be able to save her.

"Seriously, I—"

"I can't tell you, Jason."

"You can't? Or you won't?"

"We go back a ways. You've got to trust me on this." Falcon watched confusion spread across the doctor's face. "You're better off getting as far away from this situation as possible as quickly as possible."

"Call the authorities."

"I can't."

"Why not?"

Falcon wasn't going to tell Jason what had happened to Claire. He and Sally had agreed that they needed to keep the situation only to themselves or they'd ratchet up the risk of Claire being murdered by her captors and her body hidden from them forever.

And he wasn't going to tell Jason that Billie didn't want to go to the hospital. That she'd pleaded with Falcon not to take her because then someone might find her. She still hadn't told him who she thought might find her, and Falcon hadn't pushed—yet.

"Listen to me, Jason," he demanded in a gritty voice. "You've got a wife and two beautiful kids. Don't get them involved in this by sticking your nose into something that smells as bad as skunk roadkill. I'm convinced these people I'm up against are very powerful. I'm convinced they'll take revenge on anyone who—"

"OK, OK," Jason interrupted as they shook hands. "I get it."

Falcon relaxed. Bringing Jason's family into this had struck a nerve for the young doctor, as Falcon had anticipated it would. *Always make things personal for people when you're really trying to make a point*—another one of his father's mantras. That's when they understood the fastest.

"Be careful, A.J."

"I owe you dinner at Sparks," Falcon offered, nodding toward Jason's car, silently urging him to get the hell out of here. Sparks Steak House was Sanchez's favorite restaurant in Manhattan. "A *big* dinner."

"I'll take you up on that offer," he called over his shoulder as he walked to his car. "And how about a few stock tips while we eat so I can finish paying you back for my practice? The sure-thing kind of stock tips. You know what I mean?"

"Sorry," Falcon muttered to himself as he closed the door and hustled back down the hallway. "I've got enough people after me. I don't need the SEC chasing me, too."

"What are you going to do with me?" Billie asked softly when Falcon was standing beside the bed she was resting on.

"Torture you until you tell me everything I want to know."

Her mouth fell slowly open. "I . . . I . . ."

"I'm keeping you here," Falcon said as he moved to the end of the bed. He noosed a red wire band he'd pulled from his pocket around her ankle and locked it in place. "So I can keep an eye on you."

"What is that?" she asked, rising up on her good arm to look.

"A homing device. Now I can find you anywhere you go," he explained. "You can't turn it off, and you can't remove it. Nothing you'd try to cut it with would work. So don't leave here," he warned her. "If you do, I'll find you. And, when I do, I won't be happy, and that's an understatement."

"Where'd you get that thing?"

"Santa Claus."

The same technology company who'd supplied him with the spy software on his phone had also provided the human homing device, hand delivered by one of the IT bloodhounds who had hooked him up with the West Coast inventors six months ago. A week later he'd invested $30 million for 20 percent of their company through the Sutton hedge funds he managed, so they could accelerate their expansion dramatically. His $30 million investment would be worth more than a billion in less than a year, maybe less, given the incredible devices they were inventing.

He'd make sure his bloodhounds shared in the wealth for introducing him to the company—he figured he'd give them at least $50 million of the billion the West Coast firm would be worth in a year.

Always make money for your partners, his father had counseled him over and over.

Falcon took a deep breath. He still didn't believe his father had jumped from that window. He still believed something else had happened in that office overlooking Wall Street from on high— something criminal—even if no one else in the world did.

Falcon moved to the side of the bed again and touched her good shoulder gently. "People are trying to kill you." He kept telling himself Billie could be his fastest and most reliable path to Claire. And he had to treat her well so she'd cooperate with him. He didn't want to, because she was involved with Claire's kidnapping. But he had to take emotion out of this situation—for now. "Hole up here and get some rest while I figure all this out," he said sympathetically. "I'll take care of you."

"By now they're probably after you, too."

"I'll be just fine."

"But I'll be a sitting duck," she said, gesturing around. "They'll find out you own this place. They probably already have. They'll show up here after you leave."

"No one will figure out I own this place. I bought it with an LLC. All the utilities are paid by the LLC. The property taxes, too. My name is nowhere near this house."

His first day at Sutton, Michael Mattix had recommended he make all major purchases using front companies. In the Internet age, Mattix had counseled, the harder you made it for people to find out about you, the better. Falcon would make a lot of money at Sutton, Mattix had said matter-of-factly, so the young man needed to fly as low under the radar as possible from then on, to avoid making himself a target. Besides, Mattix had chuckled as he went on, secrecy was the Sutton way. Better to get used to that as soon as possible.

He'd never told anyone else about his place on the trout stream, never brought anyone here. Sanchez was the only other person in the world who knew about it—besides Billie.

"You're going to hand me over to the cops when this is done," she said.

"Given what you told me back at that place in the Adirondacks and what happened after I left there, we'll both be lucky to be alive when this is done. Stay in the present, Billie."

"I'm screwed either way."

"As long as I get Claire back unharmed, I'll move past my problem with you when this is done."

"Where's my phone?"

"Where's my niece?"

Billie's phone was in the Mustang. It wasn't like Falcon needed it. He'd wasted no time in getting the data he'd pulled from it to his IT guys. They would have the identities of every contact on her device by later this morning. But he sure as hell wasn't going to hand the phone back to her.

"I mean it. Where is she?"

"They took her someplace outside Charlotte. I don't know where. I wasn't told."

"Then you're going to call your contact and—"

"He isn't going to tell me anything, A.J. That's not how this works. My job was to meet with you and tell you what he wants. He's very careful."

"Who is very careful?"

She shook her head.

Falcon stared at her hard.

"They aren't going to hurt your niece," she said softly. "I was promised that."

He didn't believe her for a second. And she was probably right about her contact not telling her where Claire was. But the data from her phone should lead him to the person who would know, maybe directly to the kidnappers themselves. As furious as he was with Billie for being part of the group that had kidnapped Claire, he had to let his bloodhounds do their work.

"Who had you put in the trunk of that car?" he demanded. "Why are you so worried about going to a hospital?"

She looked away.

"Tell me."

She recoiled at his sharp tone. "I don't know."

For a devastating moment, he actually considered causing Billie pain so she'd tell him what he wanted to know. But he clenched his jaw and put the terrible idea out of his mind. He had limits to his desperate measures. It was bad enough that he wasn't following Jason's advice and taking her to a hospital to get her checked out the right way.

"Then tell me who's pushing Paul to get the information you want from me."

Billie's eyes raced to Falcon's even faster than they had when he'd spoken her real first name as she stood on the cabin porch.

"He's your boyfriend," Falcon spoke up before she could ask. "You wouldn't send a picture like that to just anyone. So I read your texts back and forth. He's the one running the outfit you're part of."

"You bastard! Reading my private—"

"Versus kidnapping my niece. Get real, Billie."

"I'm sorry," she whispered, her eyes falling away from his.

"Who's pushing Paul?" Falcon asked again.

"I honestly don't know who the person is. All I know is that it's a very senior US lawmaker."

Falcon inhaled slowly. His assumption was correct. This thing went so high. If a US congressperson or senator was trying to unveil a conspiracy that involved Sutton & Company, then whoever was atop that conspiracy would most certainly think nothing of taking any steps necessary in order to keep it behind the curtain.

He wasn't willing to torture Billie to get out of her what she knew. But whoever was running the conspiracy probably would—which made him pause. There might come a time when he'd have to change his attitude, if he wanted Claire back.

"I have to go," he finally said in a low voice.

"Please don't leave me here alone," she begged. "I'm scared."

"You'll be fine."

"Please don't go."

"And don't try to get away," he warned her, ignoring her pleas. "You'll be very sorry if you do," he called as he headed out the door and down the hallway. "Believe me."

Ten miles from the cabin, Falcon turned his phone back on. Right away it buzzed with a VM message from Penny Luzerne.

"Call me," she pleaded on the recording, as if she was on the brink of tears, "right away, Monsieur Falcon. *S'il vous plaît.* Oh, *mon dieu, s'il vous plaît.*"

He touched the "Call Back" button on the phone's screen immediately.

"What's wrong, Penny?" he asked even before she could say hello.

"Oh my God, I'm so glad you're all right."

"What's wrong?"

"I've been so worried about you."

"What's wrong?"

"It's . . . it's Michael Mattix. He's dead."

For an instant everything in front of Falcon dashed to slow motion. "Jesus . . . what happened?"

"He was murdered in his place uptown."

"Murdered?" Just as a car came around a curve ahead of him, he whipped the Mustang back into his lane. *"Murdered?"*

CHAPTER 11

The Bronx, New York

James Wallace and Philip Rose were in the Bronx this morning, a place they were foreigners to, a place they would typically avoid like the plague. But it was for a good cause. They were here to open an academy for orphans, which they'd personally funded fifty-fifty to the tune of twenty-eight large.

They sat side by side in the front row of a wide stage as other, less important people filed in behind and before them. Waiting for the brand-new auditorium they'd financed from their own chasm-deep pockets to fill to capacity with the new school's teachers and administrators, New York City dignitaries, many members of the city press corps, as well as the most important attendees of all—the four hundred kids aged six to eighteen who were being given the extraordinary chance of a lifetime.

Rose hadn't wanted to go $14 million deep into his pocket, but Wallace had strong-armed him into it. Now he was glad Sutton's CEO had been so forceful. This was going to be quite an event and provide significant positive results for many, many people.

By all accounts, this school would be one of the finest in the nation, outfitted with only the best of everything when it came to its facilities. The classes would be small, and each teacher had been carefully screened and handpicked for being a recognized leader in the education field.

Going forward, this academy would be the gold standard for others of its type.

Despite their busy schedules, Wallace and Rose had overseen many of the organizing details, from construction all the way to which children would receive the fortunate nod and be accepted for admission. Today would serve as a celebration of a wonderful beginning for all these children who hailed from many different ethnic backgrounds—as well as a thank-you to the two men who'd made dreams come true.

Classes wouldn't begin for a month, but the school also had dormitories where the kids would live full-time. Now that construction was complete, it made complete sense for them to move in immediately, to begin taking advantage of the tremendous facilities. And, in most cases, even more important, to escape unimaginable poverty.

"What do you think about this Prosperity for All initiative President Hilton announced this morning at her press conference?" Rose asked Wallace over the growing hum of conversation. The ceremony would start in just a few moments.

"I think it's unequivocally un-American."

"Well, of course it is, but what I meant was—"

"You and I would literally owe billions of dollars in taxes thanks to our ownership of Sutton & Company," Wallace interrupted, "if PFA passes."

"We'd be forced to take Sutton public to pay those taxes. That would be our only option."

Wallace nodded grudgingly. "Yes, I believe that's right."

"Then we'd have state and federal regulators all over us all the time. We would have a much more difficult time hiding the things we now hide and, therefore, making the money we now make." Rose gestured toward the audience. "We might not be able to fund things like this. The government would have to do it, and we both know how inept the government is at anything financial, especially Katrina Hilton's administration."

"That's why I said it was un-American. It defeats hard work. Why work hard to accumulate generational wealth if it's going to be taxed away from you even *before* you die? Why work hard at all with the rates she's proposing?"

"Why would she do this?" Rose asked, as if his question couldn't possibly have a rational answer. "She's worth a decent amount of money, right? Especially after taking her last tech company public before she went into politics."

"She's worth more than three hundred million, according to our people."

"That's why I don't get her angle," Rose said incredulously. "With the tax rates she's proposing, she'd owe sixty to seventy million dollars herself . . . *immediately.*"

"She doesn't think like we do, Philip. She thinks . . . irrationally."

Rose grimaced, as if he'd actually endured a sudden and unexpected stab of pain in his stomach. "I picked up some more bad news as I was coming here to meet you."

Wallace glanced over. "What was it?"

"You know that slavery reparation bill the senator from Michigan tries to have passed every year? The one that would require each and every Caucasian adult in this country to pay into an escrow fund for African Americans until the end of time as compensation for something that happened almost two hundred years ago."

"Yes?"

"I'm hearing it actually has a chance to pass within a few years. The vote is getting closer and closer."

"That would be the tipping point," Wallace muttered, shaking his head.

"Tipping point?"

"A war would start the moment that bill passed. Hell, look at what's happening right now with these protests and the tension between police and their communities."

"You really think it would come to that, James, to an actual guns-and-bullets race war?"

"Absolutely."

"The military would restore order very quickly," Rose said confidently.

"You're thinking in the present, Philip. If PFA passes, the military will be a shadow of itself within a few years, with Pentagon funds dropping eight hundred billion every year. The military won't be able to restore order when the race war breaks out. The whole thing is terrifying."

"So what do we do?"

Wallace looked up from his phone, put his hand on Rose's arm, and squeezed hard as the woman who'd been named headmistress of the school approached the podium just ahead and to the left of where the two men sat, smiling widely to them as she walked across the stage. The ceremony was about to begin.

After shaking hands with both of them, she moved to the podium and began her opening remarks.

Wallace subtly placed his phone on Rose's knee.

When Rose read the headline on the screen, he was barely able to control his shock. Michael Mattix had been found murdered in his Manhattan penthouse.

Slowly his eyes rose to Wallace's grim expression.

◆ ◆ ◆

Near Charlotte, North Carolina

Claire turned her head and braced for punishment when she sensed the closet door swing open. She was blindfolded, but she still closed her eyes beneath the material, anticipating a hard smack to her face. Her only clue to their presence was the cool, refreshing air that had just rushed into the stifling heat of her tiny, makeshift prison. The remote farmhouse had no air-conditioning.

She hadn't heard the room's hallway door squeak on its hinges, giving her a warning that they were coming. They must be leaving it while they were awake because it didn't make sense that they'd lubricate it. The squeak would serve as a warning that she'd managed to loosen her bindings and was trying to escape again.

Unfortunately, escape wasn't happening. Her three captors were being very careful about the knots since her last attempt, checking and rechecking on her much more often. She'd been trying for an hour but hadn't been able to loosen any of the knots at all. Now they were back again. Even if she had made progress, it wouldn't have mattered.

Fingertips touched her forehead, and she recoiled hard and shrieked as she sat with her back to the closet wall opposite the door.

"Easy, easy," the man said quietly. "I'm not gonna hurt you."

Claire recognized his voice. Of the three, he hadn't smacked her yet. He hadn't been nice, but he hadn't been mean. He'd been matter-of-fact. And he was the only one who didn't stink of cheap cologne.

After the man pulled the blindfold down, he reached around for a tray of food. Her eyes opened wide when she saw the plate full of a delicious-looking breakfast of scrambled eggs, bacon, grits, and biscuits. When the wonderful aroma filled her nostrils, her stomach went wild and her mouth actually ached for the first taste. She was starving. They hadn't fed her since yesterday morning.

"I can't cook nothing but breakfast," he admitted, chuckling loudly. "But I cook it real good." He picked up one of the bacon strips and held it to her lips. "Go on, eat."

As much as she craved the bacon, she turned her head. "No."

"What? Are you out of your mind?"

"I'm not eating until you let me go," she said bravely, "or you kill me."

CHAPTER 12

Manhattan, New York

After telling Falcon what had happened to Michael Mattix, Penny had given him a second message. Charles Cain wanted to talk, and he was furious.

Of course, that wasn't unusual. Cain was easily the most mercurial person Falcon had ever dealt with. It seemed Cain was always mad about something. He'd been divorced three times. The "why" was no mystery.

Cain was the seventh-most senior partner at Sutton, and he ran several of the firm's most important departments. That included the Worldwide Funds Transfer Department—which made him crucially important to Falcon if Falcon was going to get the information Billie's people wanted. So maybe Cain being angry with him wasn't a bad thing this time. Once he'd calmed Cain down about whatever was wrong, he could transition gracefully to the favor he needed without seeming suspicious.

"Where the hell are you?" Cain shouted into the phone the instant he picked up Falcon's call. "That Asian whale you were supposed to meet with stormed out of here an hour ago ranting and raving about how he'll never do business with Sutton & Company. Along with him went ten million dollars in fees riding on the billion dollars of his assets you were going to manage."

"A billion here, a billion there, and it all starts sounding like pocket change, Charles. It's not going to make or break Sutton & Company."

"What? Listen to me, you—"

"Relax. I'll call the man and apologize. I'll fly to Hong Kong to see him if I have to. I'll take care of everything."

"This is not the way to start your tenure as a Sutton partner, A.J. Men have been kicked out of this partnership before. James Wallace is a vindictive son of a bitch. You have no idea what he's capable of, son."

Certainly not everything Wallace is capable of, Falcon thought ruefully. But if what Billie had told him was true, he might be starting to get a hint.

Falcon took a deep breath as he swung toward the exit for the FDR Drive. What he was about to suggest was a dangerous gamble if Cain were involved in the conspiracy Billie had described. But, at number seven, Falcon figured he wasn't. Seven was high but not high enough. If this thing were real, the people behind it would keep the circle very, very tight. And he had to start somewhere. Another hour had passed, but he was no closer to finding Claire.

"I need to talk to you, Charles. I need your advice. You always said I could call on you if I needed to talk."

Despite the way the conversation had begun, Falcon knew the older man cared about him in a paternal way. They'd been out late one night at dinner last year, and Cain had said it straight up as he was opening his second bottle of Pinot. He'd told Falcon how sorry he was about his father, and he offered to talk anytime day or night the younger man needed to. As angry as Cain could get, he could also be a very caring man.

"What's the matter?"

"I've got another firm pushing me hard to join them."

"Goldman Sachs. Wallace mentioned it at your initiation. But why in the world would you even consider that opportunity now that you're the youngest partner in Sutton history? Why would you mess all that up?"

"They've made me an offer." Falcon had no intention of jumping ship. At this point there were bigger issues. The Goldman offer was simply the excuse to seek Cain's counsel. "It'd be tough for me to turn it down."

"Nothing they could offer could ever match what you have now."

"Meet me at that diner down on Broad Street," Falcon suggested. "Let's have an early lunch."

"You always said lunch was for the weak, A.J."

"Not today, Charles, not today."

"What does G2 stand for?" Falcon asked.

He pointed up at the company's tiny, neon-illuminated G2-Data moniker, which hung unobtrusively and at a slight upward angle just above the plain wood door of the understated reception area—where you wouldn't see the sign until you were leaving. Maybe most people wouldn't even see it then.

As far as Falcon knew, it was the only place the company's name appeared. There was no letterhead on written correspondences from them. E-mails weren't identified as coming from the firm. The twenty-two IT bloodhounds here didn't even carry business cards. They were all about flying below the radar and moving in the shadows.

"I've always wondered."

Basil Slicke, G2's CEO, grinned for a quick moment. "Why'd you wait so long to ask me?" he asked in his thick British accent.

"For once, Basil, just answer a question without my having to—"

"We get information on your friends *and* your enemies. We get data on *both* . . . even when you don't ask us to . . . because you never *fucking* know, Andrew."

"You're so right," Falcon agreed. "You really don't ever know."

He'd heard Basil's emphasis on the obscenity loud and clear. There was a tale hiding in there somewhere. Someday he'd ask. But he didn't have time today. He had to get to lunch with Cain, get to the Funds Transfer Department, and then, armed with what he hoped to discover there, find Claire.

"I hate not knowing," he murmured.

"*And* you hate my moniker hanging at that little angle," Basil said, nodding up at the wall over the door. "Don't you, Andrew?"

Despite the urgency of the situation, Falcon nodded his head and grinned as he glanced down at the threadbare seventies carpet covering the floor of G2-DATA's midtown offices. It seemed like Basil knew everything about everything. Of course, that was his business. Thank God he was an ally.

He checked the clock on the wall beside the door. He still had a little extra time before he needed to leave for Wall Street. And he didn't want to sit around in the open in case those guys who'd confronted him the night before last on the Street decided to do so again. He figured Paul was desperate to know what had happened to Billie.

"How do you know that bothers me, Basil?"

"You're the ultimate perfectionist, Andrew. Everything in your office at Sutton lies, sits, or stands at right angles."

"How do you know that?"

"I've hopped on your phone a few times and checked out your office through the camera."

Falcon rolled his eyes. "Jesus."

"Come on." Basil motioned for Falcon to follow. "I've got what you wanted, everything about the names on Billie's phone." He glanced over his shoulder. "I've got something else for you, too. Something you can use after your lunch with Cain."

◆ ◆ ◆

Cain had been sitting in a booth in the back of the Broad Street diner for ten minutes, and he was fuming. He never waited for *anyone*. Finally he banged both fists on the table, so the silverware clattered about. "That's it," he muttered furiously, starting to come out of his seat, "I'm—"

"Sit down," Falcon ordered calmly, sliding into the bench seat opposite Cain. From here he could keep an eagle eye on the door. He'd been watching the place for a while and was convinced no one in here was working with Cain. "Sorry I was late."

Cain was snow-haired like Wallace, but the physical similarity ended abruptly right there. Cain was overweight, and his face was a bright red. Despite his inherited high blood pressure, which his doctor warned about at every six-month visit, he loved washing down big rib eyes and fat baked potatoes drenched in butter and cheese with expensive red wine and top-shelf scotch. And he adored sweets, especially chocolate.

In between meals, Cain dealt with the nonsexy, nuts-and-bolts chores required to make the massive investment bank run smoothly. He made certain all forty thousand Sutton employees in thirty-seven countries around the globe were paid on time every other Friday at 3:00 p.m. by wire transfer in the correct currency. He made certain the hundreds of billions of client funds that poured through Sutton offices every day made their way to the correct destination. He made certain everyone had their benefits—medical plans, insurance, and so on. Then, at the end of each day, he made certain to drink heavily.

"Are you really thinking about going to Goldman?" Cain asked before Falcon had even settled into the booth. "You look like you've been up all night, A.J. Is this really about Goldman?"

Cain was addicted to gossip of any kind. So Falcon had made up a better story on the way over. "Nah, it's not about Goldman."

"*I knew it.* What is it?"

"I'm having a problem with a woman. That's what I really need to talk about. I don't have anyone else I can turn to."

Cain smiled broadly and eased back into his side of the booth. "Mr. Emotionally Bulletproof is finally opening up to me," he said happily. "I've been waiting a long time for this day. You know that, right?"

"I guess."

"So what's going on?"

"She's pushing me to—" Falcon stopped short. This was the perfect moment to ask. "Before we get to all that, who's the best person for me to work with in your Funds Transfer Department?"

Cain made an irritated face. "What's that got to do with anything?"

"Just tell me."

"What's the problem?"

"I've got a hundred-million-dollar wire that keeps bouncing back at me. It's for a very special client, and he's getting furious. I need to work with someone in Funds Transfer to make sure it gets there."

"A special client?"

"*Very* special," Falcon said quickly. It seemed like Cain had come alive when he'd heard the word *special*. Maybe somehow he'd hit on a Sutton code word. "You know what I mean," he pushed, "one of those clients."

"Of course I do." Cain shook his head. "They didn't waste much time pulling you inside the circle, did they?"

"No." Falcon had no idea what Cain was referring to, but he made certain to seem as if he did.

Cain grabbed his phone and tapped on it for several seconds. A moment later, Falcon's phone pinged. "I just sent an e-mail to you and Annie Greenberg in Funds Transfer. She'll help you." Cain grinned as he put his phone down on the diner table. "Now tell me about this woman and what she's doing to you. She got you wrapped around her little finger or what? She pushing the marriage-or-else button?"

Falcon was about to answer when his phone pinged again. But it wasn't another e-mail. It was an alert telling him that Billie had just tried stepping outside the house in the Connecticut woods. An alert that she'd just received a nasty shock to her ankle and had quickly gone back inside.

Richmond, Virginia

Paul Treviso didn't want to make the call. He knew this would be taken as a serious sign of weakness if he played this card. One, he couldn't keep track of his people. Two, he couldn't keep emotion out of the process.

But he had no choice. For the first time in his life, his heart was winning.

"Hello."

"It's me," Paul said loudly, above the noise of the downtown Richmond traffic. He'd gone outside TARC's headquarters and walked several blocks down from the entrance to make the call. He couldn't have Chalice or Thigpen overhear this conversation.

"I know who it is. What do you want?"

"It's . . . it's Billie," he explained, his eyes darting around. "I haven't heard from her."

"So?"

Paul swallowed hard. "I'm worried."

"Given your criminal background, you have a surprisingly big soft spot in your chest."

"I look out for my people."

"There is more to this than that."

"No," he lied. He was separating Bones and Talia for exactly the same reason. He should expect the same reaction from this person.

"Admit it to me," came the demand.

"All right," Paul finally agreed, "I care about her."

"This was to be just about the money. You promised me that."

"I know. I'm sorry."

"Have you made any progress at TARC?"

"Chalice is flying to Chicago this afternoon. That's the other reason I'm calling. To let you know that. It could be important. You and your boss may want to monitor that trip." He paused. "Anyway, while they're gone, I should be able to make some progress. I'll call you tomorrow morning to let you know. Hello," he muttered when there was no response. *"Hello?"*

"I'll look into the situation. Now get back inside. Chalice and Thigpen cannot suspect anything."

Paul ended the call but lingered on the street, going back and forth on his next move. He had to call them. He'd fallen in love with her.

"Yes, sir?" came the response after one ring.

"Find Falcon," Paul ordered tersely, "right now. Then you'll find Billie. Falcon has her. He *must*." He took a deep breath. "Find Billie for me. *Please*."

CHAPTER 13

Washington, DC

"Good afternoon, Senator Stiles."

"It's going on three years since you started running the White House, Dennis!" Senator Stiles exclaimed loudly and firmly in her animated Georgia accent. "That's almost three years we've been working together. Call me Patty from now on. And don't make me have to tell you that again." She smiled broadly as she held out her jewelry-less left hand. "Want a peppermint?"

Jordan shook his head with a grin as he welcomed Patricia Stiles into the Oval Office. Every meeting with her always began the same way, with her offering him a peppermint candy. It was her well-established calling card, her tradition at the beginning of every meeting, which dated all the way back to her freshman year in Washington, DC—1997. So the now–Senate majority leader was affectionately known inside and outside the Beltway as Peppermint Patty.

Peppermint Patty bore no resemblance to the *Peanuts* character of Charles Schulz's imagination. She was African American, in her early fifties, slightly overweight, and actually reminded Jordan of Oprah Winfrey with her facial features. In fact, there was a prominent picture in Patty's office of the two women standing side by side, and the resemblance was striking.

"Thank you for coming to the White House on such short notice, Senator—"

"I'm not going to tell you—"

"*Patty.*"

"Now was that so hard?" she asked in a high-pitched, faux-angry tone as she removed the clear plastic and slipped the red-and-white candy between her full lips. "You know, all these devil treats do is add inches to my waist," she grumbled. "But I can't help myself. We all need our diversions and distractions, don't we?"

"Well, I—"

"Oh, right, I almost forgot. You're a man of unquestioned discipline and principle when it comes to your diet. You never stray from your no-carb, sugarless regimen."

"He's a rock when it comes to that," Katrina confirmed as she moved into the large room from her private office. "He always has been. It can be very irritating," she kidded.

"I hate him," Patty muttered, shooting Jordan a disdainful look, "at least for that. Otherwise," she said, her expression regaining its typical sunshine, "you're very fortunate to have him."

"Don't I know it," Katrina agreed, gesturing at the chairs in front of her desk. "I appreciate you being available so soon."

"Of course, Katrina."

"Please have a seat."

Jordan grinned again as he and Patty sat down in front of the big desk. Patty Stiles was the only person in Washington who consistently addressed Katrina by her first name in private. But Katrina never said a word about it.

Patty didn't stand a lick for pomp and circumstance. Those who demonstrated a consistent need for it were no longer allowed an audience with her and after that had a rough road getting any bill they were sponsoring approved. It seemed to Jordan that Katrina didn't want to find out if Patty's anti-arrogance attitude extended to the president of the United States.

But those who assumed Patty was as casual about her job as she was about titles and formality quickly found out how wrong they were. She was the hardest-working senator on the Hill. Routinely in her Russell Building office until midnight, she was usually to her desk again by six o'clock the next morning—when she wasn't traveling the world on US business. She had no children and had never been married. Her life was politics and the betterment of the country—for all. If she called you to a meeting at seven o'clock in the morning or ten o'clock at night, she expected you to post. As the second most powerful woman in Washington—some would argue the second most powerful *person* in Washington—she had no time for those who were not as committed to the life as she.

"Isn't this wonderful?" Katrina asked as she sat down behind the desk, gesturing at Patty and Jordan, then to herself. "Sitting here in the Oval Office are two women and two African Americans."

"And the only man in here is gay," Jordan spoke up.

"Not a straight white man on the horizon," Patty observed. "Not that I have a problem with an honorable straight white man," she made clear very quickly. "But the scenery in this office today tells me our country has come a long way in the last few decades."

"But we still have a long way to go," Katrina spoke up firmly. "Patty, I must get Prosperity for All enacted as soon as possible. I know there will be some objections to it, but I must—"

"*Some* objections? This morning you proposed an eighty percent cut in military spending, Katrina. A lot of states depend on their share of that eight-hundred-billion-dollar cash flow you want to hack from the federal budget at the speed of light, including mine. States that are home to the contractors, forts, and naval yards that suckle mightily off that huge federal nipple. Millions of civilians will be affected by your plan, not to mention all the active military personnel and their families who will be displaced. I have thirteen military bases in my state alone. All branches of the military but the coast guard contribute to Georgia's fiscal well-being. Fort Benning is one of the highest-profile military facilities in this country, with twelve thousand people in some way directly connected to it. At eighty percent, that's nearly a hundred thousand individuals who would be negatively impacted by your PFA initiative."

"PFA will be an incredible transformation for this country. And, at least initially, it will cause some discomfort," Katrina agreed. "Even some pain. But think of all the good that will ultimately come of it. Think of all the people who will be helped, especially the children. I need you to bring Congress home to me on this. The House will follow the Senate's lead. We still hold a slight majority in both. You can do this, Patty."

"Of course I can do it," Patty snapped confidently. "But it would have been damn helpful if we'd coordinated your announcement. Dennis should have called me. *You* should have called me, Katrina. We should have met before you sprinted out there in front of the press corps, especially after the shootings in Baltimore. You should have waited at least twenty-four hours to let that hysteria simmer down. You gave the press corps right-wingers a perfect opportunity to undermine the gravity of what you were announcing." Patty glanced at Jordan. She never pulled any punches. She was always direct. "Your chief of staff should have advised you on that."

Jordan's eyes dropped to the floor.

"He did," Katrina admitted.

She always takes accountability, Jordan marveled. She never used him as a shield—only when he ordered her to do so. Only when it made sense for both of them—not just her.

"You should have listened to him," Patty counseled.

"I needed to get my message out fast. As I'm sure you're aware, my approval rating isn't where it should be," she admitted, her voice dropping. "And I felt I had to neutralize what happened in Baltimore with something positive."

Patty sucked on the peppermint for a few moments. "I think I can get it done but not as fast as you're hoping. I can get the act passed quickly, but such a mammoth reduction in the DoD budget like this will have to be implemented over a longer period, probably five to ten years. And I doubt I can get you an eighty percent cut right out of the gate. More like fifty, at least on this go-round. Maybe more as we get into it and people feel the positives." She glanced up. "But with the tax increases you're proposing on the wealthy, the tax cuts for the middle class, and the hits you want to make to Wall Street, you should have enough firepower to turn around your approval numbers and win the White House again in sixteen months." She held up her hand. "I don't want you to be a one-termer, Katrina. I want you to have two full terms. I'm willing to take some heat in my home state to make certain that happens."

"Believe me, Patty, when I tell you I know I can't be a one-termer. The thought haunts me every night while I try to fall asleep."

"Prosperity for All is an enormous initiative, Katrina. And it will come with huge risks in the short term." Patty gritted her teeth. "But it's necessary. And it's the right time in history to make this move, to change the course of this country for better and forever. I'm with you, Katrina."

A lump rose in Jordan's throat as Patty put Prosperity for All into historical perspective. His front-row seat to a nation changing course from a military power to one of true inclusion for all humbled and awed him. He felt blessed to be a small part of what was happening. The moment sent a shiver racing up his spine.

"Of course, you're waging war on the Pentagon, Madam President. That always strikes me as an iffy proposition."

Jordan's eyes snapped to Patty's. It was the first time he could ever remember her addressing Katrina so formally in private. She'd wanted to get their attention, Jordan realized. And she'd done it very well. Katrina was instantly riveted as well.

"They report to me," Katrina replied defiantly. "They protect me. They must do what I say."

"Don't be naive."

"What do you mean?"

"That's what John Kennedy thought. And then he went to Dallas in November of 1963."

"Don't go there, Patty. To this day there is still zero proof that the Defense Department was in any way involved in JFK's—"

"With all due respect, Katrina, *don't you be stupid, child.* You're proposing a budget cut that will blow up the Defense Department and scatter its ashes into the Potomac. The generals across the river will not take this lying down." She hesitated. "In fact, it wouldn't surprise me if they didn't take it at all. And I'm being absolutely serious when I say that."

The office went quiet for several moments.

"Exactly what do you mean by that?" Jordan finally asked.

Patty took a deep breath. "A president needs to be very careful at a time like this, at such a crucial pivot possibility in history. There's so much at stake here. Eight hundred billion dollars a year is a lot of money. It's a lot of tanks, fighter jets, and aircraft carriers. But, more important, it's a lot of stars that won't be awarded and a lot of promotions that will wither and die on the vine. Careers of very senior people will stall, even snuff out. These are people who might be willing to go to great lengths to destroy Prosperity for All, people who might be desperate enough to try anything to keep their careers on track. Do you know what I mean, Katrina? These are people who have committed thirty to forty years to a certain way of life. Their entire self-worth and self-perception are tied directly to that way of life. And they're accustomed to getting their way. Worse, they're accustomed to getting their way by using weapons. Firing bullets to achieve their goals doesn't bother them in the slightest. Killing doesn't bother them in the slightest. In fact, a lot of them probably like it."

The office went quiet again.

Katrina ran her fingers through her hair—three times.

"What are you saying I should do?" Katrina finally asked. "Limit the number of people who can have contact with me? Make my schedule more unpredictable? Increase my Secret Service detail? What?"

"How would you know if they were loyal to you?" Patty asked. "How would you know if they did or didn't have ties to people at the Pentagon?"

"How do we know if *anyone* is loyal?" Jordan asked.

"Exactly," Patty said, "thank you for making my point, Dennis."

"So what do we do?"

Jordon was out of his league here. He'd always monitored the actions and plans of the Secret Service, of course. But now that Patty was forcing him to dig deep, he realized he had no real way of knowing who he could trust in the face of Prosperity for All.

Another shiver tingled up his spine. This one was driven by an overwhelming feeling of helplessness and a healthy shot of mortal fear. It was time for Katrina to open the Black Book—which he would recommend Katrina do as soon as Patty was gone.

"Well?" he asked expectantly.

Patty glanced at him, then at Katrina. "Pray," she whispered, "even if you're an atheist."

CHAPTER 14

North of Billings, Montana

John Brady had studied detailed architectural drawings of the shuttered specialty-steel plant during the entire three-hour commercial flight out to Montana from Minneapolis. While sitting squeezed into row 23's middle-right seat of the Delta 737 like any other average American, which he clearly was not, so he looked like any other average American, which he clearly was not. Now he knew the interior of the factory like the back of his hand.

And he'd been glassing the seventeen-acre facility located twenty miles north of Billings in the high desert of eastern Montana from a bone-dry bluff fifteen hundred meters away for the last several hours through high-powered binoculars. Now he knew the exterior of the factory and his possible approach tracks as well as he knew the interior.

Of course, you could study target drawings until the bulls came home. But drawings could end up mattering oh so little when everything went haywire and the bullets began flying in the scorching fireball of battle. He knew that from experience all too well.

General Fiske's intelligence indicated that the team would meet "little to no resistance" when they entered the factory to kill the Muslim cleric—who was supposedly using this facility as a secret base of operations to carry out terrorist activities in the United States. But little to no resistance seemed counterintuitive to Brady. Quite the opposite seemed more likely. There would indeed be a protective force embedded here, he believed.

Radical Muslims loved their weapons. Firing wantonly into the air with no regard for where bullets fell was a favorite pastime for them. More to the point, they loved to kill. Even *more* to the point, they desperately wanted to *keep from being killed* regardless of their loud and ridiculous religious PR about getting to the next life as quickly as possible to bed down with forty virgins.

"Fight to the death" was their mantra, so they figured the other side would fight the same way. If they had no weapons, they couldn't defend themselves against enemies who had no intention of taking them prisoner.

Once again, Brady knew all of this directly from experience.

"There will be bullets," he muttered under his breath as he spat out a sunflower seed. It was a lot of work to get to the tiny seed. But it was so worth it when you did. "Fiske and Lewis are wrong on this one."

General Fiske had grown naive—as had General Lewis—he was convinced. They'd been away from the battlefield's front line too long. And they'd never fought on this kind of battlefield.

Fiske had claimed to Brady that the cleric didn't want to draw attention after quietly purchasing the mothballed facility for pennies on the dollar when the company had gone bankrupt due to a barrage of cheap Chinese imports. Fiske had claimed the cleric was worried that local authorities would take a keen interest in him and his facility if there was any hint of illegal activity going on here, if there was any hint of arms and a heavy resistance force. And local authorities in the wilds of Montana were well trained on spotting odd, paramilitary activities. Typically here it was white supremacists. But the same basic tip-offs applied to radical Muslim locations.

The cleric was using this desolate location specifically as a storage, staging, and training center. Only five cars and a single box truck were parked in the dusty two-acre lot. So everything seemed to fit Fiske's assessment.

But Brady wasn't fooled.

He'd been prepared to attack an hour ago. However, he was waiting for the last member of his team to arrive, the man who'd carried out Michael Mattix's death sentence for his crime of treason against the United States.

Brady wanted his five-member team at full strength for this mission. He had a vibe . . . and it wasn't a good one.

He got them every once in a while, typically every six or seven missions. So it wasn't unusual for him to be wary. In fact, he'd become accustomed to it. And nothing major had ever gone wrong before.

But this time the vibe was more intense. It was more like a *haunting*.

He brought the binoculars down when he glanced over at the boys. The three of them were sitting in the dusky shade of a rocky overhang, playing poker. It was hot as hell out here in the middle of the summer.

He grinned as he watched them laugh and poke fun at each other. They looked like everyday, ordinary men. They were all very average physically, all individuals who blended into crowds easily—which was exactly what he wanted, what he *required*. It allowed them to slip through the world unnoticed.

His focus flashed back to the boulder-strewn landscape before him, and he raised the binoculars back to his eyes. Something had moved out there . . . to the left.

He grinned again when he realized it was the fifth member of the team coming toward them. In a few minutes, they'd be at full strength. At that point they'd go over everything one more time—then penetrate the structure, kill the cleric, and get the hell out of here.

He moved his focus back to the facility and grimaced as he glassed the approach options one more time. He should be able to get to within three hundred meters of the facility without being noticed. But after that, they'd become vulnerable to being spotted. And waiting until tonight and the cover of darkness wouldn't do them any good. Everyone had night-vision technology these days.

◆ ◆ ◆

Twenty minutes ago, Troy Jensen had spotted five individuals advancing stealthily toward the facility across the high desert at four hundred meters out. The men were clearly trying to mask their approach, darting from boulder to boulder as they came, then lying low at alternating intervals.

They were good at what they were doing—though not good enough. Most lookouts would never have spotted the invaders out there in the rocks and the sand and the cacti and the rattlesnakes. But Troy had been trained by the best on the planet in every discipline of his chosen profession.

He moved silently behind his first victim, who'd been posted just inside a factory door—apparently as a sentry—clamped a steely hand over the man's mouth, and twisted the chin violently to the right so the neck snapped instantly. The man was dead without a gasp or a gurgle even before Troy eased his limp body to the sawdust-covered concrete floor.

Troy grabbed the man's pistol off the floor where it had fallen and was about to drop it into a nearby fifty-five-gallon drum half-full of oily sludge, when he stopped short. The pistol was a Glock 17, the preferred weapon of US Special Forces. He'd been expecting a Browning or something made in China or Russia.

He dropped the gun in the drum, and then dragged the body behind a stack of rusting I-beams.

Troy held a special license, the most special and deadly license anyone could hold in his line of work. The most special license anyone could hold at all, he believed. The lanky, thirty-two-year-old Brad Pitt doppelgänger was empowered to do *whatever* he and he alone decided to do—literally. His license included the approval to kill anyone at any time for any reason when he believed that action was necessary to protect the well-being of the United States of America. He didn't need to call anyone. He didn't need an act of Congress. He didn't even need to call his boss. He just needed to make the decision.

It was that simple and straightforward when it came to Troy's charge: do whatever you believe is necessary to protect the United States of America. You will never be prosecuted. And, if you are detained for any reason in a friendly country, we *will* get you out. If you are detained in an unfriendly country, we will do *everything possible* to get you out.

The key to all of this was the "we" involved. It wasn't any of the federal government's intelligence units. It was much more powerful than that.

Troy had allowed all five men to make it inside the facility's perimeter in order to make absolutely certain he killed them all. If the oncoming assault team had consisted of three men or less, he would have used his .300 Win Mag and picked them off quickly from long range, then buried the bodies where they fell before daylight. He was one of the deadliest snipers in the world.

But with four or more targets bunched together only a few yards apart, the odds were better than fifty-fifty at least one of them would belly-down and find cover in the boulder-strewn terrain out there before Troy could kill him. The survivors would quickly realize what was happening when others of their unit began to fall, and they'd go to ground behind one of the boulders out there before he could get them all. And he had to get them all. There could be no survivors.

He didn't want to be forced into setting off into the desert to track down the last one or two. His clear advantage would be gone. The odds would edge closer to even. So he'd let them all come inside the plant, where the advantage of shock and surprise remained with him.

Troy stole through the dimly lit factory, illuminated only by early-morning sunbeams shimmering through thick windows around the top of the plant's forty-foot cinder-block walls, sprinting past several huge furnaces that hadn't been fired in months. The remaining four men he was stalking had split into two teams, and they were probably all in constant contact. Which meant those remaining four might already understand that a comrade had fallen, because he wasn't making his required minute-to-minute check-in.

Troy quickly caught up to the first team of two. They were moving deliberately toward the executive offices of the facility, toward the location they believed the cleric was working—a cleric who was working with radical Muslims who believed the cleric was loyal to them but really wasn't. The cleric was actually whispering everything he was learning from the radicals to Troy and, therefore, to Red Cell Seven. He was an invaluable double agent.

Red Cell Seven was the most covert and deadly intelligence cell in the entire US arsenal. Officially, it did not exist—which wasn't unusual for deeply buried US intel cells. What made RC7 different from all the others was that its fifty-two members reported to no one but themselves on a day-to-day basis. *And* they took no funding from any government department or agency. A tiny, wealthy, ultrasecret cadre of angels privately funded them. So there was no funds-transfer trail for enemies to uncover.

RC7 had been founded in the 1970s by the Central Intelligence Agency, during the Cold War with the Soviet Union. The powers that had been at that time named it Red Cell Seven to confuse their Soviet counterparts—and the strategy had worked perfectly. The Soviets had spent years and years as well as billions and billions attempting to find cells one through six. But they never could . . . because cells one through six never existed.

In the mideighties, when the Iron Curtain disintegrated under an economic tsunami, Red Cell Seven broke away from the CIA and buried themselves even deeper underground. Assigned with keeping the country safe in any way it believed necessary, now it reported to only one individual inside the US government: the president . . . by way of the Black Book.

And *that* was what made all this so strange for Troy. The sentry he'd killed a few minutes ago had been a member of US Special Forces. The Glock 17 was absolute proof. But why would US Special Forces have been sent here to assassinate a cleric who was providing so much good information to the United States? And there could be no mistaking what these men were here to do. The Pentagon had to know what was really happening at this facility.

It made zero sense.

Making sense of it all would have to wait. He had to kill these people. He had to protect the cleric, who was holed up in another area of the facility after Troy had ordered the man to get away from the executive offices once he'd spotted the approaching assault team.

The first team Troy was stalking hesitated at the end of a long corridor that led away from the plant floor directly to the executive offices. Troy made certain neither man was the leader—none of the other men in the unit had saluted that individual. The leader knew everything about this mission. That was the man Troy wanted alive.

Troy knelt behind two pallets of stacked sheet steel, pulled his phone from his thigh pocket, and slid icons around until he got to the one he needed. He was less than fifteen feet from the two men as they conversed quietly in muffled voices. From his other thigh pocket he removed what resembled a sleek, thin, silver hockey puck. Without hesitation he slid the device across the cement floor—at this location there was no sawdust—so it came to rest close to the right boot of one of the men.

Both of them glanced quickly down at it.

Before either could react further, Troy pushed the bomb icon on his phone, and the device sent deadly nerve gas billowing up at them. They staggered several steps before tumbling to the floor.

Troy waited thirty seconds for the gas to dissipate, then moved to where the men lay and inspected their weapons. Again they were the preferred handguns of US Special Forces.

And then the possibility dawned on him.

◆ ◆ ◆

Brady and his wing—the young man who'd murdered Michael Mattix in Manhattan—crawled the last dozen yards across the bristly, dirty carpet to the office door under which a faint stream of light was shining. Brady was convinced that, after their exhaustive search of the facility, he'd finally located the cleric. The language and accents of the voices coming from within convinced him he'd hit pay dirt.

So far, Fiske and Lewis had been exactly right—no resistance. But Brady was taking no chances this close to executing his mission.

One on one side of the door, one on the other, the two men slowly rose to their feet, pistols clasped in both hands.

Brady signaled to his young wing, and then nodded down. He grabbed the knob and flung the door open. The other man dashed inside, firing away.

Brady knew the sound of gunfire very well after so many years in the field and so many close-combat struggles. An instant before he'd actually penetrated the office, he recognized that two different weapons had fired. Even before he saw his young wing slumped on the office floor in front of a dark-wood desk, he'd discerned the sound of a second gun.

He whipped around, in the direction of the enemy fire. But before he could bring his weapon to bear, fingers that felt like eagle talons wrapped around his throat, his weapon was knocked cleanly away, and something composite pressed to his temple. Then his gray eyes met the piercing crystal-blue ones behind an all-black ski mask covering the face of his attacker.

In all his years, Brady had never experienced anything like this. Even as the Arabic words of some long-ago recorded conversation kept coming from the phone on the desk, he accepted that he'd met his match. Accepted that whoever this enemy was, he was incredibly talented when it came to the art and talent of killing.

"Who sent you here?" the attacker demanded.

"God," Brady managed despite the viselike grip on his neck. He'd been expecting a foreign accent from behind the ski mask. But he quickly assessed the accent as US Northeast, though only slight.

"God has nothing to do with this."

"He has everything to do with this."

"Answer me."

"I can't remember."

The attacker brought the gun smoothly down and fired a bullet through Brady's thigh.

Brady collapsed to the floor, groaning loudly as he grabbed his leg and constricted tightly into a fetal position.

The attacker kicked Brady in the face with his steel-toe boot, then stepped directly on the wound. "Who sent you here?"

Brady screamed uncontrollably. The bullet had to have been laced with something awful because his entire leg suddenly felt as if it were on fire, as if a white-hot blowtorch were burning out of control inside it. And the fire was creeping past his groin toward his stomach. It was by far the worst pain he had ever endured.

"*Who?*"

"I . . . I . . . ," Brady gasped.

"I can stop the pain . . . if you tell me."

Brady had never been taken prisoner, but he'd played out this moment in his mind over and over. How would he react to torture? Could he stay strong and give away nothing even in the face of agony? Did he have that ultimate will inside him? A warrior never really knew until he was thrust into that situation.

"Very quickly that fire will consume your entire body, and then I won't be able to stop it."

"I . . . I . . ."

"Tell me."

"General George Fiske," Brady gasped, unable to bear the pain any longer.

The attacker nodded, very familiar with that name—not simply because General Fiske was head of intelligence for the Joint Chiefs of Staff.

"Thank you," he said as he pressed the barrel of his weapon to Brady's temple—and fired.

As Brady tumbled to the ground, quite dead, the attacker's phone buzzed. When he glanced at the number on the screen, his heart began to pound. He'd been trained to recognize the number immediately. Every morning he silently recounted it several times as soon as he came to consciousness. But in seven years as a member of Red Cell Seven, this was only the second time those digits had ever appeared before him.

He had to get east as soon as possible.

CHAPTER 15

Manhattan, New York

Falcon glanced at his watch as he emerged from the diner, leaving Cain behind to finish a mountain of greasy bacon and a double helping of biscuit gravy. It was a few minutes after noon in downtown Manhattan, thirty-six hours since Claire had been kidnapped. But now he believed he was finally closing in on what he needed, what Billie had demanded he get. There was just one more hurdle here in the city, and then he could head south toward North Carolina and Claire. It was a daunting hurdle, but with Basil Slicke's help, it was doable.

As the diner door swung closed behind Falcon, he spotted them standing on the corner directly across Broad. They were the same three men who'd come at him on Wall Street thirty-six hours ago.

They spotted him at the same moment.

Falcon bolted left, north, toward Federal Hall, as one of the men jammed his hand inside his jacket, presumably for a gun. He sprinted ahead, dodging pedestrians on the sidewalk. He glanced over his shoulder when he'd sprinted thirty yards, to check if the men were following.

Both enforcers were. The smaller man had stayed back.

Just as Falcon looked ahead again, he plowed into another man carrying a briefcase. Both of them went sprawling to the sidewalk.

Falcon jumped back to his feet like a big cat as the other man shouted obscenities and struggled to make it to his hands and knees. His pursuers were only a few strides behind.

He raced past the Stock Exchange, zigzagging to make himself a tougher target for a bullet.

He turned left when he reached Wall Street and kept going toward Broadway, still zigzagging. The men chasing him had been armed the other night. He had to assume they were now.

Falcon dove into the 4-5 subway station at the corner of Broadway and Wall, leaping down four steps at a time. Once into the station, he hurtled the subway turnstile, dashed to the south end of the platform, and then jumped down onto the tracks to the terrified shouts and screams of those awaiting trains. He didn't need to look back to see if the two men were still chasing him. He could hear their heavy breathing and their footsteps pounding the platform behind him.

As he headed into the tunnel's darkness between two glistening, shimmering rails of steel, he was hit by a wave of stiflingly hot air laced with the sour stench of mildew. One stumble and he could plunge into the charged third rail to his right, which would kill him instantly.

He thought he heard a gunshot, then another. The next station was Bowling Green, and it was half a mile away. There wasn't another stop after that until Brooklyn. He was praying he could make it to Bowling Green before a train came at him.

His prayers quickly disintegrated. Two faint headlights rose up and then sparkled ahead of him in the distance. He glanced back as he ran, searching between the closely set, sludge-covered steel support girders separating the uptown and downtown tracks. A downtown train had just pulled into the Wall Street station. The headlights were suddenly brilliant beside him, so he couldn't jump onto that track. And the men were still chasing him.

He gritted his teeth as he looked ahead again, sprinting hard. The oncoming train was closing in.

◆ ◆ ◆

Chicago, Illinois

"Good morning, Reverend Taylor."

"Call me Chalice," Taylor ordered as the two African American men shook hands across the cluttered desk of the cramped office.

"You feel like we've known each other long enough now that there's no need for formality anymore," Ben Carter said as he eased into the chair behind the desk with a wide grin on his broad face. That made him happy. He'd always felt a distance between them but had always wanted their relationship to be closer. He had to know this man had his back if things ever turned nasty. So he wanted to feel there was a bond—not a distance. "Am I right?"

"No," Taylor answered stiffly as he sat down carefully in the small chair before the desk with a groan, small at least for his huge, NFL-battered frame. "I like Chalice better. It befits me. Reverend Taylor makes me sound old."

Carter's grin faded. Chalice Taylor was the most arrogant son of a bitch Carter had ever known. And Chalice's self-adoring condition wasn't a result of being an all-world tight end for a decade. Carter had known other professional athletes who'd been loved by fans equally if not more, and they hadn't suffered this fate—at least, not to the degree Chalice had. No, Chalice was just naturally and completely self-centered, convinced the world revolved around him, convinced that the sun's name was Chalice . . . or Reverend Taylor.

Before today, Chalice had always specifically wanted to be called "Reverend." Now that edict had suddenly turned 180 degrees. Chalice simply enjoyed being difficult, Carter figured. He got a thrill out of imposing his will, even with something as trivial as what he would be called. Their relationship wasn't improving after all.

Still, Carter needed the reverend. More specifically, he needed the seemingly limitless fire hose full of money Chalice apparently had access to and could readily shoot out as he decided. Carter wasn't sure if it was ultimately Chalice's cash or not. His gut told him it wasn't. But the reverend had always delivered on all promises made. If it wasn't his money, he was sure as hell the trustee.

So Carter would put up with the petty games. He had to. He always had to keep the big picture top of mind.

"How was your flight here to Chicago?" he asked, forcing himself to be polite as much as he hated himself for it.

"A pain in the butt," Chalice muttered. "Like some pansy-ass white-boy safety who keeps elbowing me in the balls when the ref isn't looking because he knows he can't run with me without giving me the dirty play. The little plane I took out of Richmond at seven a.m. this morning didn't have first class. I can't fit in the seats average people sit in. I won't ever take a plane like that again. I won't sit with the common people like that. It doesn't fit who I am." He pointed a long forefinger at Carter. "From now on, you come to Richmond to see me."

"You said you wanted to come out here," Carter reminded Chalice. "You said you had other business."

"Are you disagreeing with me, Ben?"

"No, I'm just—"

"Don't do that. Don't ever disagree with me. You should know not to do that by now. You may be the coach here in Chicago, but I'm the GM of the entire outfit."

Carter stared across the desk. It was all he could do to keep his temper checked at the door. "Of course you are," he finally managed.

"Update me," Chalice commanded. "Tell me all the things about the game you can't tell me on the phone."

It irritated the hell out of Carter to be continually lying down and taking orders from Chalice. But he had no choice.

"We're planning another attack," Carter spoke up in a low voice, as if someone outside the closed office door might be eavesdropping. "As we agreed we would the last time I was in Richmond."

"When will it happen?" Chalice asked.

"Within a few weeks."

"That's too long. We need it sooner."

"Well, I—"

"Where will it happen?"

"Philadelphia."

"I like that play," Chalice agreed, nodding emphatically. "Philadelphia's another good city for a racial tornado to hit. It's dead center of the northeast corridor. We'll get tons of press, and it'll convince the authorities that WOW is headquartered in that area because the Baltimore attack was so close. It'll make them think the next attack will be in New York City. The trend will be that way, and people always think the ultimate goal is Manhattan. All that should deflect interest in Chicago. It's good misdirection. Nice play calling."

"Yeah, that's what I was thinking."

"What have you promised our assassin?"

"Two million dollars."

"We only paid Quentin Jefferson's widow-to-be a million five."

Carter nodded. "Yeah, so?"

"Why are we paying two million this time?"

"That's what Donny Hill says he needs to take on a mission he knows he won't come out of alive. Like Quentin Jefferson didn't. That's Donny's death price, for lack of a better way to describe it. I think it's pretty cheap, considering that—"

"All right, all right," Chalice interrupted with a wave of his big hand. "Two million dollars it is. But you make sure the attack happens within a week. Not a few weeks. You got me? For the extra half million, Donny Hill lives two weeks less."

Carter relaxed into his chair. This was incredible. The negotiation was over that fast, and now more white police officers would die. It had taken him less than thirty seconds to convince Chalice to pay $500,000 more as compensation to the assassin's widow. Whoever was behind Chalice wanted these killings to happen very badly.

And so be it. Carter didn't give a rat's ass how much money it cost as long as it wasn't his money. All he cared about was that the attacks would go off. He hated white people every bit as much as Chalice and his money people apparently did—probably more, in fact, now that he thought about it, and for a damn good reason.

"One week, Ben, you hear me?"

"I hear you, man," Carter snapped, unable to curb his attitude this time. "I heard you the first time."

"Excuse me?"

Carter's eyes narrowed. "I heard you the first time . . . *sir*."

"Chalice."

"Yes, sir, *Chalice*."

"All right then. The war on whites continues." Chalice held up for a few seconds. "What about the Kelvin James situation?"

"I moved the man, our man, who actually shot and killed Kelvin James, out of New Orleans to a small town near Tuscaloosa. It's a nice house. He and his family will be very happy there, and no one will ever find him or link him to the James murder." Carter was taken aback when Chalice burst into a barrage of deep, rolling laughter that sounded like thunder. "What's so funny?"

"I just pictured Officer Breaux. That fat, slobbering bubba-cop in New Orleans we framed for the Kelvin James murder. I pictured Breaux all those times he roughed up and abused our brothers and sisters when he was out in their neighborhoods on patrol, just for his own entertainment. He always has that snotty smirk on his face in all the photos you showed me. But when I saw him on the news last night, the smirk was gone. He looked like a redheaded stepchild covering his face with his hands as he ran from the mob of reporters and cameramen who were chasing him."

Carter smiled. "Yeah, we tracked Breaux like a trophy water buffalo that night after we lured him into the neighborhood with the fake domestic violence call. We had three people on his ass during his entire shift. We knew exactly when he got to Gallier Street and encountered Kelvin James on the street. So our man could shoot Kelvin thirty seconds after Breaux drove off. Police records will show that Breaux was undoubtedly in the James neighborhood when our people demand the records of his shift that night under the Freedom of Information Act. And we stole Breaux's personal revolver from his home to kill Kelvin. Ballistics will prove Breaux's gun is the murder weapon. Officer Breaux has a very bad problem on his hands."

"When's that revolver showing up anonymously at police headquarters with Breaux's fingerprints all over it?" Chalice asked.

"About ten minutes from now," Carter answered, checking his phone for the time.

"Who'd you send it to? Somebody friendly, I hope."

"It's going to a black female officer on the New Orleans police force who hates Breaux. They got into it in the middle of the precinct a few months ago. Her name's Latonya Jones. Latonya will make certain that murder weapon gets into the right hands. And she'll make sure the press hears all about it. I guarantee you."

"Good."

"You think Breaux will ever see the inside of a courtroom on this, Chalice?"

"Probably not, but it doesn't matter. The liberal media will grill the hell out of him just like they'll grill the rest of the New Orleans police force. They'll all be guilty in the court of public opinion, and that's the only thing that matters. That's the only court we care about. It'll be just like what happened in Ferguson, Missouri, a few years ago."

Carter winced. "I feel bad about Kelvin," he murmured.

Chalice shrugged. "We're at war. Sacrifices must be made."

"Maybe we should send something to his mother. You know, as compensation for the loss of her son, like we compensate the families of our WOW assassins."

"No chance. I don't want any hint of anything going on behind the scenes with the Kelvin James murder. Nothing anyone could say shows that maybe someone other than Officer Breaux was involved. I feel bad about Kelvin, too. But there's nothing we can do. We have to put the good of the whole in front of the James family."

"I guess." Carter had wanted to ask this question for a long time. "Where does all the money come from, Chalice? Is it yours?"

"You don't want to know."

"Well, obviously I do, because I just—"

"I'm not going to tell you, Ben. Don't ever ask me that question again." Chalice stood up and headed for the door without shaking hands. He did have other business in Chicago. But he hesitated with his hand on the knob, then turned back around. "Where does your hatred come from, Ben?"

"What hatred?"

"Your hatred of whites."

"The same place yours comes from," Carter replied, as if the answer was obvious. "Our ancestors were enslaved, lynched, and falsely imprisoned for centuries. Our brothers and sisters are still being abused by white police officers, especially in the inner cities. Here in Chicago it's ridiculous; it's out of control." He hesitated. "It's payback time, Chalice. And that's what all this is about. That's what you and I are carrying out."

Chalice shook his head. "You're not telling me everything, Ben."

"What do you mean?"

"There's something that makes this more personal for you. You've never told me what it is, but I've always sensed it. And that's made me wonder about our relationship. If you really respected me, you wouldn't hold back. Teammates have to trust each other." Chalice's eyes narrowed. "Tell me what it is. Tell me what drives you, Ben. Tell me about your *passion*."

Carter blinked several times. Maybe there was more to this man than Carter thought. Maybe he had a divine gift after all. Still, he didn't want to admit what really drove him. He was afraid to allow it to the surface. He never had before. "No, I . . . I—"

"Tell me, damn it."

Carter slowly raised his leg until his right foot was resting on the desk. Then he pulled his jeans up to reveal a prosthetic above his Nike. "Both my legs were blown off up to the knees. I stepped on an IED in Afghanistan when I was in the army."

"So?" Chalice asked without a trace of sympathy in his tone.

"I was out on patrol with four white guys when it happened." Carter clenched his jaw as the scene and the awful words echoed back to him. "As I was lying there, they said, 'Fuck him. Let him die.' And they walked away."

Chalice stared intensely at Carter for several moments. "Bless you, son," he murmured. "Now I understand."

Manhattan, New York

At the last second, Falcon dove down into the filthy, narrow crevice running between the rails and covered his head with both hands. Horn blowing and brakes screeching, the train tore over him as the engineer desperately tried but failed to stop in time. Blistering hot air roared over Falcon like a hell-sent hurricane along with the deafening sound of ten subway cars racing past only inches above his prone body.

The instant the last screeching car passed over him, he was up and running again. He snuck a glance over his shoulder but couldn't make out the silhouettes of the two men through the dim light. He couldn't tell if they were still chasing him or if they'd even made it past the train. But he kept churning his legs as hard as he could, ever wary of that powerfully charged third rail to his right.

As Falcon neared the Bowling Green station, he leaped over a pile of burning newspapers—the train's contact with the third rail had caused sparks to fly and trash discarded by passengers to ignite. Instead of climbing up onto the north end of the platform, he ducked into a small space beneath the waist-high overhang—and waited. It was cramped here for his big frame, but he was able to hide himself from view. And there were no passengers this far up the platform. So no one had seen him slip beneath the overhang.

Seconds later, he heard pounding footsteps and heavy breathing rushing toward him. He strained his ears for the sound of a second set of footsteps. But he was almost certain he heard only one person coming down the tracks. His two pursuers must have split up after the train had roared past—thinking Falcon might have somehow gotten onto the downtown track and was doubling back toward the Wall Street station.

As the legs of the man bolted past, Falcon burst from his hiding place and quickly caught the man as he started to climb up onto the platform. From behind, Falcon grabbed the man's right wrist—the hand holding a pistol—and slammed it against the yellow-painted edge of the overhang twice so the gun skittered and clattered across the concrete platform to the wall.

Falcon began to hoist himself up onto the platform, but the other man grabbed his legs and pulled him back so they both tumbled onto the tracks, heads barely missing the crackling third rail. Before the other man could swing, Falcon did, nailing the man in the chin as they were both scrambling to their knees. As the other man fell back onto the rails with a groan, Falcon climbed onto the platform, dashed across it, grabbed the gun, and swung around so he was aiming at the other man, who was almost up onto the platform.

When the other man realized Falcon had the gun, he eased back down onto the tracks, not taking his eyes from the barrel of the pistol.

Falcon glanced up the tracks toward the Wall Street station. There was still no sign of the second pursuer. "Tell Paul I don't have anything yet," Falcon said. "But I'm close. When I have it, I'll be in contact."

The man's eyes rose from the gun to Falcon's.

"And tell Paul one more thing. If anything happens to my niece, *anything at all*, I won't sleep until I've taken my revenge on everyone involved . . . including him."

◆ ◆ ◆

New Orleans, Louisiana

"Officer Huey Breaux has absolutely no knowledge of anything that happened to Kelvin James on the night in question. I cannot say that more emphatically or with more conviction. Our investigation concludes that Officer Breaux had nothing to do with this terrible tragedy. Our investigation indicates that someone else murdered Mr. James. At this time we are diligently following up on all leads. We will use all department assets available to find and successfully prosecute Mr. James's killer."

Despite the oppressive heat and humidity of the delta morning, the New Orleans police chief wore his dress uniform—replete with stars on the shoulders of his black coat—as he stood behind the dais that had been quickly erected in front of city hall for him to address the worldwide media blitz. The chief was flanked by two lieutenants who also wore their dress uniforms and hats—and who were also visibly perspiring . . . and not just from the temperature.

Conspicuously absent from the news conference were the mayor and members of the city council—all of whom were black.

Officer Breaux stood off to one side, hands clasped before him, eyes glued to the ground.

"The New Orleans police force supports Officer Breaux one hundred percent," the chief continued in his scratchy Creole accent. "He will return to active duty as of this morning. We appreciate his patience as we carried out our investigation."

The all-black protesters amassed behind the media line hissed and booed loudly at the announcement.

"Justice for Kelvin!" someone shouted.

"Police brutality must stop!" another screamed.

Five hundred protesters stood behind the assembled media, which included reporters from as far away as Japan and Moscow. But none of these activists were from TARC. These weren't Riot Actors. These were all locals, mostly from area church congregations. Organized by Paul to take over the fight from TARC long before the Kelvin James shooting had actually occurred. The three hundred Riot Actors were all on their way back to Richmond on their four freedom buses—except for Talia and Bones, who were standing on a far corner, ready to run in case they were recognized. They'd flown down late last night without telling Paul. They'd been told what was about to happen, and they wanted to see it. They *had* to see it.

"Officer Breaux is not guilty of this heinous act," the chief proclaimed loudly. "There is no doubt as to his innocence."

"What about the revolver with his fingerprints all over it?" someone shouted from the crowd. "The gun you just got, man."

Talia grabbed Bones's arm as everyone's eyes shot to the person in the crowd who had just shouted out—including all of the cops behind the dais.

"It's registered to him personally," the man bellowed in a voice that carried as much electricity as a bolt of lightning. "It's not his service weapon, either. He owns this gun personally. And the bullet that killed Kelvin James was shot from this gun. Ballistic tests prove it."

"They really did have it," Talia whispered, awestruck. "Chalice was telling the truth."

"How do you respond to that accusation, Chief?" a CNN reporter demanded from just below the dais. "What other evidence are you holding back? What else are you covering up?"

He was about to respond but was cut short by a roar from down the street. A mob of people had just turned the corner. Their drums beat a powerful, thumping cadence and the Ku Klux Klan flags they carried waved in the morning breeze.

"*White power, white power!*" came the pounding refrain timed to the drumbeats.

More and more people hoisting more and more Klan flags came pouring around the corner toward the news conference. What had initially appeared to be only a few was quickly growing into a mob of a thousand.

"Holy shit!" Bones yelled, pointing. "Look at this."

Talia pressed her body to Bones's as the protesters turned away from the dais and strained their necks to see what was happening. Most of the protesters from the local congregations were women. Only a few were young men.

The white mob was mostly young men—*angry* young men.

At a hundred yards, the white mob broke into a sprint straight for the protesters.

Panic surged through the crowd behind the media as they began looking for any way to escape. Some even broke through the line of reporters and climbed the steps onto the dais, pleading for protection from the police.

But the officers hurried back inside city hall just as the Klan members reached the protesters.

Bones took a step toward the one-sided battle.

But Talia grabbed him and held him back. "We've got to get out of here," she yelled.

"I have to help these people. They're going to be massacred."

"You'll be killed," she said, tears filling her eyes. "I can't lose you."

◆ ◆ ◆

Near Charlotte, North Carolina

"Get up, bitch," the man demanded after yanking the closet door open.

Claire was starving and thirsty. But the last thing she wanted was attention from them, especially this one. She recognized his voice.

Her hands were tied tightly behind her back, and the blindfold covered her eyes completely. Still, she pictured him in her mind without ever seeing him—a despicable, grotesque human being devoid of compassion for anyone or anything.

She struggled to her knees as he pulled her up roughly by one arm.

"Right there," he said, beginning to breathe hard with anticipation. "It's just you and me in the house right now, missy. The other two are gone for supplies. You will do exactly what I tell you to do when I tell you to do it. And you will never tell them what happened when it was just you and me here. If you do, I'll kill you. Do you understand me?" He grabbed her chin and shook it when she didn't answer. *"Do you understand?"*

Claire felt tears rising to her eyes. But she didn't want to give this man the satisfaction of seeing her cry. She had no idea what was happening, no idea why she'd been abducted. But she was going to fight whoever they were as hard and as long as she could.

He slapped her face viciously, so she screamed as she tumbled to the floor.

Then he was on her, pushing something that smelled awful against her mouth.

"Open your damn mouth," he ordered. "Open it!"

She clamped her teeth shut, but he pinched her nostrils together as he sprawled on her petite frame. Finally she could no longer bear the two hundred thirty pounds of his body pressing down on hers, his foul breath and the lack of oxygen. When she gasped for air, he jammed the cloth down her throat and secured it in her mouth with a piece of twine.

He rolled her onto her back and ripped her shirt from her body with one powerful motion.

She knew what was about to happen. Still, she didn't cry.

"*Goddamn it, Reese, get away from her.* How many times do I have to tell you?"

"I was just—"

"You were just nothing. If I catch you doing this one more time, I'll kill you myself."

"But—"

"Hey, if we get the order to kill her, we'll all take a turn. But not until then."

Someone picked her up and literally tossed her back into the closet. She knew because the door slammed behind her and this tiny room had a moldy scent she'd become accustomed to.

Now she could cry.

Where was her uncle? He'd always been her knight in shining armor. Why wasn't her knight here now?

◆ ◆ ◆

Manhattan, New York

"Hello, Mrs. Greenberg," Falcon said politely as a middle-aged woman with dark, curly hair moved through the glass double doors and extended her hand. "Thanks for seeing me on such short notice."

She was heavyset; walked with a noticeable limp; wore a long, poorly fitting dress; and had two pairs of spectacles hanging from her sturdy neck. One pair affixed to a thin silver chain, the other to a gold chain.

When their hands parted, she stepped back and eyed Falcon up and down suspiciously. "It looks like you've had quite a day," she said in a thick Queens accent, "and it's not even lunchtime."

Falcon grimaced. "I slipped as I was getting out of the cab." It sounded lame, but he couldn't think of anything else to say.

"You don't look like the clumsy type."

Falcon had been an excellent lacrosse player at UVA. "Hey, I'm no—"

"I really don't care, dear," she said, patting his arm. "You're so pretty it doesn't matter to me if you can't walk and chew gum at the same time. I just want to look at you."

Falcon grinned. He liked Annie Greenberg. He liked people who didn't take themselves too seriously. "Dust to dust" was his mantra. Everyone met the same fate at the end. There was no reason to pretend you were better than others along the way.

"And, according to that e-mail I got from Mr. Cain earlier, you're probably the newest Sutton partner. Though I must say you look awfully young for that."

Falcon had been copied on the e-mail Cain had sent from the diner. Cain hadn't mentioned anything about him being a partner in it. Cain must have sent another e-mail or placed a call.

"That makes you worth at least a hundred million." She waved for him to follow as she headed back toward the glass doors. "I'm happily married for thirty-one years. But I could make an exception for you, dollface."

"Sounds like an offer I shouldn't refuse."

"Not if you know what's good for you."

Falcon followed Annie into the sixth floor of the Sutton & Company operations center. This building was located on Tenth Avenue and Fiftieth Street, where New York City commercial rents weren't as fierce as they were on Wall Street and Fifth Avenue.

Sutton's high-profile clients never saw this building. This was the blocking and tackling site. No spectacular catches or last-second shots here. Employees here performed the mundane. They made absolutely certain all buy and sell orders were executed cleanly, that client accounts were maintained perfectly, that all employees around the world were paid properly, and that the billions and billions of currencies that flowed through Sutton on a daily basis found their destinations correctly.

This was the funds-transfer floor—just a sea of four-foot-high cubicles in all directions.

"So what's your problem?" Annie asked when they reached hers, which was located directly in the middle of the huge room. She pointed to a chair on the other side of her laminated cubicle desk and nodded for him to sit. From here, he couldn't see her computer screen.

Falcon slid his hand into his pocket and pulled out his phone. But he kept it in his lap so she couldn't see it from the other side of her desk. "I have a *special* client, Mrs. Greenberg, who hasn't received several *very special* wires." He pushed a button on the phone and then dragged his fingertip around the screen to set in motion the nifty piece of tech he'd gotten from G2.

"Oh, really?" Annie asked as if this wasn't the first time she'd heard the code. "What's the name?"

Falcon hesitated, allowing her time to log onto the Sutton system. "The name?"

He waited as her fingers continued to work, not answering on purpose.

"Mr. Falcon, I need the name."

Still, he remained silent.

"Mr. Falcon, give me the—"

"It's Chalice B. Taylor at The Alliance to Reform Communities."

She continued typing for another thirty seconds, then suddenly stopped.

He glanced down at his phone to check progress.

Just as she glanced over the desk at him.

He looked up, sensing her glare. "Yes?"

"What are you doing here, Mr. Falcon?"

"I don't understand."

"How did you get Mr. Cain to put you in touch with me?" she asked in a grave tone, grabbing her landline as she spoke.

Falcon pushed another button on his phone to retrieve the microdrone. But now he had to wait ten seconds to make certain it was home again—because he couldn't see it.

"Don't move, Mr. Falcon."

"What's wrong, Mrs. Greenberg?" he asked, counting down the seconds in his head.

"You know exactly what's wrong."

"What I'm hearing is that you aren't going to help me."

Three, two, one, he counted silently.

"Don't you go anywhere!" she yelled as Falcon bolted from her cubicle. "Hey, get back here!"

Once again he was a man on the run.

CHAPTER 16

Connecticut

Billie rolled over on her broken arm and was screaming even before her eyes fluttered open, awakened instantly by the searing pain shooting up into her shoulder.

Falcon moved quickly across the floor to comfort her—his natural instinct. For the last thirty seconds he'd been watching her sleep from the bedroom doorway. She was startlingly beautiful with her long, dark hair and exotic facial features. And she had a sparkling charisma that radiated everywhere, even while she slept.

He was attracted to her, he couldn't deny it—which was less than convenient given the situation. But he never lied to himself about anything. And he was unimpressed by people who did.

Worse, he distrusted them. If they weren't honest with themselves, why would they be honest with him—especially when it really mattered?

As much as he relied on analytics to make his investment decisions, he trusted his instincts when it came to people. As hard as it was to follow that mantra when it came to Billie, he had to trust himself.

Still, his decision bothered him. If there came a moment when she had to make a crucial choice between good and evil, between him and the wrong side, would she go for the easy wrong—or the difficult right?

He'd felt his attraction to her immediately, the instant they'd met at the cabin in the Adirondacks. The image of her leveling that shotgun at him still lingered in his mind and remained oddly arousing—and maybe that ought to be disturbing. But it wasn't, and somehow that was OK. She had an edge to her. He liked people with an edge, people who were different. Not many were.

He hadn't felt anything like this in a long while. There hadn't been time for it.

But he was feeling it now.

Was the attraction brought on by the tornado of events swirling around them? Perhaps he was suddenly vulnerable because of all that had happened to them. Perhaps his emotions were playing tricks on him. And when this was over, if he were still alive, he wouldn't find himself so into her. He'd read about these things happening when two people were enduring incredible pressure together. What could be more incredible than knowing people were trying to kill you?

He reached out to stroke her hair, then stopped and pulled a vial of pills from his pocket. He had to keep reminding himself that Billie was involved in Claire's abduction, even if her involvement was indirect. He had to keep reminding himself that Billie was the enemy.

Or was she?

"Take these." He held out two yellow painkillers from the vial the doctor had given him before leaving, before demanding but being denied those insider trading tips. "Jason gave them to me."

Billie moaned as she struggled up onto her good elbow. "Thanks," she gasped as he handed her a glass of water from the nightstand. "What time is it?" she asked after swallowing the pills.

"Seven fifteen."

She looked at him quizzically, as if she still wasn't clear.

"P.M."

"Wow. I've been asleep for a while."

"Because there was nothing else for you to do after you tried leaving."

"Thanks a lot for warning me about the shock factor," she snapped sarcastically, holding out the now half-full water glass. "That hurt."

"I told you not to leave," he reminded her, taking the glass and putting it back on the nightstand.

"The word you meant to use was *escape*, wasn't it?"

"Nope. I meant leave."

"You could have at least—"

"Tell me everything about Paul Treviso."

Billie stared at Falcon for several seconds before easing back onto the mattress. "Why should I tell you? I'm a hostage here. What's in it for me?"

"I'm protecting you by giving you a place to hide," he countered firmly. "That's what's in it for you."

"According to you."

"Listen to me, Billie, and listen well. Dangerous and powerful people are trying very hard to find us both. You should appreciate the safe haven I'm providing you." He stared at her intently, wondering how high up in Sutton this went. "They killed a partner of mine, Michael Mattix. They abducted you, and I'm sure would have killed you, too, if not for that accident. They're after us, and we need to work together, not against each other, if we're going to make it to the other side of this. You know, where we end up living."

She said nothing.

"And now I think I know *why* they're after us."

Her eyes flashed to his. "Why?"

He shook his head. "Nah, you first. Tell me all about Paul Treviso . . . other than he's a man you text nude photos to."

"How do I know this isn't bait-and-switch time?"

"You don't," he answered candidly. "You have to trust me."

"There's no chance of that ever happening."

"Never say never, Billie."

"I care about Paul."

"I understand."

"I don't want to be responsible for putting him in danger." She glanced at Falcon furtively, then away. "You strike me as a very capable man, Mr. Falcon. I figure things don't turn out well for people you don't like."

"I asked you to call me A.J. And who said anything about not liking Paul? I don't even know the man."

"He's one step closer to Claire's kidnappers, and you don't like anyone on that staircase."

"It bothers me that you'd like someone on that staircase."

"Don't try manipulating me, Mr. Falcon. I'm on that staircase."

"I can forgive you if you help me."

"If you're going after Paul, I'm not helping you catch him."

"Maybe I'm going after him, maybe I'm not. But if I do, in the end you and Paul will both thank me for it . . . if he's still alive when I find him. Unless I've totally missed my guess, he's in serious trouble, too. The same people who are after you and me will probably figure out he's also involved, if they haven't already. If they haven't, I may be able to save him."

Billie grimaced as she struggled to sit up on the edge of the bed. "You just want me to get you to him so you can find your niece."

"And you should do that any way you can."

"But as your helper?"

"No, as a human being."

"So you can turn me over to the authorities when this is done."

"I won't do that if you help me."

"You're lying about everything."

"Maybe, but I'm the only chance you've got right now. So I'm a chance you'll have to take."

"I don't have to do anything I don't want to. I never have. I never will. And I'm no gambler."

"You could have fooled me." He half grinned. "And I kind of like it."

She gave him a quick sidelong glance. "You've been told about that grin, haven't you?"

He shrugged innocently.

"How that dimple in your right cheek should be registered with women as a deadly weapon."

"Maybe once or twice."

"More like a thousand, I'm betting."

"I thought you weren't a gambler, Billie."

She took a deep breath. "Have you always been this good at manipulating?"

"Unfortunately," Falcon admitted as though he regretted it, "I'm a natural at it. I inherited the gift from my father."

"At least you're honest."

"Well, most of the time."

She managed a wry smile. "Maybe I should meet your father."

"That'll be tough."

"Why?"

"He's dead."

"I'm sorry," she murmured.

Falcon began to say something, to urge her on, because every second counted at this point. But he caught himself. She was going to start talking, he could tell. At her core, she was a good person. He just had to give her time. He had to let the water build behind the dam, to allow her common sense to take over. If this turned into her volunteering information, rather than being forced to give it, she'd tell him much, much more.

He just had to fight his natural impatience.

Fortunately, he didn't have to fight it for long.

Billie exhaled heavily. "Paul and I . . . we both have . . . well, sketchy pasts. I guess that's the best way to describe us. We met at the bottom of the barrel, helped each other out when we met each other there, you know? That's our bond."

"Spin that out all the way for me, Billie. I want details."

"Paul was a made man in the Gambino Family. That's a mafia—"

"I know about the Gambino Crime Family. Anyone who knows anything about New York City knows about the Gambinos." Falcon shook his head, like he found what he'd just heard very hard to believe. "Give me a break, Billie. A made man?"

"I'm not kidding. Look Paul up on your phone. You'll find him. Except his name was Paul Fellini then. Not Treviso. He changed it after he left the Family." She nodded at the pocket where he kept his phone. "The *Post* did several stories on him. Look. You'll see."

Falcon reached for his pocket, then stopped. He'd turned his phone off coming out of New York City. He wasn't going to turn it on again, not while he was here. "Don't try tricking me."

"I wasn't." She rolled her eyes. "Wow. Talk about trust."

"I don't trust anyone," he muttered, "until I do."

"What does that mean?" she demanded.

Falcon waved her off. "So let's assume for a minute that I believe you about Paul being in the mob. So what?"

"So my boyfriend at that time, Vito, was a soldier in the Family. Vito wasn't a made guy or anything. He was just another wannabe at the bottom of the organization carrying out orders from the captains and the lieutenants. I overheard him talking to another soldier one night, when Vito thought I was asleep, about how they were gonna hit Paul. Paul was a captain, and the underboss told them Paul was a snitch. You know, working with the Feds. So the underboss gave the order to have Paul killed."

"Was Paul working with the Feds?"

Billie shook her head. "No," she said quietly. "The underboss just didn't like him. He was worried because Paul was being promoted in the Family quickly, and he thought maybe Paul was going to replace him. So he made up the story about Paul being a Deep Throat for the government. I warned Paul about what was going on, that there was a hit out on him."

"Why did you care? Why didn't you just stay out of it? You put yourself in a dangerous line of fire by telling him."

"I was paying off a debt." She shut her eyes tightly. "Paul stopped by my boyfriend's house one night, where I was living. He came to give Vito an order and he saw that . . ." She glanced at Falcon as her voice trailed off, then past him into a distance only she could see. "He saw that Vito had been beating me. So he pummeled Vito and told him if he ever touched me again, he'd kill him. It worked, too. Vito never raised a hand against me after that. Paul's kind of like you. You push him so far. Then you better run."

Falcon gazed at Billie for a long time, trying to gauge her sincerity.

"What?" she demanded, struggling to sit up on the side of the bed.

"Tell me about yourself," he said, sitting down beside her.

"Don't you want to know what happened?"

"You were attracted to Paul for whatever reasons. You and Paul went on the run together before he was hit. And now we're up to date, at least about that situation."

"You think you're so smart."

"Tell me about yourself," he repeated.

She shrugged. "There's not much to tell."

"Oh, I'm sure quite the opposite is true. Start talking."

"I grew up in a rough area of Detroit with my mother and four sisters. I was a juvenile delinquent at thirteen and in a foster home at fourteen. I bolted from there at fifteen and hitched a ride to New York City with a trucker." She laughed like what a fool she'd been. "I was going to be an actress. But I—"

"Fell in with a bad crew when you got to the city," Falcon interrupted, "started stealing, was probably arrested a few times on minor misdemeanor theft charges, got into drugs, and ended up with a two-bit soldier in the Gambino Crime Family."

"No drugs," she said emphatically. "I've never done drugs."

He raised both eyebrows at her.

"Well, maybe I've smoked a joint or two, but nothing more than that."

"Uh-huh."

"And you?"

"We're not talking about me."

"What did you do today while I was asleep?"

"I got what Paul wanted. What you demanded I get while you were pointing that shotgun at me in the Adirondacks. Before those men grabbed you and threw you in the trunk of their car."

"Seriously?"

"I found wire transfers going outbound from Sutton & Company to an organization called The Alliance to Reform Communities, to TARC, in care of Chalice B. Taylor, the man who leads TARC. For tens of millions of dollars," he added.

"Directly?" she whispered, as if she found that impossible to believe.

He shook his head. "No, each of the wires we researched went through at least eight banks before they finally landed in a TARC account. And they all went through at least two dark holes."

"What are—"

"Numbered accounts. No names, just numbers."

"When you say 'we researched,' who is 'we'?"

"I have a group I use to do my diligence before I make investments. They can and will find anything of interest to me, if it's there to find." He raised one eyebrow. "Did you know that your youngest sister had her first child two days ago? And, BTW, your credit score is 531. You're three months behind on your Discover card. You should pay that—531 sucks."

Billie's mouth fell open in shock.

"Our lives are an open book these days, Billie. At least for people who know what they're doing. And the people I work with are *the* best."

"Of course they are," she murmured. "You wouldn't work with anyone who wasn't. But how did you pick up the money trail? You had to have a starting point."

Falcon reached into his pocket, pulled out his phone, pressed several buttons, and then manipulated the tiny device that had just launched from his phone by passing his index finger around the screen—exactly as he'd done in Annie Greenberg's cubicle. When he was finished, he held out the phone so Billie could see the screen.

"What the—"

Her image was right there on the phone's screen—sitting here on the bed. Something was filming her right now from the far corner of the room, near the ceiling. But she couldn't see a camera when she glanced in that direction.

"Where's the cam—"

"Inside a micro-drone over there," Falcon explained, pointing toward the spot she'd been looking. "You can't see it. It's way too small."

"What's a *micro*-drone?"

"It looks just like the regular drones you see flying around, but it's microscopic. You'd need a high-powered magnifying glass to see it if it were on the nightstand."

"My God, where did you get that?"

"From a firm called G2-DATA. They got it from the same company in Silicon Valley who developed the technology I used to look into your phone at the cabin." He grinned. "By the way, I erased that picture of you before I gave my bloodhounds your data."

"Sure you did."

"And the other fifteen you'd taken . . . all for Paul . . . I assume."

"Not before giving each one a good, long look, I'm sure."

"Well, I wanted to make sure I wasn't erasing a picture my people could use."

"Yeah, you just—"

"I didn't look at them, Billie."

She raised an eyebrow at him. "Maybe that's not the answer I wanted."

He raised an eyebrow back. "Maybe you could—"

"So you spied on someone using this thing, I'm guessing."

"A woman in the Sutton & Company Funds Transfer Department. I recorded her finger strokes on her keyboard."

"Because she wasn't going to just tell you about the wires when she realized what was happening. When she realized what and who you were looking for."

"Of course not."

"She's probably in on the whole thing," Billie said disgustedly.

"Probably," Falcon agreed, thinking back on Annie's tone when she realized who the mark was. It had been angry but desperate, with a little fear mixed in. "I assume she was told not to give out any information on certain marked accounts. So when she saw the flag, she knew there was a problem. But by that time, I'd recorded her keystrokes to get there."

"And you took that recording straight to your information bloodhounds."

"Yes, I did."

"So they could start tracking the wires."

"Exactly. That's where I've been for the last few hours." His eyes narrowed. "Does Paul work at TARC?"

After a few moments, she nodded. "Yes," she admitted quietly. "He changed his name, and then a friend introduced him to Reverend Taylor. He's Chalice's right-hand man."

Falcon nodded. "I see."

She put a hand on his arm and looked up at him. "Are you convinced now?"

Falcon clenched his jaw. "It's so hard to believe, Billie. So hard for me to think that Sutton & Company has been funding TARC in order to stir up white resentment in this country."

"To incite a race war," Billie said firmly. "It hasn't been just to incite bad feelings within the white population. Are you kidding me?"

"I think that's over the top."

"I think you're naive."

"Hey, if there's one thing I've never been accused of, it's being—"

"The man who ran against Katrina Hilton in the last presidential election brought up all the situations TARC was involved in. He did it in all three debates he and President Hilton had. And he brought them up at all his press conferences. He didn't specifically mention TARC when he mentioned the events because TARC goes to great lengths to hide its involvement, according to Paul. But Paul has all of TARC's history. And he told me that the guy running against President Hilton was citing each and every one all the time. In the debates and to the press, the guy went on and on about how in each situation he was talking about, blacks were simply taking advantage of and manipulating what had happened to further their cause. That in each and every case a white person had been accused of murdering a black. But there was no proof in any of the cases that the white person who the rioters were accusing of murder had actually been involved in any way. It's too coincidental that he would identify each TARC target."

"You're saying that the candidate knew what was going on. That he knew what TARC was doing."

"Yeah, because Sutton & Company's senior partners were telling him what they were doing because they were funding TARC. They were manipulating everything, including the damn election, and it almost worked. That Hitler disciple from Atlanta almost beat President Hilton. Can you imagine what would have happened if he had?" Billie's eyes were electric with rage. "And your partners at Sutton are still trying to control everything."

"With Paul Treviso's help."

"Paul thought he was doing right when he took the job at TARC," Billie retorted angrily, understanding where Falcon was going with this.

"He took the job at face value. He had no idea what was really going on with Reverend Taylor at first. But then he started getting suspicious. Now he's trying to help bring it all down."

"By kidnapping a sixteen-year-old girl," Falcon retorted right back, "probably with the help of people he knew when he was in the mob. Does that sound like the right way to go about bringing down TARC?"

Falcon stared hard at Billie for several moments before finally looking away. As he'd been waiting in a G2-DATA conference room, waiting for them to track the Sutton wires, he'd watched CNN on the conference room TV. One of the stories the broadcast had been following was a protest in New Orleans that had turned bloody. A white cop had been accused of murdering a young black man late one night six months ago. But the New Orleans police force had exonerated the cop because there was no proof the cop was involved—at least, according to the police chief.

A crowd of mostly black protesters amassing in front of city hall had suddenly been attacked by an all-white group charging at them from down the street wielding KKK flags. Suspiciously, it had taken the New Orleans police force an hour to restore peace.

And then it hit Falcon as he was sitting there on the bed next to Billie trying to make sense of it all. The news story following the report on the New Orleans melee had been about President Hilton's news conference announcing Prosperity for All. An initiative that would mean huge tax increases on men like James Wallace and Philip Rose. Huge taxes on not only their income but also their accumulated wealth—while they were still alive. And, as part of PFA, President Hilton was going to attack Wall Street . . . along with slashing military spending by 80 percent.

A chill crawled slowly up Falcon's spine, so cold and eerie he actually shook involuntarily when it reached the base of his neck. Wallace and Rose would consider all three PFA initiatives insidious, the initiatives of a traitor president. Not that Falcon welcomed 70 percent tax rates on his income or the president of the United States taking direct aim at destroying his livelihood. But he wasn't going to do anything drastic. He wasn't going to take extraordinary measures to stop Prosperity for All. He wouldn't know where to start even if he wanted to—which he didn't.

But Wallace and Rose would. And they had the connections, the means, and, most important, the arrogance to try. They were the men behind what was going on—Sutton funding TARC. Falcon doubted the conspiracy went any further than that. Wallace wouldn't want it to. He'd be too afraid.

"There's one more thing you need to know," Billie spoke up, "one more thing Paul told me that I didn't tell you at the cabin the other night."

"What?"

"You probably won't believe me."

"At this point," Falcon muttered, "I might believe anything."

"You know these shootings where cops are lured to a fake 911 call and then ambushed?"

"Like the one in Baltimore the other night, executed by that group that calls themselves the War on Whites."

"Paul thinks TARC is funding them to stir up even more rage and bitterness in the white community. He's trying to find evidence of that."

"So, by extension, T. U. Sutton & Company is funding the War on Whites," Falcon said quietly.

The idea seemed absurd, yet the evidence was mounting.

And then the awful reality hit him. Some of the profits from his hedge funds were probably being used to kill innocent civilians and police officers. He swallowed hard.

"Who's pushing Paul to find out what's going on?" he asked.

"What do you mean?"

"No offense, but I don't see Paul trying to bring down TARC all on his own. Someone's pushing him, someone with a much bigger agenda." He reached over and gently lifted her chin. "Who is it?"

"I don't know," she whispered.

"But you know I'm right."

She didn't nod right away, but then she did.

"The three men who confronted me on Wall Street. Were they old associates of Paul's?"

"Yes."

"Why did he send you to the Adirondacks to meet me instead of them?"

"Because he trusts me more than anyone else . . . A.J."

◆ ◆ ◆

Richmond, Virginia

As far as Paul could tell, TARC's headquarters were empty. He'd checked all eleven offices, and everyone seemed to have gone home for the night.

He'd turned off the security system, including the surveillance cameras that covered every room except the lavatory. Chalice wasn't aware that he knew how to manipulate the alarm and the cameras, and neither was Thiggy. At least, he assumed they weren't aware.

They'd just figure there was a system malfunction of fifteen minutes, because he was going to turn everything back on again as soon as he found what he was looking for—or didn't. They wouldn't suspect the glitch was intended, if they even checked the tapes, which Paul doubted they would. Chalice and Thigpen were not as diligent about security as they should have been. In fact, they were stupid about it.

Fortunately, what Paul was looking for ought to be in a file cabinet, not buried in a computer system requiring a password to gain access. Chalice didn't like computers. He loved his phone, but as far as filing things electronically, he wasn't into it.

His rationale for staying with paper was that electronic files were more vulnerable. Some mysterious hacker from the Internet darkness could easily steal him blind with just a few clever keystrokes. But if he kept his files under tight lock and key, Chalice believed he was safe from intrusion.

His real reason for refusing to use twenty-first-century technology, Paul knew, was simply that he hadn't taken the time to learn. He was lazy.

Paul picked the lock and entered Chalice's office easily, then stole through the dim light of the poorly furnished space to the file cabinets in the secretary's office, which was connected to Chalice's by a short, narrow hallway. It was only eight-by-eight in here, half the size again of Chalice's cramped quarters. It was barely big enough to accommodate the desk of the elderly woman—who coddled Chalice all day long—and his file cabinets. They had to put on a show of poverty for the world while they hid the tens of millions of dollars that flowed through TARC every few months to support its expanding operations.

He checked the row of *T* files first, then the *W*s.

"And there it is," Paul muttered to himself triumphantly, as if he were the smartest guy in the room when the scrawled "War on Whites" file tag appeared. He snickered to himself as he leaned down and pulled the manila folder from its resting place in line. "It's like I'm back in the eighties or something." He opened it. "A man named Ben Carter is WOW's leader," he murmured. "And WOW is based in Chicago, and we sure as shit are funding it." He smiled widely. "She's gonna be ecstatic when I call her to tell her what I've found. She's going to keep me protected after—"

"What the hell are you doing in here?"

Paul whipped around. Bones stood five feet away. Talia Seven Feathers stood beside and slightly behind him, an accusatory glare chiseled into her broad face.

"You're not supposed to be in here, Paul. No one is when Reverend Taylor's out of town. In fact, no one other than his secretary should be in here at any time if he isn't."

Paul's gaze fell deliberately down to the revolver that Bones was leveling at him. "Be careful with that thing," he said calmly. "You might hurt yourself." He could tell by the way Bones was holding the gun that the other man had little experience with firearms. "And what are you doing here, anyway? I thought you two went back to New Orleans." The barrel was shaking hard along with Bones's trembling hand. More clues to his inexperience with weapons—and his fear. "Without getting approval from me," he added.

"Call Reverend Taylor," Bones ordered over his shoulder to Talia, ignoring Paul. "Right now, Talia. Let's find out what he wants us to do with Paul."

"I know what I want to do," Talia hissed, pulling out her phone.

"Put the gun down, Bones."

"Shut up, Paul, just shut the hell up."

"You're not gonna use that thing. Believe me."

"Oh, I'll use it if you even—"

Paul whipped a .9 mm from the small of his back and fired once. The single bullet blew through Bones's chest and out his back—killing him instantly—before slamming into Talia's spine, paralyzing her.

Paul was on Talia in an instant, cupping a hand over her mouth and pinching her nostrils tightly together as she lay sprawled on the floor beside Bones's corpse.

She was dead sixty seconds later, unable to defend herself.

He stood up slowly, controlled adrenaline still coursing through his veins. It had been almost a year since he'd killed anyone, but it was like riding a bike. Once you got good at it, the skill never left.

CHAPTER 17

Camp David, Maryland

"Things are looking very positive on the Hill for PFA, Madam President," Jordan spoke up when he heard the door creak open behind him. It could only be one person coming into the room. "Already."

"That's excellent news," Katrina said, her high heels clicking closer and closer to him on the hardwood floor.

She patted Jordan on the shoulder as he relaxed on the floral-pattern couch in the middle of the cabin's great room. Then he heard her move to the window to look out onto the cool dusk that was settling into the western Maryland forest surrounding Camp David.

The evening cooldown was a welcome relief. It had been a swelteringly hot and humid day in the Mid-Atlantic.

"You know how much I appreciate all your hard work, Dennis. Not just on PFA."

She was always positive, always recognizing and applauding hard work. He'd been on the phone nonstop since five o'clock this morning pushing Prosperity for All. At this level and after being with her this long, being recognized shouldn't matter to him anymore. But it did. No one at any level wanted to be taken for granted.

"It's early yet, of course. As we know, it'll be difficult to get Prosperity for All passed in the exact form you've proposed." Jordan recognized the perfume she was wearing. It was her new favorite. "But Senate Majority

Leader Stiles is putting on a full-court press everywhere, even in the House, which technically isn't her purview."

"Peppermint Patty doesn't stand on pomp and circumstance, Dennis. That's one of the reasons we love her. That's one of her greatest attributes as a lawmaker."

"I've spoken to a number of senators friendly to us, and they've confirmed Patty's efforts on the matter," he said, glancing over at her standing by the window. She seemed expectant. "She's already got everyone in her office working overtime almost solely on this bill."

He liked her new favorite perfume. But he wasn't a fan of her heels—they were an inch too tall—or the slim-fitting azure dress she was wearing tonight. It was *too* slim-fitting and rose *too* high above her slender knees. It wasn't lewd clingy, by any means. She wasn't poured into it, and the hem only ended a few inches above her knees. Still, the look wasn't presidential—not in his opinion.

"Patty's putting the nation's needs before her native Georgia's immediate economic best interest," he said, rising up from the couch and moving to where Katrina sat. She'd done her nails, too, he noticed, in red and white. To match the blue dress, he assumed. She always did her own nails, which he found fascinating. "Patty is a true patriot."

"Yes . . . she is. She's, um . . . a, uh . . . a tribute to this country."

She seemed distracted tonight, too. She wasn't entirely engaged, and she was usually "in the moment" no matter the situation. "Are you all right, Madam President?" Something was up.

"I'm fine. Why?"

"You got a hot date tonight?" he joked.

She turned to look at him. "Where did that come from?"

"Why are you so dressed up?"

She held her arms out and twirled once. "I just felt like putting on something nice."

"Wow, well, thank you. Are we having dinner brought in here or are we going to the dining room? What's on the menu? Scallops? That's your favorite out here at the Camp. Bobby always makes them perfectly."

She gave him a quick smile.

A smile he recognized after so long with her. They weren't having dinner together. "What's going on?" he demanded, his voice automatically clicking into chief-of-staff tone.

"I need to be alone tonight."

"Why?"

"I just do." She pursed her lips, as though she regretted what she was about to say. "I need you to leave."

"Madam President?"

"Chief of Staff Jordan."

She so rarely called him that anymore—only in meetings with his people so they knew how much she respected him. "Now, Madam President?"

"Yes . . . now."

"Fine," he snapped, turning away and heading for the door.

"Dennis," she called.

"What?"

"I . . . I'm sorry. I know you don't understand. But you can't. It isn't allowed."

"Yes, Madam President."

She gazed at him for a long time. "Do something fun tonight," she finally said. "Give your mind a rest. You've been working so hard. We all deserve time to decompress."

He nodded stiffly before turning and heading for the door. Was he irritated at her for not confiding in him? Or was he jealous?

The answer would bother him for the rest of his life.

Every few minutes, Katrina walked to the window to gaze into the darkness outside Camp David's main cabin. Then she walked back to the floral-print couch, sat down, and tried hard to read a biography of Winston Churchill. But she couldn't keep her mind on the words. Several times, she realized she couldn't remember anything of what she'd read in the last few pages. Her mind was a million miles away, thinking about him.

It was almost ten o'clock, and she was still feeling bad for how she'd treated Dennis. He didn't understand why she'd dismissed him abruptly without any explanation. He was ultimately loyal and dedicated. He had been for twenty years. But she couldn't explain what was happening tonight. This was one of those presidential moments she couldn't explain to anyone. She'd pushed Dennis out of here like she'd pushed him off a cliff. But that was protocol for this situation.

She found it odd to be alone this way. No pressing engagements, no places she *had to be* in five minutes, no being guided along from appointment to appointment by a bevy of aides with names and titles she couldn't keep track of. She couldn't remember the last time she'd had an hour alone to herself like this.

Yes, she went to bed alone at night, *every night . . . night after night . . .* wherever in the world she was. But this was different. This seclusion and privacy was happening during time outside the bedroom.

Her eyes narrowed, as if she were trying to convince herself she could see him moving toward her in the shadows out there.

Where was he? It wasn't supposed to take this long. This was unacceptable. He was her last line of defense, a knight in shining armor who could not be bought or influenced to go against her under *any* circumstances. He was one of four line items in the Black Book. One of four presidential secrets only she and those former presidents who were still alive knew.

Well, he and his commander knew about this one, obviously. But they probably didn't know about the other three. They knew only that he was one of four. Perhaps, she realized, they didn't know of the three others. Maybe they didn't even know there was a Black Book.

She made a mental note to ask.

There are so many *things I want to ask him,* she thought as she kept clasping and unclasping her fingers in and out of fists.

Why was she so damn nervous? She was the president of the United States. She made everyone else nervous just with her presence in a room, even if they were fifty feet away from her. So why were her palms perspiring?

How could he keep her waiting like this?

"Good evening, Madam President."

Her heart skipped several beats when she finally heard his voice. As she turned slowly to face him, she wondered if her heart had jumped that way out of surprise or anticipation. "Good evening, Colonel Jensen."

When her eyes found Troy Jensen for the second time in her life, she had her answer. It hadn't been surprise.

For several moments, she stared at him, finding extreme comfort in his handsome appearance and fearless aura. The way he stood there with his hands locked behind his back; posture naturally ramrod straight though somehow still relaxed and confident; chin pushed out defiantly as if daring, almost wanting, someone to confront him; light-blue eyes flashing. He was an apex predator.

She'd called that special cell number during her first week in office, simply to test, simply to see how quickly he arrived and what he was like when he did. Being president of the United States was an increasingly dangerous job, and she wanted to gauge her last line of defense. She had no interest in being assassinated. She loved life too much.

She hadn't been disappointed when she'd seen him the first time, when he'd slipped into the White House undetected, as stealthily then as he had at Camp David tonight. Her reaction had been quite the opposite. She'd been attracted to him. What woman wouldn't? The thing was, he'd stuck with her even after leaving an hour later, obviously frustrated by being called to a false alarm. She couldn't stop thinking about him, and she couldn't pinpoint exactly what it was with him that caused her to think about him at least once a day. Perhaps it was those flashing blue eyes.

Whatever it was didn't matter. What mattered was that she felt safe again. Suddenly she realized how terrified she'd been since Peppermint Patty had warned her so solemnly about taking all possible precautions with her personal safety after proposing to blow up the Pentagon's budget.

Katrina's shoulders slumped slightly with relief.

"Are you all right, ma'am?"

He'd noticed her relief. "Ma'am?"

"Sorry. I meant, Madam President."

"That's no good, either."

"Excuse me?"

"Call me Katrina from now on. When we're alone, anyway."

He turned his head slightly to the side. "What?"

His profile was so strong. "I want you to call me Katrina while you're with me. No *ma'am*s, no *Madam President*s . . . just Katrina. Your obligation in the Black Book is to do exactly as I order. That is what I'm ordering you to do right now."

"It is a pretty name."

"Thank you." She hesitated. "How did you get in here without the Secret Service knowing? Or do they know?"

"They don't. Not yet."

"So how—"

"Unfortunately, there are now two less Secret Service agents patrolling your world. But one of me more than makes up for two of them."

"Oh my God, you can't be—"

"The two men are fine. They're just taking unanticipated power naps. When they wake up in a few minutes, I imagine this room will suddenly be swarming with their associates. I'm hoping you'll stick up for me at that point. Otherwise, I may actually have to kill a few of them."

"Of course I'll stick up for you. But I don't know if I should be impressed with your ability to get past them or terrified that I'm that vulnerable."

Troy grinned. "Probably a little of both."

"Oh, great—"

"If those men were the best, they'd be members of Red Cell Seven. They'd be on my team. But they aren't the best."

"Now I really am terrified."

"You shouldn't be. They're very good at what they do." His eyes glistened. "But, as I said, they aren't the best. Of course, only fifty-two are, Katrina."

He'd called her Katrina. "I like the way you take orders." She wondered if he'd understand what she meant. "Will you do everything I ask of you?"

For the first time, his expression betrayed a tiny ray of discomfort.

"Don't answer that," she recommended. "Not yet, anyway." She beckoned for him to come close. "I need to tell you why I called you here."

"Technically," he said, moving to where she stood, "you don't."

"All right, Colonel Jensen, I *want* to tell you why." She found it interesting that she wanted him to call her Katrina, but she liked calling him Colonel Jensen.

"Can I take a crack at the answer first?"

She smiled a surprised but approving smile. She liked that he'd thought about why he'd been called. "Yes."

"First, you just proposed an eight-hundred-billion-dollar cut in the Pentagon's annual budget. Let's call that exactly what it is—a perfect recipe for making a lot of very high-ranking generals furious. You need to understand something. These are people who still sleep very soundly at night even after dropping MOABs on thousands of innocent women and children in the name of killing bad guys.

"Second, you're raising tax rates on the wealthy to percentages this country hasn't seen since the Jimmy Carter administration. And you're not going after just their incomes. You're going after their wealth, too. What generations of their families have worked to save for decades, in some cases centuries.

"And you're going after Wall Street." He shook his head. "It doesn't take a genius to understand why you're looking for a safe harbor to anchor up in while the hurricane fires up. I don't know if the rich or Wall Street really have the stomach to come after you personally. But they'll back up the generals when the generals do."

"You actually believe the Pentagon will try to do me harm physically."

Troy's eyes narrowed. "Yes. And you will do everything I tell you to do when that happens."

She didn't like his assessment of the situation.

"But remember," he said, "I'm paid to think the bad things will happen so I'm ready with countermeasures when they do."

His admission made her feel at least a little better. "What do you think of PFA?" she asked.

"It doesn't matter what I think."

"I order you to tell me."

He pushed out his lower lip. "It will make my job harder, Katrina, and I don't mean my immediate job of protecting you."

"Then what do you mean?"

"I mean when I'm keeping this country safe from enemies outside our borders. Those really bad guys the generals you're trying to put out of business are trying to kill. And believe me when I tell you, *Madam President*, the bad guys the generals are trying to kill are that bad. They don't care about anyone's life but their own. They are animals of the lowest order." Troy gestured for her to stay quiet when she started to speak up. "I don't give a rat's ass about the super-wealthy or the I-bankers. In fact, there aren't many adults in any walk of life I care much about, especially the older I get. Just my family and the forty-eight other men and the three women of my Red Cell Seven command. But if Prosperity for All helps homeless and hungry children, then I'm all in. That's why I put my life on the line every day, to help children, to keep them safe." He gestured for her to stay quiet again. "But an eight-hundred-billion-dollar knife blade to the Pentagon's budget will embolden those bad guys I fight every day. It won't affect me personally or RC7 as a unit, in terms of the weapons or the training we get. As you know, Katrina, we're privately funded. But it will affect the men and women of the military who I fight with."

"Will all that affect your ability to protect me? Does it change how you feel about me?"

He stared at her for several moments. "Not at all," he said firmly. "I will die protecting you if I have to. And I will do it gladly." He chuckled. "But I'm not planning on dying anytime soon."

"Thank you," she whispered. "And I . . . I hear what you're saying about—"

The loud banging of the great room's doors bursting open interrupted her.

"Get down, Madam President!" the lead agent shouted as he dashed into the room, followed by more agents with weapons drawn. "Get down!"

"Black Book Code Red!" she shouted back, exactly as she'd been instructed to do only minutes after taking that solemn oath on that cold January day. "This is my Knight! Stand down, and that is an *order*!"

"Who is this person, Madam President?"

"Stand down right now or I will have you prosecuted!" When she glanced over at Troy, he was nodding approvingly.

"That's the fight I want to see, Madam President. Because that's the fight you'll need to have."

CHAPTER 18

McLean, Virginia

"As of now, John Brady and his team have officially gone missing."

Fiske reported the bad news as he eased into the same chair he always sat in when he came to General Lewis's home in McLean.

He wondered if Betsy was in the house. Lewis had said nothing about her when he arrived, whether she was out with friends for dinner or upstairs. Betsy was a strong-willed woman with a mind of her own. She might despise Project Sundance. She might despise that she would be forever linked to it, whether it succeeded or not. And she might do something about her hatred of it, even if it was her husband she was accusing of treason.

At this point, Fiske believed he couldn't trust anyone other than the man sitting across from him. And, as much as he hated to admit it, he was beginning to wonder if even that was a good idea. What they were planning was unprecedented and getting very real very quickly.

"There's no trace of them anywhere."

"When you say 'officially,' you mean—"

"Per the protocol Brady and I established a long time ago, one way or the other he should have checked in with me by now. That hasn't happened. So I anonymously alerted the Montana State Police to a potential problem at the facility. The police responded by sending five squad cars to the plant, which is a lot of cars to send anywhere in

Montana. But they found nothing out of the ordinary when they got there, just the cleric in his office working. He seemed shocked when they banged on his door and came busting in. He told them he planned on reopening the place in several weeks, which would mean at least fifty jobs for the area. The police apologized for bothering him and left."

"Did Brady and his team penetrate the facility?" Lewis asked tersely. "Did they at least get into the site?"

"All I know for certain is that they landed at the Billings, Montana, airport on a commercial flight. After that . . . I . . . Well, I'm not sure what happened after that."

"What could have happened to them?" Lewis's voice was calm, but Fiske noticed the other man's fingers trembling slightly. "They're the best assassination unit you have. That's what you're always telling me."

"They are the best. I stand by that."

"Then where are they?"

Nerves were suddenly strafing up and down Fiske's body from his fingertips to his toes, revealing to the world his obvious agitation, exacerbated by that slight tremble of Lewis's fingers. Lewis was never one to show what he was feeling. He was always the ultimate ice man.

Up to now, Fiske wasn't certain Lewis had ever actually felt fear—he knew he'd never seen the man feel it. But the conspiracy ocean they were now swimming in far from any shore was filled with enough huge and hungry megalodons to make anyone feel uncomfortable. Project Sundance was unprecedented. Punishment for participating in it would be unprecedented.

"I don't know, General."

"Could someone have intercepted our order to send them to Billings?"

"No chance. I gave him the order face-to-face."

"Could Brady have turned on us? Could he and his four men have gone rogue?"

"Absolutely no chance. They are all as committed to me as they possibly can be."

"Did you tell Brady what was going on out there? That the cleric is actually serving as a double agent? That he's warning people on our side of possible terrorist attacks? Or did you just tell him to kill the cleric?"

"I told Brady exactly what was going on, and he was completely on board with stopping it. He agreed that it was necessary for some terrorist attacks on this country to succeed so America would stay scared. He doesn't give a shit about tax hikes on the wealthy or attacking Wall Street. But he's a hundred percent against cutting the DoD budget by eighty percent."

"Then the only possible explanation is that someone stopped him," Lewis said gravely, "and that someone must be extraordinarily talented if Brady's as good as you claim he is." The general shook his head. "We could have a problem on our hands, George, especially if someone tortured him."

There was that use of his first name again. "Brady would never give up anything."

"You don't know that."

"Oh, I know—"

Lewis's cell phone pinged.

"You're about to meet the two civilians who know something about Project Sundance," Lewis said after reading the inbound text. "And we're about to bring them in on the rest of it."

"*What?*" Fiske asked unsteadily.

Lewis stood up. "I'll be right back. Stay put. Trust me on this."

Fiske's mind was suddenly racing, his panic soaring to an almost unimaginable level. Lewis hadn't warned him about civilians being involved. Yes, the most senior people at the Joint Chiefs now knew about Sundance. And, according to Lewis, were completely behind the plan. That was fine.

But civilians? He didn't trust civilians to keep secrets. He didn't trust civilians in any capacity.

The image of being led before a firing squad exploded in Fiske's mind. For several seconds he considered sprinting for the back door.

He started to rise shakily from his chair. But by then it was too late. Lewis was back with two more conspirators.

"General George Fiske, meet Mr. James Wallace and Mr. Philip Rose." Lewis gestured for the men to shake hands, then pointed to chairs. "James runs Sutton & Company, the premier investment bank in New York," Lewis said when everyone was seated.

"In the world," Wallace corrected.

"I know Sutton," Fiske said.

"Philip is James's right-hand man."

"And an old marine," Rose said. "I fought in Desert Storm."

"James and Philip are as diametrically opposed to Prosperity for All as we are." Lewis grinned at the implication. "Well, you all know what I mean."

Everyone chuckled. It was a good icebreaker, Fiske figured. Suddenly he felt much better about the conspiracy growing. These were serious men. He didn't know much about finance. But he knew Sutton & Company to be the most powerful investment bank on the globe. Wallace didn't need to tell him that. Having Sutton squarely on their side in all of this might actually be a significant advantage.

At some point, he just had to trust Lewis completely.

"Katrina Hilton must be stopped," Wallace spoke up impatiently, driving right to the heart of the matter. "We need to kill her," he said matter-of-factly.

Suddenly Fiske liked Wallace a great deal more. And Rose was a marine. He exhaled deliberately. General Lewis knew what he was doing. Fiske had to keep reminding himself of that.

"My concern with that simplistic an approach," Lewis answered, "is that if President Hilton were to drop the PFA ball because her head was blown off by a well-aimed sniper bullet, her vice president would pick up that ball and run with it. Killing her won't be enough."

Fiske glanced at Wallace and Rose when Lewis described the assassination. They didn't flinch. Lewis had obviously been speaking to them for a while.

"And Patricia Stiles already has senators on both sides of the political aisle all heated up and in a sweat about PFA. She is a formidable Senate majority leader and, therefore, a formidable enemy.

"She doesn't see her job stopping with the Senate, either. She considers herself the true Speaker of the House, not just the Senate leader."

"What is our plan?" Wallace asked bluntly. "How do we stop President Hilton and PFA?"

"The US military will execute a coup," Lewis replied directly. "We will take over the White House using all necessary force, James. President Hilton will be removed from office, stripped of her powers, and the Joint Chiefs of Staff will take charge of this country until a new president can be voted in after a special election, which we will control and manipulate as necessary. President Hilton, as well as several high-ranking members of her administration, will be immediately charged with treason.

"We're also working on framing her for planning to profit from the redirection of wealth associated with PFA," Lewis continued. "Specifically with skimming proceeds of funds sent to certain liberal humanitarian groups, which we will show she secretly owns pieces of. We're still working out details of that misdirection, but it really won't matter. It'll simply be icing on the cake, as it were, because she will be quietly executed within seventy-two hours of the coup taking place. As will her vice president, after they are both found guilty of treason by a military tribunal. We will not allow her to become a martyr to a certain sector of the US population. At this point, gentlemen, President Katrina Hilton is as good as dead. So is Prosperity for All."

As Lewis's words faded into the ether, the image of Katrina Hilton tied up tightly before Fiske appeared to him. It was like a premonition, as clear as day in his mind, and suddenly he didn't care how risky Project Sundance was. He didn't care that if the coup broke badly and turned into an attempted, unsuccessful coup, he would be executed—not the president. His overwhelming desire to play God to the most powerful woman ever to walk the face of the earth, to decide himself when she would die, suddenly became his all-out obsession. He would be President Hilton's executioner. He was confident that his friend and mentor, General Lewis, would gladly hand that job over to him. And it would not go quickly for the woman.

"I love it," Wallace said firmly. "You can count on whatever you need from Sutton & Company. For starters, we will provide you any and all funds you need in any place around the world. And we will keep the US markets stable."

"I was thinking the other way," Lewis said thoughtfully, "at least at first."

Wallace's eyes widened. "You want panic initially. By God, that's exactly right. That's exactly what should happen."

"Yes. I want a major run on the banks. I want chaos in the streets of small-town America. And then I want T. U. Sutton & Company to save the day, to be regarded as the cavalry. Along with the Pentagon, of course," he added.

"We can do that," Rose spoke up. "We can convince the financial world that liquidity is drying up faster than a puddle in the Sahara at high noon. The world financial markets are driven by rumor, and we have ultimate credibility. So what we whisper to other trading floors will instantly be taken at face value. All other major financial institutions will follow our lead."

"We can do better than that," Wallace said. "We can actually make the chaos happen, and not using rumors."

"How?" Lewis asked.

"We invest more than a trillion dollars every afternoon on an overnight basis with thousands of smaller banks around the country so they can fund their loan portfolios. We'll shut off that money supply to Middle America as soon as the coup is in progress. Those thousands of smaller banks we make liquid every day will have to close their doors because they won't have any money to give the people who are banging on their branch doors screaming for their deposits, screaming for their cash. When the time is right, when President Hilton is dead, we'll turn on the money hose again. We'll definitely be seen as the cavalry, especially to Middle America."

"What if the Federal Reserve steps in when you shut off your supply?" Fiske asked, still thinking about the different rope knots he would use to secure Katrina. How good she would look standing there in front of him, her hands tied to a hook in the ceiling, her ankles strapped to hooks embedded in the floor. "They might step in like they did a few years ago when the real-estate market cratered."

"Good point," Wallace agreed, motioning to Lewis. "Your people will need to take over the Federal Reserve as well. The Fed chairman is a close friend of the president's."

"What about Treasury?"

"No need for that. Hilton nominated Treasury Secretary Reed, but they've had their differences in the last few months. Besides, the Treasury Department can't really do anything about the country's liquidity. That's the Fed's job. The fewer targets the coup has, the better. The fewer news clips out there of the military storming DC government buildings, the better off we are."

"That brings up an interesting question. What about the media? Do we lock them down for a week or so after the coup?"

"Twenty years ago I would have said yes. But with all the cell phones littering the landscape, everyone's a reporter these days. Putting the media in the penalty box would do us more harm than good. We'd look like the Kremlin."

"I still say we shut off the Internet," Fiske spoke up, "at least for a week. Let the TV people do what they will, but don't let social media get out of control. I've been working on a project for the Joint Chiefs for the last six months." He kept going. "I've been having my people research how terrorists could manipulate the web. With what I know from this project and having military force at my beck and call to carry out a plan, I could interrupt service for at least a week, especially service coming in and out of this country. There are only a few places on each coast where cables come out of the water. We'll cut those cables, and the rest of the world will only know what we tell them."

"Good," Lewis said approvingly. "I want you to start developing a plan to control the Internet first thing in the morning. I want to discuss that plan with you no later than eighteen hundred hours tomorrow. Understood?"

"Yes, sir."

"The military invented the damn Internet. We should have the right to shut it down when we want to."

"Hear, hear," Wallace agreed. "The less the population knows, the better. And if we let the media keep reporting, we won't look like Communist Russia."

Lewis pointed at Wallace. "We'll need The Alliance to Reform Communities and that War on Whites group to ratchet up their activities in the coming days. Ultimately, we'll need that segment of the US population a hundred percent behind what we're doing."

"The *white* population," Rose said loudly. "Black leaders will consider the coup an opportunity to consolidate their own power, an opportunity to incite blacks to rise up, to use violence. So we'll need the white population furious at what's going on in the country from a racial perspective. We'll need rural America ready for bear, ready for war, ready for a *race war*. Then we'll need to make it clear that this coup isn't just about saving the country from President Hilton. We'll need to make the white population understand that we have a much greater social agenda. That we're taking America back and we're doing it for them. That's how we ultimately win this thing. At that point, we won't need to control and manipulate a special election."

"Wait a minute," Fiske said, leaning forward. "We control TARC and WOW?"

Lewis nodded. "Sorry, George, but I had to keep that piece of this very complex puzzle compartmentalized as long as I could."

"But how?"

"We fund them," Wallace replied. "How else does anyone control anything without a gun?"

"But someone at TARC and WOW must realize what's happening. That their money is coming from a group that's using them to stir up hatred against them."

"Chalice B. Taylor is the biggest mercenary ever to walk the face of this earth. He'd sell his mother down the Mississippi if he had the chance."

"*Chalice Taylor?* As in the Chalice Taylor who played in the NFL all those years?"

"That Chalice."

"But he made a ton of money playing football. At least, I assume he did. He was All-Pro, wasn't he?"

"He also had a posse of hangers-on that was probably the size of our European Command all those years," Rose explained. "When he got to the end of his career, he was bankrupt. His personal balance sheet was a train wreck. He was upside down by about ten million bucks. We saved him. He's still paying us back. He's ours."

"Jesus Christ," Fiske whispered. "No wonder."

"Are you sure the military rank and file will fall into line on this?" Rose asked, gesturing at Lewis.

"The hell with the rank and file," Wallace said, "what about the Joint Chiefs? Is everyone there on board?"

Lewis nodded. "They've been irate with her ever since she took office. She's always taking shots at them in her speeches. When she talks about how they have too many toys, how they have no appreciation for the real problems of this country, and how they exaggerate the terrorist threat to this country. There's always been a fundamental hatred between this administration and the Pentagon. But when she proposed cutting the DoD budget by eighty percent, she signed her own death warrant as far as the Joint Chiefs *and* the rank and file are concerned."

"When will Project Sundance commence?" Wallace asked.

"Soon," Lewis answered coldly. "Very soon we take America back from President Katrina Hilton."

He'd been waiting in the woods near the Lewis house for three hours. He'd watched Betsy Lewis arrive home from dinner with her friends. He'd listened to the neighbors get into a huge fight over money. But he hadn't gotten what he came for. He was worried that somehow he'd failed.

Then it happened. The door opened and two men slipped out into the night and headed directly for cars. He photographed each of them several times with a special night-vision camera.

Now he had to figure out who they were—and why they'd been meeting with Generals Lewis and Fiske for the last several hours. Then he'd report back to his boss—Troy Jensen.

CHAPTER 19

Richmond, Virginia

Chalice checked his phone for the sixth time in the last two minutes. "Where are Bones and Talia?" he fumed as he sat at the head of TARC's spindly conference room table. "I need them here, *right now*. I need to talk to them before they go. We all need to huddle up."

"Are you OK?" Paul asked innocently. He'd never let his expression or his tone give anything away. He was far too experienced when it came to death—especially when he was causing it. "You seem a little—"

"He's fine," Thigpen interrupted. "Aren't you, Chalice?"

"Call me *Reverend Taylor*, damn you."

"But yesterday you wanted me to call you—"

"Shut up, Thiggy." Chalice pointed at Paul. "Update me," he demanded curtly. "Where are we with the game?"

"Tomorrow we're starting protests in Dallas, Atlanta, and Tuscaloosa."

"All white cops shooting blacks civilians, correct?"

"Yes."

"What's the evidence level?"

"Not very good," Paul admitted. "In fact, it's pretty thin."

"What's the Fox News factor on this?"

"Ten out of ten. They'll be all over each one of these situations, especially The Five. At least, four of the five will be. They'll claim each protest is bullshit." Paul held up his hands. "Well, maybe not the one in Dallas. There's some evidence in Dallas that a cop might have been involved. But there's no evidence of anything like that—no evidence whatsoever—in Atlanta or Tuscaloosa. They're both Hail Mary situations." He couldn't resist the sports analogy in front of Chalice. "Like a quarterback throwing a bomb with time running out."

"Are we sending a hundred of our people to each place?" Chalice asked. "Three hundred divided by three."

"I'm sending a hundred and *fifty* to each city."

To Paul it seemed like Chalice didn't care that the evidence of racial brutality by police in those cities was lacking, at least in the murder cases they had targeted to protest—which struck him as odd. Before this, Chalice had always wanted it to at least look like the cops had been involved. There was suddenly a sense of urgency combined with a recklessness that hadn't been present before.

"I had to recruit people around Richmond quickly, but I got them."

"Homeless people?"

"Mostly."

Chalice groaned loudly.

"What else you want me to do that fast, Reverend Taylor? I thought we were going to start these protests over the next six weeks, not start all three of them tomorrow." Paul hesitated. "And why is that, Reverend Taylor, why are we fast-tracking these things?" He assumed the answer was linked to Chalice not minding that the evidence in the three protests they were about to light the fuses for was lacking. And that the answer was probably also linked to the fact that TARC was supporting the War on Whites group in Chicago. "What changed?"

"What about local support?" Chalice asked, avoiding the question. He grabbed his phone and tried Talia again. "Where are we with that?"

"We're good in Atlanta. I've got fourteen churches lined up to help us there." Paul shrugged. "But I haven't had much time to organize people to back us up in Alabama or Dallas."

He put his cell back down when the call went straight to Talia's VM. "Get on the phone and get people excited."

"Getting on the phone isn't enough. I have to go there."

"You're not going anywhere, Paul."

Paul's eyes shot to Chalice's. He had no intention of going to Atlanta or Alabama. He had a very special meeting in Washington, DC, he *had to* make. If he didn't get there, he was risking everything. He was looking at serious prison time, where his former Family members could find him and kill him. The senator who'd been blackmailing him had the power to follow through with each and every one of her threats.

The flip side: if he came through with the information he'd found, his criminal record would be erased and he could start his life over— with Billie.

"You're spending the day with me, Paul."

"But I—"

"Goddamn it, don't—"

"Reverend Taylor?"

Everyone glanced at the conference room doorway. Alice Green stood there. She was a frail, elderly woman who was Chalice's personal assistant.

"Yes, Alice?" Chalice asked.

"I'm sorry to interrupt your meeting, sir."

"No problem, Alice. What do you need?"

"It's . . . it's the oddest thing."

"Yes?" Chalice urged impatiently.

"Someone moved a file in my cabinet, an important file."

Paul tried hard to resist the reflex, but without success. His eyes shot to Chalice's for the second time in the last thirty seconds. This time the silent accusation inside the glare from across the table was obvious.

Paul looked down when his phone began to buzz, and he caught his breath. He hadn't seen that name on his screen in what seemed like forever.

◆ ◆ ◆

Philadelphia, Pennsylvania

More than thirty Philadelphia police cars and multiple officers on foot responded to frantic calls claiming a shooter clad in heavy armor was on a downtown side street mowing down pedestrians using an automatic weapon.

As law enforcement began to arrive, they could not locate the shooter.

And then the sniper shots began to ring out from above—targeting only the responding white officers.

Fourteen officers were killed before the shooter, Donny Hill, was taken out. Once again, a hand-scrawled note was found pinned to the body. WOW was taking credit for the massacre again.

By midnight, $2 million had been transferred into the widow's bank account.

CHAPTER 20

Atlanta, Georgia

The predominantly African American crowd formed early in front of the distraught mother's home, amassing only minutes after sunrise in an economically challenged neighborhood of Atlanta, Georgia. Just as other predominantly African American crowds were forming in economically challenged areas of Tuscaloosa, Alabama, and Dallas, Texas. All three crowds were protesting the same injustice: local law enforcement refusing to investigate their own officers for the shooting deaths of three African American men, none of whom were over the age of seventeen, none of whom were armed at the time of their deaths.

Refusing to investigate their own officers for the killings despite respected community leaders claiming to have credible and substantial evidence indicating that members of local law enforcement were involved—though none of that evidence had yet been produced. And that there were cover-ups ongoing to hide the officer involvement—though no evidence of that had been provided, either.

The crowd in Atlanta was significant, more than seven hundred participants, while the protests in Tuscaloosa and Dallas were only around two hundred people. However, press coverage at all three rallies was solid. In Dallas the number of reporters, cameramen, and producers actually outnumbered protesters.

"What exactly are you protesting?" Hillary Jones asked loudly over the angry chanting going on behind her in the poor Atlanta neighborhood.

Hillary was a tall, extremely attractive black woman with swept-back hair who'd been a reporter with the CBS affiliate in Atlanta for only a short time. Two months ago she'd graduated from Harvard with a degree in journalism. No one else at the station had wanted to cover the protest this morning because a high-profile political kickback trial involving the governor was starting later today. Hillary's instincts told her this protest could end up being a much bigger story than the trial, and she'd jumped at the chance to make her mark.

"What's going on here?" she demanded of Lester Barry as the camera rolled, moving the microphone so now it was in front of his lips.

Lester had been deputized to co-lead the Atlanta uprising by Reverend Chalice Taylor in Richmond yesterday as everyone was boarding buses, after Chalice had given up on locating or hearing from Bones or Talia. Lester was originally from Cleveland, but he now lived full-time in Richmond—when he wasn't on the road at one of these protests.

He'd been with TARC for a year. He was as committed to TARC's causes as anyone could be. He never considered questioning the validity of TARC's claims. For him it wouldn't have mattered if one individual protest was based on fraudulent claims. It was only the bigger picture that mattered. Law enforcement had to be fought.

"Don't give me that crap," Lester snapped at her question, his face torquing into an angry grimace. "You know what's going on here. It's another damn case of white cops killing a young black man for no reason, and nobody in power is doing anything about it. Well, *we're* doing something about it! And as a woman of color, you should be protesting, too. Not wasting my time and yours asking me dumb, stupid questions with obvious answers. You should be committed to our cause."

"What's your name, sir?" She wanted to gauge just how committed this man was.

"I'm Donny Hill."

Hillary's eyes went wide. She recognized the name from reports describing the Philadelphia WOW attack.

"That's right," Lester said loudly, folding his arms tightly over his chest, leaning to one side and bobbing his head in time with the chants. He'd recognized her reaction to the name. "I'm a ghost. I'm the black *Holy* Ghost. I'm the white man's worst nightmare. You can't kill me. I shot fourteen white officers in Philly, and I'm gonna shoot a million and fourteen more whenever I feel like it. I'm immortal."

"Are you from Atlanta, Mr. Hill?"

She knew Hill wasn't his real name, but she went with it. This was going to make fantastic TV. Just two months in and she was going to be promoted, maybe even to the network. Executives in Manhattan were always looking for talent like her so they could say they were being racially progressive.

"You're damn right I am," Lester boasted. Hillary suspected he was lying again, but she let him go on. "A-town down, baby. I'm from one block over. Cops in this neighborhood are always harassing my boys and me. Telling us we're nothing but no-good drug dealers and how they gonna kick our asses and shoot us down whenever they feel like it. But it all stops now. It all—"

A loud and growing roar from down the narrow street interrupted Lester.

Hillary glanced over her shoulder. A mostly white crowd of men was moving steadily toward her.

"Follow me!" she shouted to her cameraman. "Try to get a good shot of those men coming at us."

"Hey, where you going?" Lester yelled after her. "The story's here with me." Then he saw the mob coming down the street. "Oh, shit."

Hillary bolted for the man in the middle of the oncoming mob's front line. He was a big man wearing a tight T-shirt who had bonfires burning out of control in both eyes. He had to be the leader, she figured.

"Get out of the way!" he shouted at her as she closed in on him. "Get out of our way if you know what's good for you."

"I'm a reporter with CBS," she yelled, backpedaling now. "Tell me your side. I know you want to get it out."

"All this protesting in our streets is pure bullshit! There's not a damn bit of evidence that any cop was involved in the shooting. It's just more lies by these radical community leaders to get sympathy from left-wing politicians so they can get more handouts. They're spreading more lies so they get more coverage from the liberal media." He pointed at her furiously as he marched on. *"Like you!"*

"What are you going to do?"

"We're gonna put an end to this protest right now!"

Hillary almost tripped over the cameraman when she shot a glance over her shoulder at the protesters. She'd lost track of where they were, how close they'd gotten to the first crowd. An equally angry line of protesters was forming only fifteen feet away.

A split second later, she was in the middle of an all-out war.

She saw her cameraman get shot in the head, and then she was grabbed and hurled to the asphalt. Someone fell on top of her, and her ribs cracked loudly. She tried to scream for help, but no sound escaped her lips when she was kicked in the face.

Two more people fell on her. She tried to roll away.

Then something surface-of-the-sun hot blasted through her chest and out her back. Her eyes fluttered shut and her body went limp.

Thirty seconds later, Lester was dead, too. Shot between the eyes.

The insanity was in full force.

◆ ◆ ◆

McLean, Virginia

"Look at this; *look at this*." General Lewis pointed as he stood in front of the wide-screen television of his living room, drinking scotch. He jabbed at the TV several times with the hand holding the glass, spilling hundred-year-old gold on the Persian rug beneath his spit-shined black leather shoes. "This is better than we could have imagined, gentlemen."

Fiske broke into a grin. He'd never seen his mentor so happy.

"We've got chaos in the streets of Atlanta. Tuscaloosa's burning. Dallas is on the brink of disaster."

"And Philadelphia's screaming for justice," James Wallace spoke up.

"So is Baltimore," Philip Rose added loudly, ending a call on his cell phone. "I just talked to a friend of mine there. It's a city on a countdown to an explosion. He said gun sales are through the roof in the past two days. They've already called out the National Guard."

"It's not like we'll have to justify the coup," Lewis said. "People are going to demand that the military take over the country to restore order."

"What about Falcon?" Fiske asked before taking a sip off his straight vodka and ice. He hated scotch and bourbon. But he loved vodka.

"We think he got some kind of information when he went to see a woman named Annie Greenberg, who works in our Funds Transfer Department," Wallace answered. "We're not sure what that information could be, but we're concerned. It might connect Sutton to TARC."

"And," Rose added ominously, "if someone was smart and got another piece of information at TARC, that could connect Sutton to the War on Whites group."

"We can't have either of those connections being made," Lewis said gravely. "If those connections were ever to come to light . . ." His voice trailed off. "We must take any and all measures necessary to preserve and safeguard Project Sundance."

"The Greenberg woman says she never let Falcon see her screen," Wallace spoke up.

"Do you trust this woman?" Lewis asked. "Could she have been helping Falcon?"

"It doesn't matter," Wallace replied.

"What do you mean?"

"It just doesn't matter."

"How are we going to track Falcon down?" Fiske asked. "That would take care of everything."

"We're watching Paul Treviso very carefully," Rose answered. "We believe Falcon will meet with Treviso soon. We believe Falcon has the girl."

"You mean Billie Hogan?"

"Yes. And we believe she'll try to get to Paul the information we think Falcon may have. Falcon's niece was kidnapped. That's probably all wrapped up in this, too. We'll take Falcon when he shows up. We have good people on this."

"We have good people, too," Lewis offered. "Why don't you let us handle it?"

"We're fine," Wallace retorted.

"I understand that you want whatever information Falcon may have in his possession to be returned to you. My people will get it to you once he's caught."

"We're fine," Wallace replied in a measured voice. "Andrew Falcon's hours are numbered."

"If only we'd been able to keep Billie in our control," Rose lamented. "But Falcon is a resourceful young man, a formidable enemy."

Wallace shot Rose a look that could have killed.

"What do you mean?" Fiske demanded.

Wallace inhaled deeply. "I had people following Falcon when he went to the Adirondacks. I had people following Falcon the instant he was made a Sutton partner, the way I have all new Sutton partners followed." Wallace had explained the Adirondacks meeting earlier. "And I had suspicions about another, more senior Sutton partner. Michael Mattix."

"Who our people helped you out with," Lewis said.

"Yes," Wallace confirmed.

Fiske's eyes flashed to Lewis. Lewis hadn't told him why he'd wanted Michael Mattix killed, only that the hit needed to happen immediately. Now Fiske understood why he'd been told to call Brady and order the colonel to direct one of his men from Wisconsin to Manhattan—before going to Montana.

"Why did you have suspicions about Mattix?" Fiske asked.

This conversation reminded Fiske that Brady and his team had gone officially missing—and that he might face a firing squad if all this tumbled out of bed. That walk to the death pole would be so difficult. Then his wrists would be secured behind the pole, the hood would come sliding down over his eyes, and a target would be pinned to his uniform over his heart. Would he hear the rifles fire?

"It had come to my attention a week ago that Mr. Mattix was subject to manipulation as a result of certain alleged insider-trading violations."

"What do you mean?"

"Mattix ran our Mergers and Acquisitions Department," Rose explained. "He would have had access to a significant amount of nonpublic information and multiple opportunities to profit illegally on that information."

"So Mattix was vulnerable to being manipulated," Wallace said gravely, "by an aggressive politician who wouldn't necessarily be sympathetic to our cause."

"Who?" Lewis demanded.

"I can't be sure at this point," Wallace answered, "but Patricia Stiles would fit that bill to a T."

"Peppermint Patty," Fiske whispered.

The room went still for a few moments.

"Anyway," Wallace spoke up again, "I had people following Falcon, but we were also on Billie Hogan. We knew she was Paul Treviso's girlfriend. We've been monitoring TARC closely. We followed Billie from Richmond to New York. After Falcon left that cabin, we snatched Billie. We were going to interrogate her. We were going to find out why she had met with Falcon, what she wanted from him, and who had put her up to it. And we were going to find out who had recommended they go after Falcon to get whatever they wanted."

"Which is where Michael Mattix comes in," Rose said. "We think he recommended Falcon to whoever is driving all this. We think he told them to use Falcon to get what they want."

"Patricia Stiles," Lewis said gruffly. "You think she could be the one at the top on the other side, the one who's driving all this."

Wallace nodded. "She could give Paul Treviso a new lease on life. His real name is Paul Fellini, and he's been accused of committing at least fifteen murders while he was a member of the Gambino Crime Family. According to people I know in the governor's office and at the *New York Times*, that's probably a fraction of the damage he actually caused. The person manipulating him must be someone who could cause him a lot of trouble if he doesn't help."

"And reward him with something very nice if he comes through," Fiske added.

"Like erasing his criminal past," Rose observed, "like giving him a chance to start his life over."

"We have to stop whatever is going on there," Wallace said sharply. "We must find Andrew Falcon and Billie Hogan and take them out."

The four men nodded as they glanced around at each other.

Lewis raised his glass, and the other three followed.

"To Project Sundance," he whispered.

"To Project Sundance," the other three echoed.

"It must succeed."

◆ ◆ ◆

New Jersey

A new day was just breaking when the ten-year-old felt the weight of the world on the other end of his thirty-pound-test, monofilament fishing line. A flash of sunlight had just illuminated the eastern horizon of the Atlantic Ocean that lay beyond the huge Verrazano-Narrows suspension bridge connecting Brooklyn to Staten Island.

The boy and his father had gotten up at two o'clock that morning to drive to the marina on the New Jersey side of New York Harbor, just below the mouth of the Hudson River, where the father kept an eighteen-foot Boston Whaler.

They'd started fishing as soon as they'd gotten out of the marina, drifting along with the Hudson's current and the outgoing tide down the harbor toward the massive bridge. A hundred yards from the span, the boy had hooked up just as the sun had broken the horizon. It had to be some kind of sign, his father figured.

"Easy, son, easy," the father cautioned after he'd reeled in his own line, "don't bring it in too fast. Look at that bend in your rod. You got yourself a huge fish." He was thinking striper, but usually they ran. The line was going straight down. "Careful now."

"It feels like I've got a boulder on my hook."

Several minutes later, Annie Greenberg's body broke the surface of the dark water.

CHAPTER 21

North of Richmond, Virginia

"Are you all right?" Falcon asked, checking his watch. Fifty-five hours since Claire had been kidnapped, but he was closing in on finding her. He could feel it now.

Billie nodded from the passenger seat. "I'm fine."

She wasn't fine. Her broken arm was killing her. She'd been grimacing every time she switched positions to get comfortable. Once she'd actually let out a muffled shriek, then acted like she hadn't, like she was angry at herself for seeming weak.

She hadn't taken any painkillers since yesterday because she didn't want to be woozy if things went crazy in Richmond—which Falcon understood and agreed with. He'd protect her as best he could, but she might have to fend for herself at some chaotic moment in the next two hours. Better to be sharp mentally and in some physical pain, especially with a cast on one arm. Better that than be slow off the mark. An instant of indecision or hesitation could make the difference, given the hurricane he believed they were heading into.

He glanced at her head. That sewn-up gash had to be bothering her, too.

They'd been driving all night. She'd caught a few minutes of restless sleep on the Jersey Turnpike around Exit 8, twitching as she navigated through an intense dream. Moaning at what was happening in her nightmare or the physical pain she was actually feeling in her sleep. Maybe it was both. He couldn't tell.

Except for those five miles of haunted shut-eye, she'd remained awake the entire time he piloted the rented Ford Explorer from Connecticut. So she had to be exhausted as well as hurting.

She was tough, belying that satin-on-the-eyes exterior. She had that willingness to keep sprinting ahead into the darkness. When it would have been so much easier to lie down, curl into a tight ball, and give up. She was a natural fighter. He loved fighters.

He glanced out the driver's-side window through the dim early light as they passed the Kings Dominion exit off I-95, thirty minutes north of Richmond. He hoped Claire had found that same drive to keep going while she was being held. He hoped Claire was a natural fighter. She'd never been through anything like this. Not many people had.

Equally as important, he hoped the people holding her weren't animals. He was worried they were old mafia associates of Paul Treviso's who would think nothing of taking out their fantasies on a sixteen-year-old if they got bored. He would kill Paul if they harmed her in any way while she was with them. He'd made that pact with himself as they were crossing from Maryland into Virginia two hours ago.

Stay positive, he told himself. If everything broke right in Richmond, he'd have Claire back to Sally soon. If not . . . well, he wasn't going there. To think that way created negative energy. Nothing good ever came of negative energy.

Falcon could feel Wallace out there, searching for him, trying desperately to stop him. Wallace had to know by now that he'd discovered the connection between Sutton and TARC. Annie Greenberg was probably on some separate payroll or had a special deal with him when it came to wiring money around. And had probably told Wallace what had happened in her cubicle—though she'd have no idea that the micro-drone had been spying on her.

Wallace must have directed Billie's kidnapping. If he and Sutton were funding TARC, he was probably watching TARC's major players carefully and would have known that Billie was Paul's girlfriend. He would have had her followed and would have known about her trip to the Adirondacks. The people keeping tabs on her could have been watching their meeting at the cabin. They'd gotten her, and then come after him with her in the trunk.

But who was leading the other side? Who was manipulating Paul? His father's voice kept telling him that uncovering the identity of that person could be the key to everything, a person who could protect him against Wallace and whoever else Wallace was working with. Falcon already had his suspicions about the identity of Wallace's accomplices. If he was right, this was going to be one tough fight.

Falcon took a calibrated breath. He missed his father so much. He still remembered getting that awful call. It had been a beautiful, clear autumn day, filled with awe-inspiring colors shimmering on trees, with the crisp, clean afternoon air laced with a hint of the winter cold that was coming. He and his girlfriend at the time had been driving through a gorgeous area of the Shenandoah Valley when the call had come out of nowhere. Autumn's beauty had evaporated in the blink of an eye. The pain and fury he'd experienced during those first few days after his father's death were still so vivid. He'd never experienced anything like it—before or since—until Claire had been kidnapped.

He'd thought about his father a lot as the miles passed. He'd wanted to drive the Mustang to Richmond, so he could feel close to Senior as he drove into the hurricane. But that would have been stupid, and his father would have counseled him that way. Wallace probably knew about the Mustang, and it was a highly recognizable vehicle. He and Billie would have been vulnerable in it. He needed to fly below the radar as long as possible.

Take emotion out of your investment decisions. Use only analytics to make them. But trust your instincts when it comes to people. Analyze their records—their achievements and, more important, their failures. Use analysis to get to that final tipping point on whether or not to partner with someone. Then trust your gut to make the ultimate decision. And never question yourself. When you lose, don't lose the lesson. But always, always have confidence in the path you've chosen, no matter how bleak or dire the situation seems.

He swallowed hard. God, he missed his father. There was just no way he'd jumped from that Wall Street window. His father was the most intense fighter he'd ever known, and suicide was the ultimate act of a coward. It just didn't make sense.

"What about you?" she asked.

Falcon's eyes shot to Billie's, surprised by the sound of her voice. He'd been a million miles away. "What about me?"

"Are you all right?"

"Of course I am."

"You wouldn't tell me if you weren't," she scoffed, then turned away and looked out her window into the gray morning light that was barely making its way to the ground through a dense cloud cover rolling up the east coast. "And that's why I could never be with you."

Very interesting, she'd actually thought about being with him. "Who said anything about being with me?"

"Nobody," she volleyed back quickly, as if she regretted saying that. "I'm only making a point."

He liked that she'd shown concern back for him, asking if he was all right. Most people were so laser-focused on themselves they didn't respond in kind to that question. "Which is?" And he liked how she'd thought about being with him. He still couldn't shake his attraction for her, though he'd tried damn hard to during the drive.

"You keep everything to yourself, A.J. You said it earlier. You keep your personal life personal. You don't open up to people. You're guarded. I don't like that in a man."

"Hey, you're the one who says you're fine when you aren't."

"I just don't want to be a pain in the ass for you. I don't want to be that anchor-girl. That's all. That's why I said I was fine."

"You're not a pain," he said quietly.

She was fiercely independent as well as being a fighter—and there was a subtle difference. Being a fighter was an in-the-moment quality. Being independent was a constant battle. Of course, why wouldn't she be independent? She'd been on her own since she was fourteen.

"So I'm very sure Paul Treviso opens up his soul to you on an hourly basis," Falcon said sarcastically. "I'm a hundred percent sure that a hit man for the Gambino Crime Family tells you all the most private thoughts running through his mind all the time, right?"

"I don't want to talk about Paul."

"Why not?"

"Were you thinking about your father just then?" she asked, turning back toward him.

How could she know?

"Tell me," she urged gently, wincing as she moved her bad arm. "Come on, open up a little. I've told you about me."

He'd caught that wince. "What do you want to know?"

"How did he die?"

"It depends on who you talk to."

She moaned, frustrated. "What does that mean?"

"He went out of a Wall Street window at midnight," Falcon answered. "A few seconds later he slammed onto the Street forty floors down. If you believe the press reports, he jumped."

"But you don't think so."

"My father never took the easy way out of a *parking lot*, for Christ's sake. He would *not* have committed suicide," Falcon argued adamantly. That familiar lump was building in his throat. Someone out there needed to be brought to justice. "My father was a fighter. Yes, he had some bad things going on at his investment firm at the time. But he would *never* have taken the cowardly way out . . . of *anything*."

Billie gazed at Falcon for several seconds. "Now we're getting somewhere," she murmured. "Now we're peeling back the onion."

"You got one layer." She had a way of getting what she wanted, he'd noticed. She was damn good at mental manipulation, too. "That's all you're getting."

"We'll see."

"Yes, we will."

"So your father was thrown out that window."

"I'm a hundred percent convinced of it."

"Who killed him?"

Falcon glanced into the rearview mirror. Somebody back there had been pacing them for several miles, passing cars in the slower lane exactly when he passed the next car ahead, staying exactly two cars back. "You'll think I'm crazy."

"I already *know* you are." She patted his arm with her good hand. "In a nice way, I mean. You took care of me when you didn't have to, when it would have been a lot easier and safer for you to abandon me."

"I had my agenda. Let's be very clear on that. I don't want you thinking it's more than that," he lied.

"You could have left me to die in that car. You had the information you needed. You have your information bloodhounds. I couldn't have blamed you if you had left me. I was with the people who have your niece."

"*Was* with?"

"I'm sorry Paul ordered the kidnapping," she said in a subdued tone, avoiding his question. "He could have figured out another way to manipulate you. He didn't have to kidnap Claire."

"I'll kill him if anything happens to her."

"You won't have to," Billie promised. "I'll do it for you."

Falcon raised both eyebrows. "I'm glad to hear you say that." But could he believe her? He was so attracted to her. But he didn't trust her, not yet. How could he?

"Who threw your father out that window?" she asked.

"James Wallace."

"*What?*"

"Not Wallace personally, of course, but people who work for him." Now that he knew Wallace was funding TARC, he was convinced Wallace was also responsible for his father's death. "It's been two years since my father was murdered. Who knows? It might have been those same two guys who got you at the cabin."

"How can you be so sure your father was murdered?" She touched his arm again. "I understand how you feel about your dad. I'm sure you're justified thinking he would never choose suicide as an option. I'm just asking if you have some piece of absolute proof connecting Wallace to the murder."

"Six months ago I was going through some old boxes of my father's, and I found a diary." Falcon shrugged. "It wasn't really a diary. It was just some notes on a page. They were scrawled, but he referenced Sutton & Company."

"I thought he had his own firm," Billie said.

"He did."

"How could he know anything about Sutton?"

"His traders did tons of business with Sutton. Everybody does tons of business with Sutton. You have to if you want to make money on the Street. Sutton's that important a firm. So my father knew James Wallace . . . very well." Falcon glanced into the rearview mirror at the car he'd been casing. It was directly behind the Explorer now. There was no buffer car in between any longer. "The thing was, he'd just had lunch with Wallace that day. That lunch was written down in his appointment book, which was also in the box I was going through. The memo his notes were written on was dated the same day." He hesitated. "That night he went out the window." The vehicle was staying back, like that Mercedes had in the Adirondacks. But now it could come at them at any time. "I always wondered why Wallace recruited me so hard out of school."

"You mean out of Harvard Business School, not UVA undergrad."

"Yeah, but how did you know that? I never told you I went to HBS."

"I know a lot about you, A.J. In this day and age it's pretty easy to find out almost anything about anyone. I researched the hell out of you after Paul asked me to go up to that cabin for him. I always want to know my enemy as well as I can."

"Enemy, huh?"

"You were then."

"And now?" he asked.

"I haven't decided yet."

"Let me know when you do."

"Stay on point," she said. "Why would you question James Wallace recruiting you so hard? Your résumé was tremendous, even then. You were an analyst at J.P. Morgan for the two years in between UVA and Harvard, in their Mergers and Acquisitions Department. That's a high-profile job. And Wallace obviously knew your father well. Everything I read about your father described him as a legend on Wall Street. If the apple doesn't fall far from the tree, it's obvious to me why Wallace would have recruited you to work at Sutton."

Falcon's gaze moved deliberately to Billie.

She winced when his eyes made it to hers, not out of physical pain this time. "OK, you got me," she admitted. "I knew how your father died. I was trying to get you to talk."

"Uh-huh."

"I'm serious. I wanted to see if maybe you'd open up a little. I thought your father would be a good topic to get that started with. So shoot me because I want to get closer to you." She stared down into her lap. "Maybe I have thought about us," she admitted. "Well, not maybe."

She could so easily be playing him. He considered himself a very good judge of people. But most people weren't at her level in terms of intelligence—or guile.

"Who's blackmailing Paul into trying to get proof of Sutton & Company funding TARC?" Falcon asked.

"Who says anyone's blackmailing him?"

She could have been a damn good lawyer, he figured. She was good at dodging questions and manipulating words. "OK, who's dangling the reward out there if Paul comes through?" He could see she was struggling. She wanted to help, but she didn't want to implicate. "Do you know?"

She shut her eyes tightly, then nodded several times quickly.

Let the water build behind the dam, he reminded himself. Let her get to the point where she volunteers the name of the person behind the reward for Paul—and probably the punishment if he failed, even if Billie wouldn't admit that there was a flip side for Paul if that happened. Maybe she didn't know.

"What's the reward?" He'd try a different angle.

She took a deep breath. "His criminal past gets erased. He gets a completely new identity. He starts life over with the slate wiped clean. Can you really blame him for going after that as hard as he can?"

"I sure as hell—"

"Other than kidnapping Claire, of course."

Whoever was pushing Paul was very powerful, if he was truly convinced the person pushing him could restart his life with a clean slate—which only made sense and was what Falcon had assumed. He had to find this person.

"Is TARC behind what's going on in Atlanta and Dallas right now?" he asked. "Is TARC organizing those protests?"

"And what's happening in Tuscaloosa," she admitted. "But they weren't all supposed to happen this quickly and at the same time. They were supposed to happen over the next few months."

Falcon's eyes narrowed. Schedules at TARC had been accelerated at the same time President Hilton had made her blockbuster announcement. The first thing that struck him about that: there could easily be a connection to the timing if his suspicions about Wallace's conspirators were correct. He'd found a few other interesting wire transfers when he'd uncovered the Sutton–TARC connection. Money was going to the Pentagon as well, and to one particular general at the Pentagon.

"You think there's any chance TARC is involved with the group that's claimed responsibility for what happened in Baltimore and Philadelphia?" He hadn't found any wires going to WOW. "The War on Whites?"

"I don't know . . . I honestly don't."

He could buy that. Paul might not even know.

He wanted to ask her again who was pushing Paul to get the information, but he held back. "Do you love Paul?" It was a crazy question to ask, especially for him. But he had to know.

"I thought I did." She stared straight ahead for several moments. "Now I'm not sure. I can't find a way to justify kidnapping a sixteen-year-old girl. Before I left for the Adirondacks, I thought I was OK with it. But now I'm not."

She was saying all the right things.

He was about to push for more when he spotted the car behind them suddenly swerve into the fast lane and accelerate quickly. "Hold on, Billie!" he shouted as he poised his right foot above the brake pedal. "This could get nasty."

◆ ◆ ◆

Camp David, Maryland

Troy followed Katrina as she walked down a narrow hallway toward her Camp David bedroom suite.

It was just the two of them now. She'd ordered her Secret Service detail to remain outside the cabin until further notice. Despite the lead agent's loud and increasingly frustrated protests, he was also familiar with the Black Book protocol—as the lead agent last night had been. And he'd finally relented when she threatened him with prosecution.

Katrina had been up all night dealing with a sudden crisis. Satellite photographs indicated that a Russian army division was heading for the Ukraine border. She and her COS, Dennis Jordan, had spent the night working the phones to European heads of state and had placed and taken multiple calls to and from the Kremlin. Fifteen minutes ago the latest images from space had arrived electronically, and they indicated that the Russian troops were turning around and heading away from the border.

At that point she'd told her staff she needed sleep. She'd asked Troy to accompany her to her bedroom.

Troy had been impressed with her ice-water-in-the-veins demeanor under pressure—as well as Jordan's, though Troy had picked up on an odd vibe from the senior staffer. It was almost as if the guy was jealous. Troy's G2 contact indicated no romantic relationship between Katrina and Jordan. In fact, his intelligence briefer had informed him that Jordan was gay—which Troy had no issue with. But it didn't fit with the jealousy vibe.

"Good night, Katrina," Troy said the moment her fingertips touched the bedroom's brass doorknob.

"What are you talking about?" she asked, turning to face him. "Good night? How does 'good night' protect me?"

He liked her perfume. He'd gotten a pleasant whiff of it while he was following her. "I'll stay out here," he said, gesturing down at the hardwood floor. And her dress was sexy—edgy for the president of the United States but not over the top. It showed off her comely figure without crossing the line. "I'm close. Don't worry. Nothing will ever happen to you on my watch."

She looked at him like he was insane. "You're going to sleep in the hallway?" she asked incredulously.

"Yes."

"On a wood floor?"

"This floor will be way more comfortable than nine out of ten other places I sleep this year."

"You're not sleeping in the hallway," she said before turning the knob and moving into the bedroom. "Get in here right now, and that's an order."

Still, he lingered outside.

"Come in here," she ordered again, leaning out of the bathroom. "Please, Colonel Jensen. I'm tired, and I don't want to deal with this."

Troy moved inside the room and eased into a large, comfortably padded chair that was positioned at the end of the king-size bed. He was facing the bathroom, and he was relieved when she closed the door so it was open only a crack.

He had to admit the chair felt good and would be better than the floor. He had no problem sleeping while he was sitting up. He'd trained himself to do so long ago.

"It's quite the life you lead, Colonel Jensen," she called when she turned off the faucet. "I'd be interested to hear about some of those other places you sleep."

"They're not interesting at all," he assured her.

"I don't know about that."

"Nice job tonight," he said, turning the conversation away from things he could not tell her about, even though she was the president. "I was impressed."

"Just another day in the life of a US president," she said, moving out of the bathroom and through the bedroom until she was standing before him. "You know," she said in a low voice, "bringing the world back from the brink of nuclear annihilation. No big deal."

"Uh-huh, sure."

Katrina's dress was gone, replaced by plain black pajamas. Still, she was gorgeous. She didn't need some over-the-top, breast-plunging negligee to make that point crystal clear. Plus, she was the most powerful and charismatic woman in the world. The entire effect was impressive, almost intoxicating. Troy couldn't deny it.

"You don't have to sleep in that chair tonight, Colonel Jensen."

"What?" Troy hated ever being shocked—and giving it away so obviously. "I . . . um . . . well—"

"Gotcha." Katrina smiled broadly despite her weariness, as though she'd gotten exactly the reaction she was looking for.

"Huh?"

"It's a big bed. You stay on your side; I'll stay on mine." Her smile grew wider. "But I like the way you were thinking. It makes an older woman feel good."

Troy's shoulders slumped, and he shook his head. She'd gotten him all right.

CHAPTER 22

Richmond, Virginia

"Can I have a gun?"

"I only have one."

"I saw you slide another pistol under your seat when we left Connecticut. You thought I didn't, but I did. Why would you lie to me?"

He tried to think of a lighthearted comeback, but nothing hit him—which was unusual. "Well, I didn't—"

"It looked like another Beretta."

Falcon glanced over at Billie. He'd pulled the rented Explorer to a stop at the curb on a quiet side street. They were a mile from the Richmond strip mall where they were set to meet Paul. "You know your guns."

"Hit men use lots of them. We have an armory at our place."

"That makes me feel good, given who we're meeting in ten minutes."

"You always know where you stand with me," she said, putting her hand on his arm. "I would never lie to you, A.J."

He wasn't convinced of that, especially a mile and ten minutes away from meeting Paul to execute the exchange: proof of Sutton funding TARC for Claire's release.

He'd stood right next to Billie the entire time she'd spoken to Paul last night. She'd been firm with him, businesslike, not at all like a girlfriend who hadn't seen or spoken to her guy in a few days' time. Falcon had heard every word of their conversation.

Paul had tried to keep her on the phone longer, after the time and place had been set. He'd tried to find out details of what had happened to her. But she'd said good-bye curtly and handed Falcon back the phone exactly as he'd instructed her.

However, he was concerned Paul might have prearranged something before Billie had left for the Adirondacks, in case she was taken and exactly this situation played out. He was a hardened criminal. He might have anticipated needing a code.

"Don't be so paranoid."

How did she always know what he was thinking? It was more than a little disconcerting, like she was some sort of savant when it came to reading his mind. The only explanation he could come up with: she was so much like him.

"A decent dose of paranoia isn't a bad thing," he answered. "It keeps you considering all possibilities."

"Yeah, sure," she scoffed, pulling her hand from his arm. "Well, your decent dose of paranoia almost got me killed back on I-95."

He'd slammed on the Explorer's brakes when the vehicle he'd been watching suddenly swerved into the fast lane of the interstate to pass them. Billie's bad arm had been compressed tightly between the seat belt and her body when Falcon had suddenly pulled the car onto the shoulder and jammed down on the brake pedal. She'd screamed in pain as the other car had hurtled past and kept on going.

"*Killed* might be a slight exaggeration, Billie."

"That guy wasn't after us."

"You don't know that because—"

"And I like it when you use my name," she interrupted, putting her hand back on him, on his shoulder this time. "It sounds good to me when you say 'Billie.'"

"I hate when you do that."

"When I do *what*?"

"When you try so hard to make me trust you."

"I don't know what you're talking about," she replied innocently, as if his comment had cut into her very soul. "I'm attracted to you. I won't deny it." She hesitated. "And I think you have feelings for me."

"How could that be possible?" he snapped, angry that she was dangling the bait—even angrier that he was biting. "I've only known you for a few days."

"You've never heard of love at first sight? Come on."

He shook his head. "In our own ways, we're both much too savvy to buy into that silly notion. Only fools think that can happen."

She took her hand away from his arm again and looked down. "Thanks."

"Don't con me."

She glanced over at him, hurt. "I never would. I never will."

The look on her face reminded him of Claire's expression when she was standing outside her father's hospital room. He had to glance away quickly or meet his own reality.

"Let's assume for a few seconds that you're telling me the truth," he said evenly. "Let's assume for a few seconds that you do have feelings for me."

"OK."

"What am I supposed to think when you can turn on your feelings for me with the flip of a switch? And, just as fast, you can turn off your feelings for Paul?"

◆ ◆ ◆

Camp David, Maryland

Troy awakened from his dream with a start. He'd been sprinting through a jungle, dodging trees, hanging vines, and snakes, trying to escape a well-armed rebel force that was chasing him. Out of nowhere the jungle had ended at the edge of a wide river. The water's surface was dotted everywhere by pairs of crocodile eyes.

He shook his head, clearing the disturbing images from his mind.

As the bedroom came into focus, he realized that Katrina was kneeling in front of him, staring up at him intently. She'd been shaking him, he now realized. He hadn't taken her up on her offer to share one side of the king-size presidential bed. It hadn't felt right, especially after she'd elicited his reaction.

"Are you all right?" she asked.

"I'm fine."

"You were calling out in your sleep. I was worried."

"You never have to worry about me, Madam—Katrina."

"It sure sounded like I did."

"I'm fine."

"Well, I'm not," she admitted, rising to her feet. "I had my own dream."

"What was it?"

"You were correct, Colonel Jensen. The military was out to get me. They captured me. They tried me in a kangaroo court. I was sentenced to die. They were leading me to the firing squad when I woke up." She ran her fingers through his hair. "That's when I heard you."

◆ ◆ ◆

Richmond, Virginia

Falcon had no choice about coming to Richmond. He'd known that all along. Paul Treviso would never release Claire on a vague promise to deliver the proof. It would have to be a face-to-face exchange.

Of course, he would never hand over the information on the flash drive that Basil Slicke had put together documenting the wire transfers

Paul wanted so badly on nothing more than a vague promise to release his niece.

The showdown was inevitable.

There was no alternative.

But it could be so dangerous.

He reached under the driver's seat and pulled out the other Beretta, the one Billie had spotted him hide in Connecticut. He held it out for her as they sat in the Explorer at the edge of the sprawling lot. He'd parked close to an exit onto Broad Street so he could get them out of there fast if necessary.

"Take it."

"You sure?" she asked.

"Yes."

"I mean it. If you let me have this gun, it means you trust me completely. You have to be sure."

Falcon stared at her for a full ten seconds before nodding deliberately and inching the pistol slightly closer to her. "I'll give it to you as long as you don't check for bullets in the clip. That's *my* condition."

"I'll know in a heartbeat if the clip has bullets in it," she said. "I've handled enough guns to feel the difference in weights." She raised an eyebrow at him. "I told you. You'll always know where you stand with me. No games, *ever*."

"Last I heard, blanks weighed about as much as the actual ones. So you won't be able to tell by the weight of the gun if the rounds are real." He gestured at the pistol once it slipped from his fingers to hers. "But if you pop it out and look at them, you'll know whether they're real or not right away."

"I get one question and one honest answer."

He grinned at her as he reached over and tapped the gun. "Shoot."

"Are the bullets real?"

"Yes."

It was Billie's turn to nod. "Then we have a deal."

CHAPTER 23

Washington, DC

"Prosperity for All is coming together!" Patty Stiles shouted to the members of her staff who were crowded together into her inner office. She sprang out of her well-padded leather chair, tightly clasped, pudgy fists raised ecstatically above her head. "We just got the Senate!"

A roar exploded from her mostly millennial staff as cell phones and landlines rang madly.

She'd just heard personally from the minority leader, Bob Burns, and he wasn't happy. She could clearly hear frustration in his voice. He'd been cornered and manipulated into going along with PFA by the blazing and intensifying riots flaring up like Independence Day fireworks across the South—not just Atlanta, Tuscaloosa, and Dallas now—and the unrelenting blitzes of daytime and late-night talk-show hosts.

It was sad for the country that a politician had to be shamed into doing something that was good for a vast majority of the population by a combination of talk-show hosts and bloody riots, but Patty didn't care. At this point, she'd take the result any way she could get it. She was on a mission for President Hilton.

"Senator Burns of Mississippi just called me himself to admit defeat. Now we've gotta get the House, people."

An even more thunderous cheer erupted.

"We still need thirty-three votes, people. Get back to work. Get on your phones and stay on your phones."

How quickly this bill had come together in the Senate chamber astounded her. Those in the upper strata had fallen like closely aligned dominoes.

Representatives weren't being as easily swayed. A greater percentage of them hailed from across the aisle than did those in the Senate. But she'd get enough of them in the lower house to sign PFA as well and make it a reality. She'd shame enough of them into voting for this to get it passed. She'd keep the talk-show hosts at it. She had her staff calling all of them constantly to encourage them. And God bless the rioters. Sometimes change had to be bloody. Unfortunately, the riots needed to go on. They would help push congressmen into making the right decision.

"Let me out," she ordered, nodding toward the doorway that led to the outer office. She had a call she needed to make, and she couldn't do it here.

Her staffers parted like the Red Sea.

She called out the same command at the doorway to those in the outer office, and, again, the staffers here made a path for her instantly. Moments later she was in the hallway, she'd closed the door behind herself, and the loud hum of conversation coming from inside her office faded.

Patty walked quickly down the hallway and then hustled down another corridor to a secluded alcove beneath a stairway, where she placed the call. It was risky not to go through her intermediary, but she had to know. She'd already been in contact with Paul once earlier. The connection was already provable.

"Hello."

"Have you gotten my proof yet?"

"I'm about to pick it up."

"What are you waiting for?"

"I . . . uh . . . can't get in touch with my partners. That's gonna be a problem."

Patty held the phone away from her face, looked at it for a second like she didn't recognize it, like she couldn't comprehend what Paul had just said.

She pressed the device back to her ear. "Partners? Who are you talking about? Not Chalice and Thigpen, I certainly hope. You weren't supposed to tell them *anything*."

"No, no, of course not."

"Who, then?" She suddenly had a very bad feeling about this.

"I needed a way to force Andrew Falcon to get the proof."

"Andrew Falcon? Who's Andrew Falcon? You were supposed to approach Michael Mattix. He was your target at Sutton & Company."

"Well, I—"

"We had him dead to rights on a massive insider-trading charge. It was a lock. That was your leverage. I handed him to you on a silver platter."

"Michael Mattix couldn't get what we needed. He told me that Wallace would suspect him right away if he started rooting around in the Funds Transfer Department. And I believed him after I checked his story out. Mattix headed the entire Mergers and Acquisitions Department. He couldn't just go walking in there and ask if wires had been sent to certain places. So I got Mattix to throw me a younger partner at Sutton who wasn't as high-profile. His name is Andrew Falcon."

An awful chill crawled up her spine. "What do you have on Falcon that's making him get what I want?"

"Well . . . I had to think outside the box. He's young and clean, so I had to make it more personal for him."

Patty swallowed hard. "What have you done?"

"Don't worry about it. I'm handling it."

Had she gone too far? Had she been blinded by her ambition? *"What have you done, Paul?"*

◆ ◆ ◆

McLean, Virginia

"Riots are exploding in four more southern cities," Fiske reported. "The insanity has spread to Mississippi and South Carolina like a virus." He and General Lewis were standing in Lewis's home study in front of the television. "And I'm getting text reports of uprisings in Los Angeles. The governor is about to call out the National Guard. Looters are at it like mad, and the crazy thing is it's spilling into Beverly Hills and Brentwood. The underprivileged are feeling empowered like never before. The more radical local leaders are actually encouraging people to go where the big homes are and tear things up. Cops are trying to take back the streets in the upper-class neighborhoods, but they're being overwhelmed."

"Switch it," Lewis ordered, gesturing at the television. He was on his cell phone, holding for his most important contact at the Pentagon. "Find an overhead shot from a chopper of the LA looting. Somebody's got to be covering it by now."

Fiske grabbed the remote off the coffee table and spun through the all-news channels until he found the shot on MSNBC. West LA was beginning to burn.

"Beautiful," Lewis murmured, as if he were looking at the Mona Lisa hanging from the Louvre wall. "I couldn't have asked for more. People won't even notice when we storm the White House and the Capitol. They'll be watching this. By the time we've restored peace to the country, the Pentagon will essentially be the White House. A certain portion of Americans will beg the military to use whatever force is necessary to keep the underprivileged in their ghettos, to keep them from rising up again. It's the opportunity of the century for us to take America back, General Fiske."

A rush of adrenaline stormed through Fiske's body. Perhaps now was the best time to ask the crucial question. "General Lewis?"

"Yes?"

The intoxicating image of Katrina Hilton hanging tied up before him rose to his mind for the fiftieth time this morning. "I'd like to personally lead the attack on the White House. I want to be the one who takes President Hilton prisoner."

"She's not even there. She's at Camp David."

"She'll be back today. She'll need to look presidential. She can't do that from Camp David. She needs to be at the White House."

"You're probably right."

"I know I'm right. I'll call her myself and tell her she needs to come back if she's not here by this afternoon."

"George, I don't know if I want you in the middle of an attack. You might get—"

"Please, sir." He'd heard Lewis use his first name, but he didn't care. "I've never asked for anything like this from you before, sir."

Lewis stared at Fiske for several moments. "All right, General Fiske, that command is yours."

A twice as powerful shot of adrenaline shook Fiske's body like an earthquake just as Lewis's phone rang. "This is my friend from Baltimore," Lewis said, gesturing at the device. "Hello. Yeah. Really? OK, thanks."

"What's going on?"

"The war is starting in Baltimore, too."

Lewis nodded and held up his hand as the person on the other end of his line came back to him. "OK. Yes, sir. That's very good news. *Yes, sir.*"

"Who was that?"

"General Jackson."

General Joseph Jackson was chairman of the Joint Chiefs of Staff. Prior to being JCS chairman, he'd been the twenty-first commandant of the Marine Corps. In his capacity as JCS chairman he was the principal military adviser to the secretary of defense, the Homeland Security Council, the National Security Council, and the president of the United States. However, *by law*, he had no operational command authority. Operational authority—the ability to order US troops to attack—went from the president to the secretary of defense to the unified combatant command.

General Jackson traced his family lines directly back to Thomas Jonathan "Stonewall" Jackson, the second-most beloved Confederate general of the American Civil War.

"And?" Fiske asked expectantly.

"He's been in touch with the unified combatant commanders. He's gone behind Secretary Wilson's back to UCC."

Secretary of Defense Gerald Powell Wilson had been handpicked by Katrina Hilton. He was a high-profile African American businessman who had experience in the defense industry but was by no means a "military man," as most of those surrounding him were. He was not well liked by those who would stand a post in the event of war. He was a civilian and never had been a true warrior.

"And?" Fiske asked, even more expectantly this time.

"General Jackson's communication with the UCC was well received. The army and the Marine Corps are in agreement with us, at least at the highest levels. Jackson will be contacting the air force and the navy later today."

A thrill like he'd never known surged through Fiske's strong frame. He was going to execute President Katrina Hilton, after he'd had his way with her. He was going to play God to the most powerful woman the world had ever known.

◆ ◆ ◆

Tulip, Mississippi

During the nineteen fifties and sixties, the small southern Mississippi town of Tulip had been an epicenter of the Civil Rights Movement. One August, four young black men had been lynched in four successive days for "violating" four young white girls simply by "casting lewd glances in their direction."

A week later, Martin Luther King Jr. had led a march of ten thousand freedom fighters into Tulip on a sultry afternoon, doubling its population in the short time it took for the marchers to enter the town limits. Dr. King had stood on the town hall steps as the FBI, state police, town deputies, and white-shrouded members of the KKK had watched. Despite the overwhelming heat, he'd pleaded racial harmony for more than three hours, so dehydrated at the end he'd passed out.

The next day, another black teenager was found hung in the woods outside Tulip. A hand-scrawled note pinned to his bloody shirt proclaimed "White Supremacy Forever."

The murders had eased in the seventies, though every few years since then a black man had disappeared into thin air and rumors of the KKK still operating in Tulip ran rampant for weeks. In the last fifteen years, when that had happened, a white man had disappeared a week later.

The town was 50 percent black and 50 percent white. Racial harmony would never be possible here. In fact, violent disharmony simmered barely below the surface at all times, especially on a hot summer morning.

Henry Buford, a white dairy farmer, was driving his Ford F-150 on Main Street toward the Southern States store when a tricked-out turquoise Chevy with gangster white walls swerved in front of him and slammed on its brakes. Henry slammed on his brakes, too, just in time to avoid careering into the Chevy's back bumper.

"What the hell!" Henry shouted, as pissed off as he'd been in weeks.

It didn't help that two of his prized bulls had died mysteriously last Thursday. He suspected his black neighbor of poisoning them—they'd always had a stormy relationship—though he couldn't prove it. He didn't have the money to pay the vet for an autopsy.

A young black woman jumped from the Chevy's passenger side, a huge red comb lodged in her Afro. She slammed the car door behind her and headed into the five-and-dime in the middle of town. The old store was right next to city hall and the same steps Dr. King had orated from more than half a century ago.

The turquoise Chevy stayed put, even after the young woman disappeared inside.

Henry rammed the 150's transmission into "Park," climbed from the vehicle, and headed for the Chevy even as other cars passed in the left lane. He'd had enough of the insolence, arrogance, and total disregard he felt blacks in general had for the decent white way of life.

"Fuck you want?" the driver wanted to know when Buford appeared at his open window.

The young black man's hair was arranged in neat cornrows. Henry hated cornrows. The idea that a man, any man, would put his hair into rubber bands was abhorrent to him.

"You cut right in front of me, you fucking asshole," he yelled over the hip-hop blaring from inside the car, "and slammed on your brakes. I almost hit you, for *Christ's sake*. This is not a parking spot. This is Main Street. You are blocking traffic because you're just a lazy animal."

"Don't call me an asshole," the young man snapped before calmly inhaling from his Camel no-filter cigarette. He flicked a burning ash out the window as he blew smoke up into Henry's face. It landed on Henry's muddy boot. "You call me Mister. And I'll call you *bitch*."

Henry reached into the car and grabbed for the man, closing his fingers tightly around the young man's neck, pressing both thumbs to the dark throat, literally trying to kill. He could see nothing but red at this point. He had no control of his actions. He pressed harder and harder, his intent to suffocate. He'd had enough of these people and their animal ways.

Even as he was being choked, the man grabbed a .44 Magnum from the console, pressed the barrel of the gun to Henry's forehead, and fired.

Henry tumbled back, dead before he hit the pavement, blood and brains spilling onto Main Street.

A little girl screamed. Dogs began barking wildly.

The driver climbed from his Chevy, pointed the .44 down at Henry's prone body, and systematically fired the remaining five rounds into Henry's body, causing it to twitch with each impact.

A friend of Henry's happened to be coming out of the diner directly across the street from the five-and-dime when the first shot rang out. He raced to his pickup, grabbed a loaded twelve-gauge shotgun from the rack in the back of the cab, and sprinted toward the man who was just firing the sixth and final round from the .44.

The black man turned as Henry's friend put the shell in the left barrel into his chest. The sickening blast hurled him back into the side of the Chevy as his girlfriend came screaming out of the five-and-dime. Henry's friend turned the shotgun on her when she dashed around the trunk of the Chevy toward him with a knife, and he put the shell in the right barrel into her face.

Moments later, Main Street was a war zone. Battle lines were drawn. More and more people were dying as an all-out gun battle erupted.

CHAPTER 24

Richmond, Virginia

"Where is he?" Falcon asked, keeping his anger in check—for the moment. "It's after eleven o'clock." He glanced around the large mall parking lot. "Paul was supposed to be here at eight. This is ridiculous." The longer this went on, the more anxious he was about Claire and how terrified she must be. "We're targets out here."

If Paul was under the sheets with Chalice as far as this meeting went, he and Billie were *already* in the crosshairs, because Paul would have told Chalice where the meeting was taking place. If Paul wasn't working with Chalice, then the danger level would ratchet up when Paul got here because whoever was following Paul would see them with him.

Falcon believed Wallace was watching everything at TARC. Wallace was far too much of a control freak not to have arranged surveillance, especially with something as sensitive and potentially damaging as his funding TARC. So Falcon was certain Paul was being followed.

Of course, Paul was a lifelong criminal. If he wasn't working with Chalice, he'd realize there was a good chance he was being followed and would take a roundabout way of getting here—hopefully losing the tail in the process. Maybe that would be Paul's excuse for being so late.

Falcon was willing to bet Paul wasn't working with Chalice. Chalice couldn't wipe Paul's criminal past clean and set him up with a new lease on life—he'd need help from higher authorities if he wanted to elude the Gambino Family forever.

"There!" Billie tapped the Explorer's passenger window excitedly, pointing toward the right and a black Suburban that had just wheeled into the lot. "That's Paul. That's his truck."

The Suburban pulled to a stop near a JoAnn Fabrics. The parking lot in front of the store was crowded with soccer-mom and -dad rides—minivans and other big SUVs—and Paul's Suburban went into hiding after backing into a spot behind an Escalade.

Falcon cased the parking lot once more. He'd been scanning it ever since they'd arrived, trying to pick out any vehicle that didn't look or act normal. That had gotten more difficult after ten o'clock, when all the stores in the mall had opened. He counted three vehicles that had been here for an hour, one of which he was certain no one had gotten out of after it stopped. That beat-up blue sedan was parked over by a Dick's Sporting Goods.

"Here we go."

Falcon slipped the Explorer into gear. Instead of going straight for the Suburban, he headed for the blue sedan. He stopped in front of it, blocking its escape, then hopped out and peered inside. An old man was passed out behind the steering wheel, head tilted back, mouth wide open. What looked like all his worldly possessions were piled haphazardly in the back, and a wide-eyed calico cat lay on the passenger seat. The man awoke with a start as Falcon turned back for the Explorer.

"Just a lost soul looking for a port in the storm," he muttered. His expression went grim. "Like me."

"Everything all right?" Billie asked as he climbed back in.

He glanced down at the pistol lying in her lap. "We're about to find out."

He wheeled the Explorer toward Paul, then turned quickly up the lane, going against the big white arrow painted on the asphalt, and skidded to a stop in front of the black Suburban.

Billie climbed from the Explorer before it had even come to a full stop, shrieking loudly when she used her bad shoulder to jar the door open.

"What are you doing?" yelled Falcon. "Get back in here!"

She jumped to the ground, ignoring him. "Get out here, Paul!" she shouted. "Let's go!"

Paul climbed out of the Suburban the instant he saw her.

Falcon had googled Paul Fellini, so he knew what to expect physically—dark eyes, dark hair, receding in the front and long in the back, slightly overweight, and closing in on forty. But Paul had a certain in-charge, confident aura about him Falcon hadn't expected. The former mobster seemed very cool as he slipped on his sunglasses beneath the clear, blue morning sky and moved toward Billie.

Falcon had been expecting more a man who exhibited the characteristics of prey—looking around constantly and quickly, hunched over as he walked. But Paul stood straight up, moved ahead deliberately, and focused straight on Billie.

Falcon jumped down into the parking lot, too, Beretta out and ready, first round chambered.

"What the hell is this?" Paul asked sharply when he saw that Falcon and Billie were both armed. He pointed at her cast. "What happened to your arm?"

"Where's my niece?" Falcon demanded, gesturing at the Suburban. "Where's Claire?"

"Where's my flash drive with all the wire-transfer evidence?"

Falcon patted his shirt pocket. The tiny drive wasn't really there. It was in the Explorer. "Let me see Claire or you're not getting anything."

"Where is she, Paul?" Billie pushed. "Don't tell me you don't have her. I promised this man you would. I promised him he could count on you, on *me*. I swore to him that you wouldn't let me down."

"What's your problem, Billie? Why'd you promise him anything?"

"What do you mean?"

"Why do you care about this guy?" Paul asked harshly. "Or his damn niece? What do you care what he thinks of you?"

"Where is she?" Falcon demanded, a bad feeling crawling up his spine. Out of the corner of his eye he spotted a gray sedan coming straight at them from the mall's main entrance. "Tell me now."

"I'm having problems with the people who kidnapped her for me," Paul admitted. "They want more money for her release. More than the fifty grand I was paying them. They want a million now. They looked you up on the Internet. They figure you can pay a million no problem."

"*What?* Listen to me, you son of a—"

The squeal of tires cut Falcon off as the gray sedan tore around the end of the line of cars by the storefronts and raced toward the Explorer.

Billie screamed in pain when Falcon grabbed her and pulled her behind the Explorer, away from the gray sedan.

Paul reached for the small of his back and whipped out a gun from his belt as he darted to and crouched down behind the Escalade.

Two men jumped from the gray sedan, pistols drawn, and disappeared into the sea of cars.

"Let's get out of here," Billie hissed to Falcon. "Come on."

"Can't."

"What do you mean?"

"I'm not leaving here without my niece."

"Paul doesn't have her."

"But he knows where she is. I'm not leaving here without finding out *exactly* where she is. The only person who can tell me is Paul."

"Who are these guys?" she asked, lifting her head just enough to peer above the Explorer's hood.

"Wallace's people," Falcon answered, just as a gun went off. "I'm sure of it."

A hail of gunfire followed.

Falcon hustled past Billie toward the Suburban.

"A.J., stop!" she shouted.

But he didn't. He dashed for the Suburban. One of the men who'd jumped from the gray sedan stepped out from behind a minivan to the left and fired as Falcon dove for cover behind the Escalade. He spotted the man's legs from under the big SUV and fired twice. The guy screamed and fell. Falcon fired again at him, then scrambled ahead between two more minivans.

Paul was kneeling ten feet away, pistol pointed straight at Falcon. "Give me the damn flash drive or I shoot."

"Screw you."

"I gave you a chance, Falcon. Now you die."

But just as Paul pulled the trigger, he was hit in the chest by a bullet fired by the man who'd been driving the gray sedan. Paul staggered forward a few steps, then tumbled to the ground gasping for breath, still clasping his pistol.

Falcon ducked behind the front of the Suburban as Paul's shooter sprinted around the back, then stopped in his tracks when he spotted Billie aiming at the shooter. She didn't hesitate, firing twice in rapid succession, nailing the man in the stomach and chest. He keeled over and collapsed.

Falcon sprinted to where he lay and kicked his gun away, then hustled to Paul, who was on his back, bleeding badly from the wound in his chest. The bullet had entered from the side, just below his left armpit. He didn't have long.

"Where's my niece?" Falcon demanded, spying the cell phone in Paul's outstretched hand. He'd called someone as he lay dying. "Where is she?"

Paul gasped, then began to whisper.

Falcon leaned down, putting his ear close to Paul's mouth so he could hear the words, memorizing the address.

When he stood up, he realized that Billie was walking slowly toward him, gun leading the way and pointed—at him.

"What are you doing?" he asked calmly.

She didn't answer. She just gazed straight at him, almost through him, he realized.

"Billie, don't do this." He wouldn't have time to pull his gun up and fire. Her finger was already on the trigger. "I didn't shoot Paul, Billie."

She stopped, gun still up and aimed. "Shut up," she hissed.

He'd misjudged her. How could he have been so stupid? "Billie, I'm sorry he's—"

"Put the gun down."

Falcon whipped around, toward the sound of the male voice. "What the—" Who was this guy? There'd only been two men in the gray sedan. He was positive. "Who the hell are you?"

"Put the gun down, Billie," the man ordered calmly but sternly, ignoring Falcon. "I'm not here to hurt you. I'm here to help."

"Who are you?" she demanded, still holding out her pistol. "How do you know my name?"

She hadn't been aiming at him after all, Falcon realized. She'd been aiming at this guy. He hadn't misjudged her. She was covering him, protecting him.

"Put your gun down and everything will be fine. Like I said, I'm here to help."

Falcon's eyes flashed back and forth between Billie and the man. This man had a smooth, competent air about him. He'd been in situations like this before.

"I need to get both of you to my commander immediately," he said. "We're wasting time."

"Commander?" Falcon asked as if he found that hard to believe. "Are you US military?"

"Don't worry about it," he answered without taking his eyes off Billie. "Now, put the gun down."

"Do what he says, Billie," Falcon urged. He had a good feeling about this. And he figured they wouldn't do well in a gunfight with this guy. "Come on."

She swallowed hard, then slowly brought the gun down and hurried to where Paul lay. She knelt down next to him and caressed his face.

But Paul couldn't feel her touch. Paul was dead.

◆ ◆ ◆

Camp David, Maryland

"I need to get to the White House," Katrina whispered as she stared at her bedroom TV screen in horror. The riots were spreading. Tulip, Mississippi, was a war zone. More and more situations exactly like it were firing up throughout the South. "Immediately."

Troy was reading a text that had just hit his phone. "You can't leave until I—"

A loud knocking on the door interrupted him.

"Madam President," Jordan called loudly. "I need to speak to you."

Troy moved quickly to the door and opened it.

Jordan brushed past after shooting him an irritated glance. "I know you were up all night, but we've got to get you to Washington. We've got to get you to the White House so the country sees you in charge." He gestured at the TV. "We may need to call out federal troops to stop these riots. The situation is getting out of control."

"It already is out of control. Let's go."

"Not yet," Troy said.

"*What?*"

"We sit tight for an hour. Important people are coming here. People I must see."

"You will not tell the president of the United States what she will or will not do," Jordan spoke up, moving toward Troy. "Not while I'm her—"

Troy grabbed Jordan by the throat as gently as he could, spun him around, and forced him against the near wall. "My sole responsibility right now is the safety of my commander in chief," he hissed. "The people coming here may have crucial information for me regarding that responsibility. We will stay here until they arrive. Do you understand me, Chief of Staff Jordan?"

Katrina gazed at Troy. She did not approve of violence in any way—neither Dennis going at Troy nor Troy's brutal reaction to Dennis's approach.

But she loved that this man would sacrifice everything for her. Suddenly she felt safe. And that good, soothing feeling caused her to understand exactly how terrified she'd been—until just now.

CHAPTER 25

McLean, Virginia

"Come in, Captain Buford." Fiske saluted back to the younger man, then beckoned inward, gesturing for the US Army captain to enter. "I'm General Fiske. I'm the one who called you."

"Yes, sir," Buford answered in his scratchy, Deep South, Tulip, Mississippi, accent as he strode confidently into the Lewis house.

Fiske glanced at the olive-green Humvee parked in the driveway. Buford had driven the menacing-looking vehicle up to McLean from his post at Fort A.P. Hill—a fort named for the Rebel general whose division had saved the Confederate army at Antietam with a last-moment, late-afternoon charge on the battlefield after an all-day, double-time march from Harpers Ferry. The fort was located seventy-five miles south of Washington, DC.

"This way, Captain," Fiske ordered as he closed the door, then brushed past Buford. Fiske prayed that Captain Buford was the man who would capture President Katrina Hilton. "Follow me." He prayed that Buford was the man who would grant him his ultimate fantasy and bring her to him. And maybe Buford would use that very Humvee that was parked in the driveway to do it. "Step lively, son."

"Yes, sir."

Lewis rose from the comfortable leather chair positioned in the corner opposite the big screen when the other two men entered his den.

"General Lewis, this is Captain Dace Buford." Fiske pointed from one man to the other as they saluted each other sharply. "Captain Buford, this is General Lewis, director of the Joint Chiefs of Staff."

"I'm aware of who General Lewis is," Buford said calmly. "As I also know that you run intel for JCS, General Fiske."

"Very good," Lewis said approvingly. "At ease, son."

Buford spread his black boots twelve inches apart, clasped his hands behind his back, stuck his chin out, and stared hard straight ahead at a painting of the Shenandoah Mountains hanging on the far wall.

Lewis nodded to Fiske.

Fiske moved in front of Buford, clasping his hands behind his back as well. He and Lewis had researched Captain Buford extensively—as they had carefully screened ten other men and two women, all captains as well—before selecting Buford to approach with their plan.

"What we are about to convey to you must remain top secret," Fiske began. "You cannot communicate any of what we tell you to anyone unless we give you a specific order to do so. I cannot emphasize that more strongly. Do you understand, Captain Buford?"

"Yes, sir."

"The fate of this nation depends on your ability to maintain the secrecy of what we discuss here this morning."

Buford's focus moved deliberately from the painting on the far wall to Fiske.

"Do you understand?"

"Yes, sir."

"Are you aware of something called Prosperity for All?" Lewis asked, moving beside Fiske.

"The initiative President Hilton recently announced. Yes, I am."

"Are you aware of PFA's primary provisions?"

"I'm aware of the only provision that really matters, General Lewis. I'm aware of the provision that cuts this country's annual military budget by eighty percent."

"I never like to assume anything," Lewis said, "but, in this case, can I assume that you are not in favor of that provision?"

"Yes, sir."

"How *much* are you not in favor of that provision?"

"Sir?"

"You should feel you can speak freely in this house, Captain Buford."

"Yes, sir, but—"

"If I were to tell you that President Hilton has enough votes in Congress to enact PFA, to make it law, how would you feel?"

"Given," Fiske added before Buford could answer, "that an eighty percent decrease in the military budget cuts eight hundred billion dollars out of it. So the odds are overwhelmingly strong that you and your command will lose their jobs. What would you say to that?"

Captain Buford blinked several times. "I'd say that whether or not I lose my job is irrelevant. The only thing that matters in all of this is that the United States would become very, very vulnerable . . . to enemies foreign and domestic."

Lewis and Fiske glanced at each other. This thing was so risky. But they were feeling better about it.

Lewis motioned to Fiske.

"Captain Buford," Fiske said, his voice dropping low, "what I am about to say may seem . . ." He hesitated. "Well, you may have a difficult time believing I've said it after I have. You see, General Lewis and I agree with you one hundred percent. If PFA becomes law and the Department of Defense is required to spend less than two hundred billion dollars a year every year, this country would quickly become a substate of China or Russia. And ISIS would run rampant throughout our country. We would be helpless. The military's annual payroll alone is more than one hundred and fifty billion."

"Yes, sir."

"We cannot allow that to happen. Do you agree with me, Captain?"

"Yes, sir, I absolutely agree with you."

Fiske drew himself up so his posture was ramrod straight. This was the edge of a Mount-Everest-high sheer cliff, the point of absolutely no return. Up until this moment, Captain Buford had said all the right things and sent all the right signals. But if he balked at the order Fiske was about to give, that could spell the demise of Project Sundance. Buford might walk out of here and call the secretary of defense—President Hilton's handpicked adviser and longtime friend—or someone else the captain figured couldn't possibly be involved with the coup and was high enough on either the US political or military ladder to stop it. In thirty seconds, Fiske might know if one day he'd be staring down the barrels of a firing squad. Even worse, he might know that his ultimate fantasy would not be coming true. The firing squad would be over quickly. He didn't fear that. But the lost fantasy would haunt him every moment he waited for the bullets. And he was so close he could taste the fantasy. So close he could smell her perfume as he garroted her while she hung before him.

He and Lewis had discussed what to do if Buford balked at the order. They'd discussed executing him if he showed even the slightest hesitation—that seemed to be the only short-term solution. But, of course, they wouldn't be able to hide the crime for long. Even if the coup were successful, they could still stand trial for murder.

They hadn't come to an agreement. Fiske wondered if Lewis had made a decision on his own.

Fiske took a deep breath. "It's time for me to tell you why we called you here."

"Yes, sir," Buford replied impatiently.

They'd quietly researched Captain Buford as well as Buford's family and strongly believed them all to be staunch racists. Captain Buford had done a nice job of hiding his strong predilection during his military career. But Fiske and Lewis were convinced that beneath a thin veneer of racial acceptance, Buford was a bigot of the highest order.

And somehow, they'd gotten lucky, *so* lucky. Buford's uncle on his father's side had just been brutally murdered by a black man on Main Street in Tulip in the middle of the day, literally setting off a war in the small town. There had been one other candidate they'd been more impressed with, who they were more certain would fall into line immediately with the coup. And they'd been just about to call that candidate—until they'd found out what had happened to Henry Buford in Tulip. That murder had tipped the scales in favor of Buford.

"Your uncle was murdered yesterday in Buford," Lewis said quietly.

Buford swallowed hard. "Yes, sir," he responded in a raspy, emotionally charged voice. "By a black man."

"We're both very sorry for your family's loss," Lewis said sympathetically, "but there's a bigger issue here. I mean, do you understand what President Hilton intends to do with all the money she's saving by cutting the military budget to nothing and taxing the hell out of the middle class?"

President Hilton had no intention of taxing the middle class, Fiske knew, and it wasn't as if the IRS could apply tax rates based on the color of a person's skin.

"She's going to hand it over to the people who do nothing for this country but feed off others," Buford answered tersely.

"She's going to give it to all these people who are rioting in the streets," Fiske added.

"And to groups like the War on Whites." Lewis sneered. "To groups who are ambushing cops. Because she feels so sorry for them, because she feels they've been wronged."

Buford glanced from general to general, anger flashing in his eyes. "What do you want me to do?"

"Take the White House," Lewis interrupted, teeth gritted. "The US military cannot allow President Hilton to run this country into the ground. We will not allow her to endanger what so many men have given their lives to protect over the last three centuries."

"Take the White House?" Buford whispered incredulously.

"That's right, Captain. And that's an order."

"You will bring President Hilton to me after you take the White House," Fiske spoke up quickly. "To a location I will give you once the White House is secure and you have taken her prisoner."

"Take the White House," Buford repeated, more loudly and confidently this time.

"Yes," Lewis said, "take the White House. And with it, America."

CHAPTER 26

Camp David, Maryland

Troy and his Red Cell Seven subordinate saluted each other smartly. The subordinate was the man who'd shown up out of nowhere at the gun battle outside the Richmond mall to save Falcon and Billie. He was also the man who'd just delivered Falcon and Billie to Camp David.

"Dismissed."

"Yes, sir."

"But stick around outside," Troy ordered. "I may need you and our other three in a little while."

"Yes, sir."

"And chat up the Secret Service boys while you're out there, Charlie. They're pretty pissed off now that I'm in charge of the president's security." He chuckled. "Make some new friends for me, will you? At the end of the day we're all supposed to be on the same team. The way things are going, we might need them."

"*Really?* Those freaking guys? Suits with guns?"

"Charlie."

"Sorry, sir."

"If I want your opinion, I'll ask for it."

"Yes, sir."

"Dismissed again."

"Yes, sir."

Charlie turned and headed out of the main cabin's great room.

When he was gone, Troy extended his hand to Falcon. "Hey."

"I'm A.J. Falcon," Falcon said as they shook.

"I know who you are. I'm Troy Jensen. I trust you have no idea who I am."

"I'm not sure about the trust issue, not yet, anyway. But you're right about the who-you-are issue. I've got no idea." Falcon gestured at Billie. "This is Billie Hogan."

"I like that name. It's nice to meet you, Billie."

"Pleasure's all mine, Troy," Billie said, grimacing as she held out her good hand. Every movement was still painful for her.

"You OK?" Troy asked, nodding at the cast on her bad arm.

Billie smiled wanly. "I'm fine. Don't worry about me."

"She means it, too," Falcon said firmly, glancing around the big, richly decorated room. The history of this place wasn't lost on him. "She's tough."

"Good to know." Troy raised one eyebrow and gave her a quick up-and-down. "Tough, cool name, *and* she's beautiful. I'm in."

"I have two questions," Falcon said quickly.

He didn't appreciate the other man's forward comment or the up-and-down glance he'd so obviously given Billie. He didn't appreciate the long look Billie had volleyed back at him, either.

Most of all, he didn't appreciate the jealousy that was suddenly piercing his chest. He was completely unaccustomed to it . . . so he almost didn't recognize it.

"Just two questions?" Troy asked.

"Not really, but I'll keep it at that for now."

"And they are?"

"How do you know who I am? And what are Billie and I doing here?"

Troy gave Falcon a perplexed expression. "I thought everyone knew who you were."

"What are you talking about?"

"You're the second Wizard of Wall Street, and son to the first. You're investment banking royalty. And you're Sutton & Company's youngest superstar of all time."

"Give me a break," Falcon muttered.

Was that "youngest" reference an allusion to his being promoted to partner? Was Troy ally or enemy? How could Troy know about the partnership promotion?

"It's true. I know all about you."

"And I'm sure a guy like you counts tons of Wall Streeters as his close friends," Falcon muttered cynically. "So I guess I shouldn't feel very good about why I'm here. Maybe that's why you're stalling on telling me."

"You could throw most I-bankers into the deep end of the ocean in front of an oncoming supertanker without a life jacket, and I wouldn't give a rat's ass," Troy admitted. "But your father was a damn good man. My father knew him well."

Falcon's brows furrowed. "Seriously?"

"Oh yeah."

"Wait a minute," Falcon said in a hushed voice. "Is your father William Jensen, chairman of the Federal Reserve?"

"He is, Mr. Falcon, one and the same. He's also a former CEO of this country's biggest commercial bank, Manhattan National." Troy's eyes narrowed. "To this day, my father doesn't believe your dad jumped out that window. He believes he was thrown."

Falcon swallowed hard. He hadn't liked Troy much a few moments ago when he'd dished Billie the compliment about being beautiful. But suddenly those bad feelings were gone. This young man had known and respected his father. How could he possibly be a bad guy?

"Why does he believe that?"

"My father says your dad would never have given up on anything, *especially* his own life." Troy glanced at Billie, then back at Falcon. "Your father was more of a patriot than you realize, Mr. Falcon."

"Call me A.J. And how do you know he was such a patriot?"

"I just do. Look, your father was involved with some very important things, things that went way past Wall Street, things that could have made him a target for a lot of people."

"Like?"

"I can't say."

"You can't say a lot, you know that?"

"I do."

"I'm guessing I ought to get used to that."

"Yes, you should."

Falcon rolled his eyes. "OK."

"You should be proud of your father."

"I already was before I met you."

"Well, put that pride on steroids."

"Who are you?" Falcon demanded.

"What do you mean?"

"What branch of the military are you in?"

"Who says I'm military?"

"You and your subordinate saluted a few seconds ago."

Troy shrugged. "Just two knights acknowledging each other on the field of battle."

Falcon groaned. "Give me at least a small measure of transparency."

"I can't. Like you said, you won't ever get the whole story out of me. It just isn't possible."

Falcon stared at Troy for several moments, taking it all in. Now he had a *million* questions. "So what are Billie and I doing here?" But he sensed that now wasn't the time to push for all the other answers.

"Of course, I can't tell you much," Troy answered, his demeanor diving to dead serious. "But while I was on a mission recently in the western half of this country, I learned that a high-ranking US general was involved in a plot to destabilize this country. He was trying to weaken our ability to detect terrorist attacks before they occurred."

"Why would a high-ranking general be involved in something like *that*?" Billie asked, her expression giving away her shock.

"That's the million-dollar question, right? Seems ridiculous, doesn't it?"

"It seems more like treason than ridiculous."

"That general's trying to show how badly this country needs our military," Falcon spoke up. "It's probably wrapped up in Prosperity for All. The Pentagon has to be going nuts about President Hilton cutting their checkbook by eighty percent."

Troy glanced at Billie and pointed at Falcon. "No wonder this guy's hedge funds are up ten percent so far this year while the market's flat."

"Actually they're up twelve percent," Billie said. "At least they were a week ago when I checked."

It was Falcon's turn to glance at Billie.

"I told you," she said softly, "I know everything about you, A.J."

"So you agree, Troy?" Falcon asked, still staring at Billie. She was beautiful. He was actually starting to believe he could trust her. "You think what you learned about the general is related to PFA?"

"I think there's a damn good chance."

"So then you should be going nuts about the budget cuts as well," Falcon observed. "Sorry, Troy, but I'm a pragmatist. I don't buy into war being romanticized. If President Hilton is cutting the DoD's budget by as much as I've heard, you and your people will feel the ax as well."

"Nice try. But you're wrong."

"Why am I wrong?"

"I can't tell you."

"Here we go again."

"And sometimes being romantic about war is the only way to make it bearable."

"Yeah, well—"

"Have you ever manned a post, Mr. Falcon? Have you ever been on a real battlefield?"

Falcon shook his head.

248

"Then shut the fuck up."

"I deserved that." Falcon clenched his teeth. "You still haven't told me why we're here."

"Once I found out what was going on out west, I put the general in question under tight surveillance, using audio and visual technology. The man I had watching the general's house witnessed an extraordinary visit there by two men you are quite familiar with, Mr. Falcon."

"Let me guess. Those two men were James Wallace and Philip Rose."

Troy glanced at Billie again while pointing at Falcon. "Please pass 'Go' and collect two hundred bucks, Mr. Falcon. Now I'm *really* impressed." He looked back at Falcon. "And maybe now you're starting to figure out why you're here."

"After that meeting, you started tailing James Wallace, too," Falcon said. "And you were able to execute audio surveillance on him as well. You overheard him talking about The Alliance to Reform Communities. Maybe even the War on Whites group and how Sutton is secretly funding TARC, which is in turn funding WOW. So, ultimately, Sutton is funding WOW." He gestured at Troy. "You probably heard Wallace and Rose mention my name several times, probably more than several times, so you know I'm a man on the run."

"Are you?" Troy asked in a leading tone. "A man on the run?"

"Seriously?" Falcon asked in a WTF, are-you-kidding-me tone. "You really think I could possibly be on the wrong side of this?"

"I always consider every possibility. A man in my position has to."

"And what position is that?"

"I told you not to expect—"

"Your guy saw those two pricks trying to kill Billie and me," Falcon snapped. "In fact, one of them would have gotten us if your guy hadn't shown up. They were Wallace's men. I assume once you heard Wallace and Rose talking about TARC, you put TARC under surveillance as well."

"How do you know TARC is funding the War on Whites?"

"Paul Treviso told me just before he died." Falcon glanced over at Billie. "I assume you know who Paul Treviso is if you've been listening to Wallace and Rose, if you've been watching TARC. That's how your guy showed up at the mall. He was watching Treviso. You probably told him to look out for Billie and me."

"Treviso was Chalice Taylor's right-hand man at TARC and a former Gambino Crime Family hit man—at least, when his name was Fellini." Troy pointed at Billie. "And he was your boyfriend before he died." This time Troy pointed at Falcon. "Do you know that?"

"Yes," Falcon admitted in a low voice, "I do."

"Is there anything going on between you two?" Troy asked bluntly, nodding to Falcon and then Billie.

"What kind of question is that? First of all, it's none of your—"

"Yes," Billie interrupted Falcon, "there is something going on."

A thin smile spread across Troy's face. "Honest, too," he murmured, "at least in the moment when it's convenient."

"What's that supposed to mean?" Billie demanded.

"It's just an observation, Ms. Hogan."

"I don't like it."

"Yeah, well, I don't much care—"

"And I'd appreciate it if you wouldn't—"

"What it appears we have going on here," Troy cut in impatiently, "is a conspiracy between and at the highest levels of the US military and Wall Street, at the highest levels of our federal government and the private sector."

"The objective of which," Falcon spoke up, "appears to be to destroy Prosperity for All. The military detests the budget cuts President Hilton is imposing, and Wall Street detests the tax hikes and givebacks on profits she's going to require. And they're doing something about it. Something I doubt most people could ever comprehend actually happening in the country."

"They must have known it was coming."

"Men like James Wallace and Philip Rose know everything that's coming."

"Maybe not always," said Troy quietly. "There was chatter on the audio surveillance of Wallace and Rose indicating that you might have come up with tangible proof of what we just laid out, a connection between Sutton and TARC. My problem is I don't have anything like that. What I have is circumstantial, nothing I can hang my hat on, nothing I can *move* with." Troy's eyes narrowed as he stared at Falcon. "Was the chatter accurate? Do you have something I can use?"

Falcon nodded deliberately. "Yes, I do. But first you're going to tell me who you are. I'm not giving what I have to just anyone."

"I can't tell you that. But do me a favor. Look around and tell me where you are."

"Fair enough, but you told me you weren't part of the military. If you're here, protecting the president of the United States at Camp David, you *must* be part of the military . . . *somehow.* If you're part of the military, I don't care how you spin it for me, you aren't very happy about the DoD's budget being cut eighty percent. In fact, you're furious. If I were the president, I wouldn't feel very safe."

"Maybe that's why I am here," Troy replied. "Maybe I'm not influenced by the DoD budget."

Falcon's eyes narrowed. That was interesting, and it made sense. "You're not getting what I have until you help me."

"Help you?"

"Yeah, help me."

"I'm not negotiating."

"Sounds like you'd better. Sounds like if you don't, you're SOL."

"You Wall Street guys think you can—"

Troy was interrupted when the front door to the cabin opened and Katrina Hilton walked in—followed by Charlie and a squadron of Secret Service agents.

"I need to get to the White House, Colonel Jensen," she said calmly. "And I need to get there *now.*"

CHAPTER 27

Near Charlotte, North Carolina

Troy, Falcon, another of Troy's command, and the pilot had flown more than four hundred miles from Camp David to North Carolina in less than ninety minutes. The brand-new Sikorsky Raider had made quick work of the evening flight to the remote, rural area that was located in the southern part of the state outside the city of Charlotte—which bordered South Carolina.

According to Falcon, Paul Treviso had gasped the specific address of the hostage house from the asphalt, as he lay dying. Troy had no reason to suspect that Paul or Falcon was lying. And Falcon had made it very clear he wasn't giving anyone any proof of anything until Claire was safe and sound, that there would be no bargaining on the issue. Once she was safe, Troy would get what he wanted, Falcon had promised.

The location Paul had identified in a whisper just before his last breath was the address of an old farmhouse that was tucked into the edge of a dense pine forest, half a mile from the nearest home, with a huge field sprawling out before its front porch. It was only twenty-five miles from Sally's Charlotte suburb house.

Claire would be home soon, safe and sound. Then Troy could get back to the business at hand with the proof Falcon had—absolute, unassailable evidence of Sutton & Company funding the Alliance to Reform Communities. With that evidence in hand, Troy hoped he could head off the riots overtaking the country. With that evidence, he hoped he could avert the possibility that the military might take an unprecedented step in US history. A step the predominantly white rural population might actually support. A step the country might never recover from. A step the *world* might never recover from.

With Falcon's damning evidence in hand, Troy believed he might be able to convince the world that the hate and conflict manifesting itself in the riots exploding around the country had been artificially manufactured by an ultra-right-wing faction. A faction that needed the hate and conflict as motivation for others not as radical to join their awful cause and their evil side. With Falcon's evidence, Troy prayed he could convince the world that a few ultrawealthy, ultraconservative individuals had psychopathically devised and executed their insidious plan to cause the strife that would enable them to take incredible steps and measures never seen before in the United States of America. And bring the country back from the edge of a situation not seen in the world since Nazi Germany.

Troy feared for President Hilton's life. But, most of all, he feared for America.

He and Falcon had to stop what was happening before it was too late. Before a few high-ranking generals and the most powerful investment bank in the world were able to change the course of world history from a bumpy path toward inclusion—directly toward hell.

He was glad his teammate in all of this was A.J. Falcon. They'd only known each other a few hours, but the man was badass.

Troy grinned to himself as the pilot began to set the chopper down. Maybe he could convince Falcon to give up his finance career and join RC7.

Troy's grin faded. Maybe Falcon would have no choice.

Troy and Falcon had scouted the target area outside Charlotte on the web, and they'd identified another field the chopper could land in. According to Google Maps there was a postage-size opening in the forest on the far side of the heavily wooded ridge the old house was built at the base of. Where the chopper could land and not be detected by anyone at the house.

Landing in the field in front of the house wasn't an option—their approach would be only slightly more obvious than a herd of elephants charging. Coming from this side, they should keep surprise with them.

But now they had to hike up, over, and down the three-hundred-foot ridge to reach the hostage house and rescue Claire.

"Charlie!" Troy called into his microphone as the three men bailed out on both sides of the Raider before the pilot could put the helicopter all the way down into the long grass, damp from the early-evening dew. "You there?"

"I'm here, boss."

"Is she still at the original location?"

"She's still here," Charlie replied from Camp David. "But I don't know how much longer I can *keep* her here. The other side of the aisle is starting to question her courage on all the news networks. She's fuming. At some point she's going to start threatening us with taking her hostage. I don't want any part of that."

"Keep her there at all costs, Charlie. Do not let her leave tonight. Use that southern charm of yours. You hear me?"

"I heard you the first thirty times, boss."

"Call me if it gets really bad."

"Yes, sir."

"I got your back on this. Don't worry."

"I'll remember you saying that when I'm sitting in Leavenworth. Ten-four."

"Ten-four," Troy shouted above the roar of the engine. "Out," he yelled as Falcon hustled around the nose of the craft, stooped at the waist beneath the spinning rotors. "I hope for your sake this doesn't turn out badly, Mr. Falcon. If it does, there will be hell to pay."

"Define 'turn out badly.' And call me A.J. while you do it."

Falcon was a damn good negotiator—which, Troy realized, he should have anticipated. That was Wall Street. On that thin strip of Lower Manhattan road leading through the towering buildings on either side from Trinity Church to the East River, you only got what you won from being better than others at the game of chicken. And his father had always called Falcon Senior the best he'd ever seen at it. Apparently, they'd gone at it a few times. And Jensen Senior hadn't always come out on the winning side.

Well, it was time for Troy to start his own negotiation with Junior.

"If President Hilton leaves Camp David to go to the White House before we get back tonight, I'll take it out on you, Mr. Falcon," Troy said when they were out from under the rotors and heading up the ridge, patting the pistol in the holster on his hip. "You think you can out-negotiate me. But I've got the ultimate say-so."

"How are you going to take it out on me? What are you gonna do?"

"Shoot you."

"Not if I shoot you first," Falcon retorted with a grin, patting the pistol Troy had given him—resting in the holster on *his* hip. "Why is President Hilton so much safer at Camp David than at the White House? From everything I've read and heard, the White House is a fortress. Jets taking off from Reagan only have ten seconds to turn left off the flight path toward 1600 Pennsylvania or the antiaircraft guns on the White House roof shoot them down."

"If history has taught us anything," Troy answered somberly, "it's that you can kill anyone if you try hard enough, if you're willing to sacrifice more assets than the other side is. So I've created a diversion, so there will be no attempt."

"What's the diversion?"

Troy had taken Falcon's cell phone so there was no risk of his ruining the cover story if somehow he'd totally misjudged the other man. "Ten minutes ago I put out a false story about her flying to the White House. She's supposed to be on her way there in a half hour."

"Some people will know she's not."

"True," Troy admitted as they climbed the slope through the sweet-smelling pines and the last rays of twilight side by side, the third member of the team following them a few feet behind. "But if a guy on my team or a Secret Service agent is the one who blows the cover story, then we've got bigger problems, right?"

"Agreed, but by midnight tonight someone on the White House staff will know she's not at 1600. You can't be as confident of keeping the fake story straight at that point."

"*Marine One* and *Two* will take off from Camp David in thirty minutes. And one of President Hilton's doubles will be aboard. In the darkness, that woman is a very convincing replica of the real one. And I'm having members of my command and the Secret Service deny the press access to the landing on the White House lawn as well as keep the staff away. The double will go right to the living quarters as soon as the presidential helicopters are on the ground."

"How many presidential doubles are there?"

"I believe four, but I'm not sure."

"Because this isn't what you usually do. Protect the president, I mean."

"No, it isn't."

"Why, then?" Falcon asked.

"Why, then *what*?"

"Why are you protecting her now?"

"I can't tell you."

"Son of a bitch!" Falcon exclaimed, coming to a stop halfway up the ridge. "The Founding Fathers thought of everything!"

"What's your problem?" Troy demanded, shooting his subordinate a quick glance as they all took several deep breaths. "What are you talking about?"

"You were telling me the truth. You aren't part of the military."

"I never said I was or I wasn't."

"Well, you aren't. You might have come from it, but you aren't officially part of it now. You're independent somehow, maybe privately funded. That way you aren't affected when something like this happens, when the president proposes something that grinds the military as negatively as Prosperity for All does. It's that way so you and your team can stay objective. *Son of a bitch!*"

Troy grimaced. Falcon was a worthy adversary no matter what arena he was operating in.

"And that chopper we took here is money," Falcon muttered. "I'm no military hardware expert, but I'm no babe in the woods, either. I've bought and shorted a good number of defense company stocks over the past few years. So I've read a ton about the cutting-edge equipment coming on line. That chopper was doing more than two hundred and seventy miles per hour."

Troy raised an eyebrow. "The airspeed on those choppers is clocked in—"

"I know how to convert knots to MPHs. And two hundred seventy miles an hour is *moving* for any helicopter. So clearly you guys, whoever you guys are, get the best military equipment available all the time, even if you aren't technically part of the military." Falcon hesitated. "Who are you, Troy Jensen?"

Troy pointed at Falcon. "Just make damn sure that evidence you have is rock solid," he snapped, ignoring the question.

"Oh, it's rock solid. But tell me what you're thinking."

"Thinking?"

"You're worried the US military might take action against the civilian side of the government, against the president of the United States, Congress, and others. Maybe even against the Federal Reserve and your father. That's it, isn't it? You're scared that if the general you've identified is willing to allow terrorists to attack US soil, he might have the balls for worse. Maybe even to put a goddamn coup into motion." Falcon jabbed the air repeatedly. "You're terrified that if the Pentagon gets control of this country, the general you identified and others will shut down the riots exploding across the South with brute force. And when the white rural population sees that going on, they'll support it. And then there'll be no stopping the coup because a plurality of this country will support it." Falcon's voice dropped to a whisper. "Then we're back into the fifties and sixties, maybe worse. Maybe the combination of ultraconservatives and the military, unchecked by a democratic process, takes this country in an almost unimaginable direction."

Troy stared at Falcon steadily for several moments. Finally, he nodded . . . sadly. "That's exactly what I'm concerned about, A.J. Falcon. Are you relieved now that you know?"

"No, I'm as terrified as you are." He grabbed Troy as the other man turned to start heading farther up the slope again. "There's one more thing you need to hear. One more thing Paul Treviso told me as he was dying."

Troy's eyes flashed. "What is it?"

"He told me he'd secretly contacted a senior political leader two weeks ago to tell her what he suspected was going on at TARC. That TARC was being funded by an ultra-right-wing group whose sole objective was to create exactly what's going on. Race wars. He told me this thing has been going on for a while. That they were backing the ultraconservative presidential candidate who almost beat President Hilton in the last election. So he called the Senate majority leader because she was liberal and black, and he figured she couldn't possibly be involved in the conspiracy."

"He called Patricia Stiles? *Paul called Peppermint Patty?*"

"Paul wanted a new life. In exchange for immunity, absolute protection from the Gambino Crime Family and a fresh start with a new name and a new fictitious personal history, he was going to provide evidence that Sutton & Company was funding TARC and that TARC was funding the War on Whites, all with the explicit objective of starting a race war. Paul told me where I can get his proof of TARC funding WOW, which I don't have. I have the wires from Sutton into TARC but nothing from TARC to WOW. Paul told me that Chalice Taylor is also being paid directly by Wallace and Rose. He told me Chalice rolled over and agreed to everything because the ex-NFLer was flat broke."

"My God," Troy whispered. He glanced into Falcon's eyes. "Come on, let's get your niece and get back to Camp David."

Minutes later, they reached the peak of the ridge and began to descend the other side.

Halfway down the slope, Troy held his hand up, motioning for Falcon and the other man of his command to stop. He pointed at the other man and nodded, then held a finger to his lips when he looked over at Falcon.

"Are we waiting for all the light to be gone?" Falcon asked, crouching down beside Troy. In another five minutes the forest would be completely dark. He gazed down through the thick forest but could make out nothing other than the trees. "Should only be a few more minutes."

Troy's subordinate had pulled a small device from his holster belt and was holding it up in front of his face, aiming it down the slope.

"What's that?" Falcon whispered. "What's he doing?"

On the flight down, Falcon had told Troy about his fascination with technology. How his father had constantly counseled him to always soak up as much of it as possible, to always embrace it and never ignore it. Falcon had admitted that sometimes he invested in tiny hatchling companies simply to better understand something that might rock the world.

"That device," Troy whispered back, "can detect anything alive within a mile, even if it's behind a rock wall. I want to know what we're dealing with before we go in."

A moment later, the man glanced over at Troy and shook his head.

"What does that mean?" Falcon demanded. *"Troy?"*

Troy grimaced. "It means—"

Falcon didn't wait for Troy to finish. He was off before Troy could, racing down the hill, dodging trees.

Troy sprinted after him, trying to keep up. But the man was fast.

Troy pulled his gun out when the dim outline of the house appeared through the forest twenty feet away. Falcon disappeared around one side of the home, and Troy sprinted after him, tearing up the front porch steps toward the now-open front door.

When Troy burst into the dimly lit living room, he stopped short and caught his breath at the horrible scene.

Falcon was on his knees, face buried in his hands.

And a young woman—who Troy assumed was Claire—was hanging limply by the neck from a hook in the ceiling, eyes open but unseeing, toes dangling a foot off the carpeted floor.

A piece of paper was pinned to the young woman's blouse, and Troy moved ahead deliberately to scan the hand-scrawled note.

It read: "This one is for Paul Treviso."

As Paul lay dying on the Richmond mall parking lot, he'd called these men and told them to kill Claire. Then he'd whispered her location to Falcon—so he could see her dead.

CHAPTER 28

Camp David, Maryland

"I'm leaving."

"You're staying."

"Get out of my way."

"I have my orders."

Katrina motioned to her lead Secret Service agent. "Get the convoy ready, Agent Mitchell. We're leaving in ten minutes. I'm going to the White House."

"Yes, Madam President," Mitchell replied, motioning exuberantly to a subordinate, as if he'd just won a great battle.

Charlie stepped in front of her as the subordinate sprinted off. "This is for your safety," he said through gritted teeth. "This comes directly from Colonel Jensen, the RC7 leader. He'll be back here in one hour. At least wait for him to get here before you make a move. *Please*, Madam President. You know waiting is the right thing to do."

"Colonel Jensen will be back here in one hour?" she asked, raising an eyebrow.

"Yes."

"And his sole job right now is to protect my life, correct?"

"Yes, Madam President."

"Then what's he doing an hour away from me?"

"He had to leave. He had no choice. So he put me in charge of your security until he can get—"

She took a step to the right to go.

Charlie sidestepped in front of her.

"If this man gets in my way again," she said evenly, gesturing toward Charlie and then Mitchell, "put him under arrest immediately."

Mitchell smiled thinly at Charlie. "Yes, Madam President."

◆ ◆ ◆

Tulip, Mississippi

The tiny town of Tulip, Mississippi, had become the lightning rod for the growing disaster that was spreading out across the United States. Atlanta, Dallas, and Tuscaloosa were burning out of control. Riots in New Orleans and Houston were beginning to burn. Ethnically diverse neighborhoods in several northern cities—Chicago, Minneapolis, and Cleveland—were erupting in violence. More and more areas were being directly affected. But the intense focus of the press, and, therefore, the nation, was Tulip, Mississippi.

In fact, it had become the press's obsession.

The reasons were clear. The conflict had begun with a black man gunning down a white man on Main Street in the middle of the day beneath a beautiful blue sky for all to see. Some networks were reporting that the shooting had begun as an act of self-defense, which the white man had aggressively initiated. Others were claiming the black shooter was laughing as he emptied his Colt revolver into the victim even as the victim lay motionless on the street.

Blacks were certain the shooting had been in self-defense.

Whites were equally as sure the shooter was wrapped inside a crystal-meth haze as he pulled the trigger of his Colt revolver over and over.

Lines were clearly drawn regarding the killing.

But the obsession with Tulip went deeper than that—much deeper.

Two thousand whites lived on the north side of Main Street. Two thousand blacks lived on the south side. Two-story colonial homes in back of white picket fences were built on the north side. Old ranch homes with scraggly yards littered the south side. Reporters had discovered that restaurants on Main Street still seated whites in the front sections of their establishments—but put blacks at the back tables. The schools still had segregated classes in all grades. And local police were doing nothing to stop violence against blacks—while cops were protecting neighborhoods on the north side of Main Street with a vengeance.

Blacks were forced to defend themselves. White attacks against blacks were being ignored.

It was as racially divided a place as could be. It seemed to be a town time had forgotten for the last seventy years—which made for compelling television and huge ratings.

The governor had called out the National Guard. Still, the war in Tulip, Mississippi, raged on.

It seemed nothing could stop it. It had gone from a lightning rod to the fuse lighting the rest of the country's dynamite.

◆ ◆ ◆

McLean, Virginia

Generals Lewis and Fiske stood side by side in the den of the Lewis house in McLean, Virginia, monitoring the intensifying situations that were exploding in front of them on the big screen. Fiske flipped channels every thirty seconds. That way they were able to get quick updates on what was happening in the big cities around the country.

However, the focus of every network inevitably and quickly returned to Tulip, Mississippi. Tulip had gripped the nation's attention—and, more and more by the minute, the world's.

Lewis switched the glass full of 212-year-old scotch he was holding in his right hand to his left, then placed his right palm on Fiske's left arm. "It's happening, my friend," he whispered in a scratchy tone saturated by emotion. "It's actually happening."

"Yes . . . it is."

"The course of this country is changing before our very eyes. We're about to take it back."

"Yes, it appears we are."

"And we're in the eye of the hurricane that's forcing the change. You and I are driving the hurricane. Nothing could be better than this."

"I spoke to him half an hour ago," Fiske said.

Lewis tightened his grip on Fiske's arm and glanced over at him. "What did you say?"

"Uh . . . I'm sorry, sir," Fiske muttered, realizing he had no idea what Lewis had just said or what had been on TV for the last thirty seconds. "I was thinking about something else."

"Obviously."

Fiske couldn't keep his mind off the fantasy that was rapidly becoming reality. As much as the country was obsessed with Tulip, Mississippi, he was obsessed with Captain Buford taking President Hilton prisoner and bringing her to him. As James Wallace had suggested at their last meeting, they were Satan's angels.

And Fiske loved it.

"What were you thinking about, George?"

There was that use of his first name. It was Lewis's code that he wanted an absolutely honest answer. So Fiske would give it to him—just not all of it.

"I was thinking about Captain Buford taking President Hilton prisoner before he and his command attack the White House. I was thinking about Buford bringing Katrina to me."

"Good," Lewis said, slipping his fingers from Fiske's uniform and returning the glass full of liquid gold to his right hand. "I'm glad."

It was Fiske's turn to glance over at Lewis curiously. "You're glad that's what I was thinking about?"

"I'm glad you've ultimately agreed with me and that you aren't actually going to physically lead that assault."

During the last few hours, Fiske had thought long and hard about the danger of leading the charge, and realized that his initial reaction had been wrong. The fight for the White House would get nasty. 1600 Pennsylvania had several powerful defense tricks up its sleeve—like *Air Force One*, *Marine One*, and the limousine the president rode in did—and taking the building would be no cakewalk. Lives would definitely be lost, and he didn't want one of those to be his.

Fortunately, the military was aware of what those White House defenses were, and Fiske had been able to get the specifics of them to Captain Buford. There would be no surprises, but the devastation on both sides would still be horrible. Buford had taken two more units as a result. Now he had more than four hundred men under his direct command—at Fiske's direct order.

And, as it turned out, Katrina would be taken before she ever reached the White House. So there was no need for him to be there and risk his own skin to absolutely ensure she was taken alive. He would be miles away when the assault on 1600 began, satisfying himself in a way he'd never thought possible.

"As always, sir," Fiske said respectfully, "your instincts were correct. Thank you for your guidance."

"So you spoke to Buford thirty minutes ago?" Lewis asked. "Is that who you were referring to?"

"Yes, sir."

"And?"

"He and his command left Fort Hill two hours ago. They will intercept the president's convoy on I-270 northwest of Washington, DC. My snitch in the Secret Service contacted me just before she left Camp David. The story about her coming to 1600 on *Marine One* was a ruse."

"I'm glad you were able to find a sympathizer in the Secret Service."

"We have sympathizers everywhere, General Lewis," Fiske said. "The hatred runs deep and wide and has for decades."

"Yes, it has," Lewis agreed.

"How old is that scotch?" Fiske asked, pointing at Lewis's glass.

Lewis took a sip and then held the half-full glass up before his eyes. "Two hundred twelve years," he answered.

Fiske whistled softly, impressed.

"This scotch comes from my family's hometown in the Highlands of Scotland. I bought the bottle a decade ago specifically for this night. It cost me thirty thousand dollars." He closed his eyes and took a long swallow. "And it was worth every penny."

◆ ◆ ◆

Tulip, Mississippi

At 10:00 p.m. Tulip's Main Street was quiet except for the military helicopter hovering high overhead. National Guard sharpshooters had taken up positions on the roofs of buildings lining both sides of the thoroughfare. But there were still sporadic reports of gunfire every few minutes.

The tallest buildings were only three stories high. So the strategic views weren't that strategic. And the NG units that had responded thus far to Tulip were not equipped with night-vision capability.

Soldiers scanned Main Street constantly with powerful spotlights, which created an eerie scene. Bouquets of flowers placed by mourners had built a mountain at the spot where Henry Buford had died. And the shadows formed by the crisscrossing rays of light made the mountain seem bigger than it actually was. No one had visited the flower mountain since nightfall an hour ago. It was too dangerous.

Most of the gunfire was coming from the south side. Small units of white militiamen were roaming the areas, searching for prey. But prey was becoming harder to find now that battle lines had been so clearly drawn. Everyone who wasn't a predator was locked behind doors with weapons loaded and drawn. Most people on both sides of Tulip's Main Street had at least two guns in the house. After all, this was the Bible Belt.

Predators were becoming prey. Those locked inside of homes were taking potshots from windows at anything that moved in their yards.

Local police and National Guard units were stationed throughout the north side, so there was little gunfire in this area. The rationale for keeping units there was that homes on the north side were more valuable and contained more valuable items. Looting was more likely on the north side, so these town blocks needed more protection.

The outcry from the press and community leaders nationwide had done nothing to move authorities into the south side. However, the governor had promised to send additional troops into Tulip when they became available, and that they would be deployed on the south side, though that deployment wouldn't be anytime soon. The governor's problem was that riots were now breaking out all across the state. The National Guard was stretched thin everywhere—not just Mississippi.

The first person to notice the little black girl was a soldier atop the Southern States store—the store Henry Buford had been headed to when the incident had occurred. The soldier called quietly to another man on the next building over and pointed down.

The girl was ten years old and beautiful. She had smooth mahogany skin and huge brown eyes. Her facial features were exotic—full lips, high cheekbones, and long lashes surrounding her gorgeous eyes. Her natural expression was a smile, which her sculpted cheekbones accentuated, and she made everyone around her feel better just by being with them.

She moved slowly and deliberately up Main Street, following the yellow lines painted down the center of the street as if she were a bridesmaid moving toward the altar. She clutched a huge bouquet of wildflowers she'd picked from a field this evening as she walked. She'd snuck out of her house on the south side despite her father's angry warning for his family to remain inside. And she'd snuck out again a few minutes ago to deliver this bouquet of beautiful flowers to Henry Buford's death scene.

Soldiers began to clap as more and more of them noticed her and she drew closer and closer to the scene. As she reached it, the ovations and the shouts of encouragement turned into a roar.

When she knelt down, kissed the bouquet, and placed it at the base of the floral mountain, the roar went deafening—not only on Tulip's Main Street but across the country as the nation watched on TV.

◆ ◆ ◆

Northwest of Washington, DC

"What's wrong?" Katrina demanded as the presidential convoy came to a grinding halt on I-270 thirty miles northwest of the White House.

She was in the main limousine in the middle of the forty-vehicle string of black SUVs, sedans, and other limousines. Accompanying her were Chief of Staff Jordan and the lead Secret Service agent, Bernie Mitchell.

"Why are we stopping?"

"What the hell is going on, Agent Mitchell?" Jordan snapped as he sat beside Katrina on the forward-facing seat.

Katrina always sat facing forward. She would suffer motion sickness facing backward, Jordan knew. She had ever since her first ride in a limousine. They'd splurged and taken one the day of that first initial public offering years ago. They'd discovered her affliction a mile from the Plaza Hotel on their way downtown toward the New York Stock Exchange to ring the opening bell. She'd become violently ill. But they'd still been on time for her to ring the bell.

"Damn it, Mitchell," Jordan piled on, "keep this train moving."

"What's happening up front?" Mitchell hissed into the microphone embedded into the leather band encircling his left wrist. He was sitting in the backward-facing seat. *"Why are we stopping?"* He glanced at Jordan when no one answered. "There's got to be an accident."

"Why didn't you get an answer from the lead vehicle?" Jordan asked suspiciously. "And I thought there was supposed to be a car several miles ahead of us monitoring our route in the event of something like this. So we didn't ever stop. We're vulnerable stopped like this."

"This limousine could take a direct hit from a surface-to-air missile and all we'd suffer would be a few bruises. The car would get knocked around good, but we'd be fine. The armor on this thing's incredible." Mitchell raised the microphone to his lips again. "This is Golden Egg to Arrowhead. What the hell's happening up there? *Somebody*—"

His transmission was interrupted by the sound of gunfire. It was close.

Jordan's eyes flashed to Mitchell's, then to Katrina's. He'd never seen her truly terrified for her life. He did now.

"Lock us down!" Jordan shouted.

"Affirmative," Mitchell confirmed, hitting a button on the panel beside his seat. "We are locked down. We are insulated." He raised the microphone to his lips again. "Take evasive action!" he ordered the driver. "Immediately!"

The limousine instantly lurched forward and left, accelerating quickly.

Katrina and Jordan tried frantically to secure their seat belts. They never used them because they never needed to. Of course it was procedure for them to use the belts, but the Secret Service agents didn't follow up. It seemed silly.

Moments after the limousine lurched forward, it screeched to a fishtailing stop.

Katrina shrieked as she and Jordon were hurled ahead into the backward-facing bench seat in front of them, Jordan directly into Mitchell.

Their heads smashed together. After Jordan had scrambled back to the forward-facing seat and touched his forehead, he realized he was bleeding. He glanced at Mitchell. The man was unaffected.

"Go, go, go!" Mitchell yelled. "Come on!"

But nothing happened. The vehicle did not move.

Then the door beside Mitchell opened, and a uniformed man leaned into the limousine, aiming a pistol.

"Good-bye, Mr. Jordan," Captain Buford said calmly, putting two bullets into Jordan's chest.

Jordan slumped over dead, his head falling into Katrina's lap.

Buford stepped into the limousine, grabbed Katrina's wrist, and pulled her screaming from the vehicle. When she was out, he stuck his head back in for a moment and nodded to Mitchell. "Thanks."

"You got it," Mitchell answered calmly. "Godspeed."

Two minutes later, President Katrina Hilton lay in the back of Buford's Humvee, tied and gagged, heading toward a remote location—General George Fiske waiting.

◆ ◆ ◆

Tulip, Mississippi

The little girl who'd placed the bouquet of flowers down at the base of the floral mountain rose from her knees and acknowledged the cheers with exuberant waves of both arms. Her smile was on full display, and the cheers grew thunderous again.

She waved and waved—until a thirty-caliber bullet smashed into her forehead. The force of the impact blew her head apart and knocked her body into the mountain of flowers.

The war was suddenly back on—more intensely than ever.

CHAPTER 29

In the air above Virginia

"I've got someone picking you up in northern Virginia," Troy hollered to Falcon over the roar of the rotor whirling above them.

Immediately after they'd discovered Claire's body, Troy had radioed for the pilot to fly over the ridge and set the Sikorsky Raider down in the open field in front of the farmhouse. Falcon hadn't said a word since they'd taken off from North Carolina, carrying Claire's body in the chopper.

"My guy is waiting outside Manassas, near the Bull Run battlefield. He's got a Humvee for you. It's yours to do what you want with." Troy received no answer. "We've got about three minutes until the pilot puts us down. We have to move fast once we're on the ground because I've got to hop back in this thing and get to downtown DC as soon as possible." Still nothing. "A.J., I said I've got somebody who's gonna—"

"I heard you," Falcon interrupted sullenly.

Claire lay on the floor beside him. A thick gray blanket Troy had found in the back of the chopper shrouded her. The note that had been pinned to her blouse when they'd found her was now crumpled in Falcon's right hand. It was damp.

"Where am I supposed to go?" Falcon asked.

"Somewhere safe."

"Like?"

"Get away from DC. Go west, into the Shenandoah Mountains. Hole up out there until things settle down. You've got a gun. Don't hesitate to use it."

"You mean run away like a coward."

"Like a sane, rational civilian."

"Like a coward."

"DC's a shitshow, A.J. From what I'm hearing, the military is badly split on this thing. Ten percent support it, ten percent don't, and the other eighty percent are waiting to see what happens. Troops backing the coup took the White House and the Capitol a few minutes ago, and we need to retake those buildings immediately. The longer the coup has possession of them, the harder it'll be to get them back. The harder it'll be to defeat the coup. We must rout the insurgents right away."

"Why?"

"The risk is that Russia and/or China recognizes the generals who've taken power as in charge of the country and, therefore, gives them legitimacy. Then the troops who've been walking the tightrope and waiting to see what happens will go with the coup, with the winning side, because this is a life-and-death situation. If you're on the losing side of a coup, sooner or later you're looking down the rifle barrels of a firing squad. So if the coup's endorsed by the other superpowers, everything quickly becomes a done deal."

"Why in the hell would Russia or China *ever* recognize a US government run by a bunch of generals? That's the last thing those two countries want. They want the troops who still support President Hilton to win. They can't wait for our military spending to drop by eighty percent."

"That would be their best-case scenario," Troy agreed. "But understand that they don't want to piss off the generals in charge of the coup, either, in case the coup succeeds. And believe me, those generals are on the phone with Moscow and Beijing right now demanding that officials of those countries recognize a new US government. They're telling the Russians and the Chinese that if they don't recognize the new government immediately and they win, they'll remember when things settle down. They're telling them they'll negotiate treaties with the first of them that recognizes the coup government. They're forcing those foreign governments to make a choice as we speak."

"Jesus," Falcon whispered. It made so much sense.

Troy reached over and patted Falcon's shoulder. "I'm sorry about Claire."

Falcon clenched his jaw. "She's dead because of me. I let her down."

"No. You did everything in your power to save her."

"She's dead," he repeated, emotion swelling up in his chest again. He bit down hard on his lower lip. He hadn't called Sally yet. He couldn't bear to do it. "And that's all that matters."

"We'll find the people who are responsible," Troy vowed. "And they will be punished accordingly. I promise you."

"How can you promise me that?"

"I just can."

"Who are you, Troy? Who do you report to?"

Troy shook his head. "I told you not to ask me those questions."

Falcon kept staring down at the floor. "I'm not getting out of this helicopter in Manassas," he said firmly.

"*What?*"

"I'm going with you to DC. I'm fighting."

"You don't want this fight," Troy assured him.

"I don't care how dangerous it is," he said, looking up and over at Troy. "I'm not afraid." He nodded down at Claire's body. "And I'm not letting her die in vain. I have to do something to avenge her suffering."

"A.J., I can't let you—"

"And get me a real weapon. I'm not going into battle with just this popgun on my hip."

Troy gritted his teeth. "What about Claire?"

"I'll take care of her," Billie spoke up from the seat beside Falcon.

She'd flown down to North Carolina with them, but she'd stayed in the chopper when they'd gone over the ridge.

"You need to fight," she whispered in Falcon's ear. "I understand why. I'll take care of Claire's body. And I'll be waiting for you when everything's over, one way or the other." She ran her fingers through his dark hair when he turned toward her. "And I'll be with you when you bury her." She kissed him gently on the cheek. "I'll be with you as long as you want me to be."

◆ ◆ ◆

Washington, DC

Peppermint Patty glanced up from her desk in the Russell Building when the sharp rap on the door to her inner office finally came. She hadn't run away in panic as most of her colleagues had. She'd remained at her desk late into the night as she always did, working for the people.

"Come in," she called, standing up.

The door swung open, and four soldiers moved smartly into the office.

"Turn around and put your hands behind your back, Ms. Stiles," the man in charge ordered. "Now."

She complied with the order. It would be stupid not to. They might have orders to shoot.

The metal cuffs clamping around her wrists felt oddly comforting. In her younger days she'd been a staunch civil-rights activist, and she'd lost count of how many times she'd been arrested. Lost count until her first political opponent had reminded her of the number—which was fifteen—in their first televised debate.

It hadn't mattered. She'd still won.

As she had no doubt she would this time as well. She'd been cuffed all those times, but she'd always been released. And she'd ended up the Senate majority leader.

She smiled at the captain as he turned her back around to face him when the cuffs were secured. "What took you guys so long?"

CHAPTER 30

Washington, DC

"You may see some things tonight," Troy muttered to Falcon as they knelt behind a Honda Accord that was parked on Seventeenth Street near the White House, "things you may find hard to believe are actually happening. It's technology that my unit alone has access to. Keep everything you see strictly confidential. If you survive, speak to no one about it. I mean that in very black-and-white terms. You'll be subject to capital punishment if you ever whisper anything about it to anyone outside my command. You would be considered a spy and prosecuted as one. Do you understand?"

"Yes, sir," Falcon answered evenly.

The "sir" hadn't been forced, not even something Falcon really thought about. It had come from his lips as a natural matter of course, without a moment's hesitation. Troy was charged with retaking the White House from a revolutionary force, from a military coup. The situation seemed otherworldly to Falcon, to the point of being almost unbelievable. He had to keep confirming to himself that he was actually awake.

But here they were, preparing to attack 1600 Pennsylvania Avenue.

Troy was leading one of the most pivotal moments in US history, a moment that would ultimately determine the course of human events into eternity. He deserved to be addressed with the utmost respect. It was that simple.

"Why not starve them out?" Falcon asked. "Why attack?"

"Same answer as before," Troy replied firmly. "The longer they hold the iconic landmarks of American government, the more they are legitimized. The more the soldiers who are on the fence switch to their side. Then it's over."

This was crazy. Military coups didn't go down in the United States of America. They went down in third-world countries run by drunk-with-power dictators who were murdering helpless populations and plundering state banks for themselves. America was the safe harbor investors ran to and hid in like frightened sheep when things like this happened elsewhere in the world. America was the rock of stability in times of panic. Not the place where panic was actually happening.

"Take this."

Falcon gazed for a few seconds at the sleek, mean-looking submachine gun Troy was holding out, reflecting on all that had happened in the few days since he'd been named a partner at Sutton & Company.

Finally, he reached for it.

The all-black composite felt good in his hands as soon as he touched it, eerily comforting against the skin of his fingers and palms. This weapon was suddenly his best friend in the world.

"It's a Heckler & Koch MP8," Troy explained, "the latest and greatest antiterrorism weapon. It's one of only a hundred in existence. It is *the* weapon you want in your hands for the nightmare you're about to endure. Thank the Germans." He nodded. "But keep a hold of that popgun on your hip just in case." He reached into a bag lying on the street beside him and tossed two extra clips to Falcon. "Fire only when you absolutely have to. You'll be out of bullets before you know it if you're trigger-happy with that thing. Then you'll be damn glad you have the pistol. Push this to eject the spent clip," Troy said, touching the top of the MP8. "Slip the next one in and you're ready to go again."

"Got it."

Troy grabbed Falcon's shoulder. "You sure about this, A.J.?"

"Yes."

"You can stay behind out here or head west now. There's a mass transit line that would take you straight to Billie, if it's still operating, of course."

"No."

"You won't be a coward in my eyes if you do."

"It's not your eyes I care about."

"If you get killed, it's not on me. I'll have no sympathy. In fact, it won't bother me at all. In a few days I'll forget I even knew you. You should understand that going in."

"I do."

"And I'm not watching over you during our assault," Troy said, gesturing in the direction of the White House. "I won't have time."

"I know."

"The odds are good you'll die tonight."

"Enough!"

The chopper had put down ten minutes ago in the darkness near the Lincoln Memorial, ground that was still held by troops loyal to President Hilton. After jumping from the craft, they'd moved down a desolate Constitution Avenue and were now several hundred yards south of the White House. They hadn't seen a single civilian since jumping from the helicopter. People were inside behind bolted-tight doors—or had abandoned the city altogether.

On the way to the White House area, they'd been joined by five hundred US Army regulars in uniform and another fifty or so men dressed like Troy—clad in desert camouflage outfits with no identifying marks, medals, or bars anywhere on them. As far as Falcon could tell, any of them could be Troy's second-in-command or just another member of the unit, whatever unit that was.

"This is the man we're looking for," Troy said, holding out his phone so Falcon could see the face on the screen. "His name is Buford. He's a US Army captain, and he left Fort A.P. Hill earlier this evening with several hundred men under his command on the direct orders of General George Fiske, who heads up intelligence for the Joint Chiefs of Staff. Apparently, they took President Hilton prisoner as her motorcade was returning to the city from Camp David. Then they took the White House. Another command took the Capitol."

"How do you know all this?" Falcon asked, committing Buford's face to memory.

"Several men, including a lieutenant, deserted Buford's force after the president was taken prisoner on I-270, after she was cuffed and driven off." Troy slipped the phone back into his pocket. "The lieutenant told a man in my command that the ultimate destination was the White House."

"What is *wrong* with these people?"

"I'm very sure I don't know," Troy replied, shaking his head in disbelief and disgust. "But if you see Buford, don't kill him. We need him alive. He knows where President Hilton is being held. Once we take the White House back, we need to reinstall her as president as soon as possible."

"I'll try to take Buford alive if I have a chance. But if it comes down to him or me, it's gonna be—"

"Him," Troy cut in. "Yes, I get it."

The man of Troy's command named Charlie jogged up to them from behind and knelt down behind the Honda on the other side of Troy. "Everything's ready, sir."

"The shock and awe factor, too?" Troy asked.

"Yes, sir."

"All right, Charlie. Be ready to fire on my signal."

"Yes, sir."

Charlie rose up and sprinted back into the night.

"What's happening?" Falcon asked.

"You stay with me if at all possible," Troy said. "It'll be chaos from the moment we break from here. You keep up with me. You do exactly as I say."

"I will." He would, too. He wasn't going to be stupid about this. No going out on his own.

"Put these on," Troy ordered, holding out his right hand.

Falcon took what looked like an ordinary pair of eyeglasses that had thick, clear frames. "Really?"

"Just put them on."

When Falcon did, a small screen appeared ahead and to the left of him. On the screen were uniformed soldiers pointing guns out windows.

"A few minutes ago we sent six micro-drones into the White House."

"Hey, I know what—"

"I know you do," Troy interrupted. "Because he works with me, Basil Slicke must obtain permission from me before he can take on any civilian work. I've known about your interest in technology and gadgets for a while and, therefore, the fact that you use G2-DATA to help you with those things." Troy pointed ahead of Falcon, out where the virtual screen was appearing for him. "You'll have six screens available to you. All you have to do is think of the number, and the corresponding screen will appear before you. So think of anything but one."

When Falcon thought of two, the screen automatically changed. He ran through the rest until six provided him a view of the roof. At least fifty men were in position, all aiming weapons down toward the ground. "Unbelievable," he whispered.

"Yes, it is," Troy agreed as he slipped on his own pair. "The left stem detects everything you're thinking and scrolls the screen to the desired camera. And it's equipped with night vision. It's a crazy-cool device that will give us the upper hand in this battle." He hesitated. "You all right, A.J.?"

"I've got a favor to ask of you."

"What?"

"When this is over and if I'm still alive, will you help me find out what really happened to my father?"

Troy hesitated a few moments, then nodded. "Yes, I will."

"Thank you."

"Now get down and cover your eyes."

"What's happening?"

"You ever heard the term MOAB?"

"Sure. Mother of All Bombs, but—"

"You're about to experience the MOAB of concussion bombs," Troy said, sending a text to Charlie.

"What do you—"

"Get down!"

A moment later, a massive burst of blinding light exploded in the darkness above the White House. In an instant, the powerful shock wave blew past Falcon like a tornado.

"Let's go!" Troy shouted when it was gone, pulling Falcon to his feet.

As they jumped up, specially designed green lasers shot out from the car line the men were hiding behind, punching fiery holes in the tall wrought-iron fence surrounding the White House grounds.

Along with Troy and fifty other men, Falcon sprinted toward the closest hole in the fence, sparks still spewing from the metal. As he ran, he kept his focus flashing from what lay ahead, to where Troy was, to the shot that was being projected on the screen by the glasses. On screen six, he saw that all soldiers on the White House roof were now down, sprawled in different positions, weapons dropped. It was much the same picture on the other five screens, which were all views of different areas of 1600's interior—hallways and offices—though not everyone was down here.

The man just to A.J.'s right tumbled to the ground with a moan, and suddenly bullets were strafing the ground and shrubs all around them.

"Down!" Troy shouted. "Cover your eyes."

Falcon fell forward, taking cover behind a tree.

Another blinding light exploded, this time directly in front of the White House's south wall. Another powerful wave blew past.

"Come on!"

Falcon's heart jumped a beat as they broke into the open and dashed for the left side staircase leading up to the huge porch. A man staggered out of the door in front of them, brandishing a gun. Falcon aimed, but before he could fire, Troy had cut the enemy down with a quick burst of fire from his MP8.

Falcon sprinted into the White House after Troy, and within sixty seconds they'd located a barely conscious Captain Buford.

"Where is President Hilton?" Troy demanded of the captain.

"I don't know," Buford gasped.

"Where is she?"

Buford shook his head. "No."

Troy reached into his pocket, removed a tiny syringe, and jammed it into Buford's neck.

CHAPTER 31

Near Great Falls, Virginia

"I don't see evidence of a protective force anywhere," Troy muttered as they stood well inside the tree line encircling the mansion at twenty yards out. During the last few minutes, they'd lapped the home to check it from all sides. "No trucks, no sentries, no nothing." Dawn was still an hour off. So it was still very dark beneath the oaks, the elms, and the overcast sky. "I think General Fiske has President Hilton alone in there. I think it's just the two of them."

The rambling colonial was set on five secluded acres near the Potomac River, not far from the town of Great Falls, Virginia, which was thirty miles west of the White House.

Troy and Falcon had driven a jeep away from the White House. But they'd left it hidden on an old logging road and hiked a mile through the woods to get here so as not to draw attention.

"Fiske might have taken her someplace else by now if he's been watching television," Falcon said. "He'll know the coup has lost the White House by now. It's been on all the news channels."

"Yeah, but he knows his people still have control of the Capitol. And the *world* knows President Hilton has been taken prisoner by the generals running the coup. So the issue's still in doubt. And if the other side makes it to daybreak still alive and fighting and still in possession of the president and the Capitol, Sutton & Company plans to start cutting off funds to the financial system."

"Really?"

"We picked up Sutton's plan to squeeze the markets during our surveillance of Lewis and Fiske, while we were listening in to their conversations with Wallace and Rose."

This was the first Falcon had heard of Wallace's plan to attack the financial system, and he had to admit it was a good one—especially because, now that he thought about it, Sutton could actually make it happen.

Jimmy Three Sticks was all-in on this action. He was going to do whatever was necessary to take this administration down and replace it with generals.

"The masses will go into all-out panic mode when they can't get their hands on their cash," Troy continued. "When Sutton announces support for the coup, when they promise to save the system like the cavalry saving the day at the last minute, I'm afraid that could swing a majority of the country to the generals' side. In the end, most people vote more passionately about their wallets and pocketbooks than they do about anything else. You know that better than I do, A.J. We've got to save President Hilton and get her back to the White House ASAP because when Sutton launches, the effects will start being felt by ordinary people almost immediately. Then dollars and cents might ultimately have more influence on this situation and this country's future than guns and bullets."

"Fiske might be worried about you doing exactly what you did to Captain Buford. He might have already moved President Hilton to another location by now as a precaution."

The syringe Troy had injected Buford with had pumped a powerful, fast-acting truth serum into the army captain's system. Within sixty seconds, he was spilling his guts, talking like he couldn't stop, answering any and every question Troy posed—including the crucial one concerning the president's whereabouts. Buford immediately admitted that members of his unit had delivered President Hilton to General Fiske's house near Great Falls.

"No chance," Troy answered. "He figures Buford's dead at this point. He figures Buford was executed on-site when we overran them. That's the one silver lining for Fiske with the White House being taken back. He figures the guy who can point the finger at him is gone, that the communication line was cut."

A gust of wind swept through the trees, rustling the leaves above them.

"Nice place," Falcon said, gesturing at the structure's massive silhouette. "It looks like we're paying our highest-ranking generals damn well. While they spend their days at the Pentagon devising plans to take over the country."

"And it sounds to me like somebody's a big supporter of President Hilton's plan to slash the military budget."

"Not at all," Falcon shot back. "The men and women who fight to protect this country should get the best of everything for the rest of their lives. And that includes their families. What I don't like seeing is the brass taking more than their fair share of the pie."

"Well, don't worry too much about that. According to my sources, Fiske's wife is the one who bought this mansion. She's the one with the money, and she's in Europe right now enjoying it."

"Tell me again why it's just you and me here," Falcon said as he slid the pistol from its holster on his belt. They would leave the machine guns at this spot, particularly because it didn't look like they'd be up against a superior force. Any shots fired near the president had to be done with pinpoint accuracy. They couldn't risk killing Katrina with a hail of bullets sprayed by the MP8. "And not an entire army division."

"We need surprise on our side," Troy answered. "News choppers are flying over DC everywhere. Even at night they'd have spotted a small convoy of military trucks headed out of Washington for Great

Falls and followed it. Fiske would have seen us coming." He glanced over. "You ready?"

"As ready as I'll ever be," Falcon answered calmly.

"Then let's do it."

But just as they burst from beneath the oaks and elms and sprinted for the closest first-floor window, the big two-car garage door began to lift up noisily. And an outdoor bulb flashed on, illuminating the first ten feet of the driveway.

"Come on!" Troy shouted, veering off from this end of the mansion to head toward the garage. "You stay on this side of the door. I'll go around."

Seconds later, Falcon was peering around the near side of the garage, and Troy had reached the other side after making certain to stay in the darkness, outside the arc of the bulb.

Fiske, clad in his uniform, was just emerging from the door leading out of the home, and he was hustling President Hilton ahead of him toward a big black Tahoe. Her hands were tied behind her back, and Fiske had a pistol to her head while he clamped her back tightly to his chest with his other arm, forearm just beneath her neck.

Falcon had been leaning forward, one eye barely around the brick wall. When he took a small step forward to see slightly better, the toe of his boot touched the driveway—and a high-pitched alarm split the quiet night.

At the sound of the alarm, Fiske went ramrod straight, then pivoted so he was facing the garage door, twisting and hurling the president in front of him so she served as a shield.

"Don't move, General Fiske!" Troy yelled above the alarm, emerging into full view with the pistol leading the way. He leaned over the Tahoe's hood, using it as a partial shield and support for the arm aiming the pistol. "Let her go."

"The hell I will!" he shouted back as she screamed in pain when he twisted her again to make certain she was between Troy and him. "Get away or I kill her. If I kill her, the coup will succeed. You may get me, but the country will be ours."

"*Let her go!*"

"*Get back!*"

At that moment, everything happened in superslow motion for Falcon. Everything decelerated to what seemed like a tenth of its normal speed.

Fiske was stepping backward, keeping Katrina between him and the garage door, dragging her along with one arm still clamped to her upper chest, trying to get into the house, where he could lock the door and call reinforcements to help him, where he might have a safe room that he could bolt himself inside until his cavalry could arrive.

As Falcon moved out from his hiding place behind the garage wall, Troy slid around the front of the Tahoe, and they both began slowly moving toward the retreating Fiske.

When Falcon appeared, Fiske's eyes went wide, and for an instant he swung the barrel of his pistol away from Katrina's head and pointed it at Falcon.

"*Duck!*" Troy shouted to Katrina.

Katrina was able to bend down only a few inches—but that was enough to give Troy a shot.

It was almost as if Falcon could actually see the bullet explode from Troy's gun, as if he could see it knife through the garage and then smash into Fiske's left shoulder. The force of the round's impact spun Fiske around and dropped him to the cement slab. Katrina tumbled to the garage floor as well.

Fiske came to rest on his stomach, gun still clenched in his right hand and pointed straight at Katrina.

Falcon felt as if he were having that recurring dream of trying to run fast but only being able to plod along as he sprinted forward.

Fiske lifted the gun up to aim at Katrina.

Katrina put her hands in front of her face.

Fiske's index finger squeezed the trigger.
Katrina screamed in terror.
Troy aimed.
Falcon dove.
A gun exploded.
A bullet tore through flesh.

CHAPTER 32

Washington, DC

Reporters moved into the White House press room cautiously, eyes flashing about suspiciously as they took their normal seats—which were based on seniority. They had a right to be nervous. After all, they weren't war correspondents. Armed members of the military had escorted them in here. But who were the soldiers backing?

They didn't have to wait long to find out.

"Good morning, ladies and gentlemen of the press, and welcome back to the White House."

Katrina moved into the room confidently, took her place behind the dais with the presidential seal affixed to it, and clasped the edges of the dais with both hands. She made eye contact with as many of the assembled press corps as possible, unable to control her million-dollar smile while she did.

"As of seven o'clock this morning, one hour ago, I was back in the White House and back in charge," she announced. "At this time all leaders of the attempted coup have been killed or captured. The United States is once again a democracy."

EPILOGUE

Fiske's throat was bone dry as he followed the captain across the courtyard toward the lone seven-foot-high post, clad in his dress uniform. His heart beat three times its normal pace. He perspired badly, despite the cold temperature. And his mind raced, as any military mind would.

How could he escape? How could he stop this from happening? How could he survive?

General Lewis had taken the easy way out by shoving the barrel of his pearl-handled Colt .45 revolver in his mouth as soldiers were coming up the path of his McLean home to arrest him. That was six months ago.

Fiske had not had the same chance to take the easy way out. After he'd shot A.J. Falcon in the garage of his home, Troy Jensen had taken him prisoner. And then he'd turned Fiske over to the army later that morning.

Thirty days ago, the court martial had concluded—and the death sentence had been handed down.

"Turn around," the captain hissed when they reached the wooden post. "Put your back up against it."

"No sympathy for me?" Fiske asked as his back moved against the rigid post.

He'd heard how pathetic he'd sounded, but he couldn't help it. He was trying hard to remain strong as his last few seconds ticked down.

But the tears were rising up.

"Put your hands behind the post."

For a split second, Fiske considered running. But that would be pointless. There was nowhere to go. And he would be forever known as the ultimate coward if he tried to run away now. Not being considered a coward in his final moments was all he had left to hold on to at this point.

"Do you want the hood?" the captain asked.

Fiske glanced over the captain's shoulder at the firing squad, at the seven men standing ten yards away who would blow his heart apart. One of the rifles was loaded with a blank, Fiske knew, so each assassin could always suppose that he hadn't been the killer. But the gun loaded with the blank wouldn't recoil nearly as much as those loaded with live ammunition when it fired. The men were experienced marksmen. They would know who was innocent—and who wasn't.

"Yes," Fiske whispered.

The hood would hide his tears.

He glanced up at the clear, blue sky sadly and took one last look at its beauty before the hood came down and ultimate darkness covered his face for the first and final time.

His tears began to flow. In those last few seconds, he thought about the women he'd tortured as he sobbed beneath the cloth, including the last one—President Hilton. He was getting exactly what he deserved, he realized.

The guns fired, but Fiske didn't hear the reports. He was already dead.

◆ ◆ ◆

Trinity Church chimed its last 9:00 p.m. bell as Andrew Blake Falcon limped slowly east along Wall Street past the New York Stock Exchange with the aid of a wooden cane carved from the pole to which General George Fiske had been strapped tightly at his execution.

Falcon wasn't above revenge—and handling this cane proved that point . . . to himself. At several levels, he hated weakness, his own especially.

But, at other levels, he loved that he was aware of his weaknesses. Most people weren't. That awareness made him stronger.

The air whipped chilly and hard past him, through the base of the sixty-story man-made canyons lining both sides of the world-famous, narrow asphalt strip where megafortunes were regularly won and lost. Falcon leaned into the cold January gusts to keep his balance. This would be the first time he'd ever been to the spot. It took everything he had to even approach it.

He'd always coached himself to remove emotion from everything. His father had, too.

But he'd failed in this instance. He couldn't remove any emotion from this. He'd been practicing—no, preparing—for almost three years.

Still, he was completely unprepared to handle it.

And he could handle *anything* else.

The lone bullet General Fiske had been able to fire—aimed at Katrina—had blasted into Falcon's right thigh instead, severing a major artery.

But his quick thinking and swift move had saved President Hilton's life when the future of the United States and the rest of the world had hung in the balance. It didn't make up for Claire's death—but then . . . nothing ever would.

Falcon stopped . . . uncertain. And he was never uncertain about anything.

He glanced down at the dirty sidewalk—candy wrappers and newspapers whipped and mini-eddy-swirled past the base of the cane.

"Keep going, sweetheart," Billie urged. "I need to meet him."

Six feet away from the location, Falcon stopped again, catching sight of a man he never wanted to see again.

James Lee Wallace III, aka Jimmy Three Sticks, stood thirty feet away, on the other side of the spot. Everything about his posture and his very presence there radiated his conviction that he was bulletproof.

Lewis and Fiske were dead. But Wallace and Rose were still running Sutton & Company, still making billions. The evidence linking them to the coup hadn't been strong enough to convict them of anything.

"We'll get them," Troy murmured, leaning in and speaking so quietly not even Billie could hear.

"Are you sure?"

"Oh, yes." Troy glanced around. "I have to go. I'll call you later."

Falcon watched as Wallace turned and walked away.

It was just Billie and him now.

"Help me," he whispered to her.

"Yes, sweetheart."

When he was standing at the spot, he knelt slowly and carefully. And then he leaned all the way down so he could actually kiss the spot where his father had slammed into the pavement.

"I love you, Dad. I miss you so much, every day." He gritted his teeth and shut his eyes tightly. "I hope you're proud of me."

AUTHOR'S NOTE

Dear Reader,

The events depicted in *Ultimate Power*'s Prologue in the fictitious town of Tulip, Mississippi, were written in April 2017, four months prior to the actual events that occurred in Charlottesville, Virginia, in August 2017. The scene in the book originally took place in Charlottesville, but I moved it to the fictitious Mississippi town in May 2017 for purposes of the story.

Sincerely,

Stephen Frey

ACKNOWLEDGMENTS

First to Cynthia Manson, who has been with me right from the beginning, twenty-three books ago. She's a fabulous business partner and a great friend. I treasure our relationship.

Second, to the wonderful people at Thomas & Mercer without whom this book would not exist: Megha Parekh, Gracie Doyle, and Jeff Belle.

Third, to Caitlin Alexander, my content editor. Awesome. Enough said.

Fourth, to my daughters, Christina, Ashley, and Elle.

And to the others who have been so supportive through the years:

The Malone Family . . . Matt, Sarah, Aidan, and Logan.

The Erdman Family . . . Big Sky, Nancy, Hannah, Henry, Emma, and Eleanor.

The Brusman Family . . . Andy, Chris, Campbell, and Aidan.

The Lynch Family . . . Pat, Terry, Joe, and Robert.

Jeff Faville, Jesse Waltz, Jeanette Follo, Andy Youngs, Barbara Fertig, Sean O'Halloran, Walter Frey, Peter Borland, Louise Burke, Alexandre and Veronique Benaim, Greg Seuss.

ABOUT THE AUTHOR

Photo © 2009 Sam Johnson

New York Times bestselling author Stephen Frey has spent twenty-five years working in private equity and investment banking at firms, including J. P. Morgan & Company and Winston Partners. He is the author of twenty-three novels, including the Red Cell series: *Arctic Fire*, *Red Cell Seven*, and *Kodiak Sky*. He is currently a partner at Succession Capital in Virginia Beach, Virginia.